WILD *hart*

HART'S BAY

E. DAVIES

Wild Hart / E. Davies. – 1st ed.
ISBN: 978-1-912245-37-6

To the bold, brave, and beautiful whose strength lies in their softness.

1

EZRA

"Don't forget to get laid!"

Ezra cringed as Aaron's voice carried down the street like a super-gay foghorn.

But when he glared over his shoulder at his roommate, Aaron just winked and pushed his tongue into his cheek, curling his fingers in front of his lips to imitate a blowjob.

Honest to God, Aaron just liked to make people squirm and blush. If he wasn't one of Ezra Carter's best friends, he would have earned himself a strong retort at the same volume.

But Ezra had a date to get to, so he was on his best behavior. He didn't even flip his friend off over his shoulder as he let Seaglass Gallery's back workshop door bang closed.

Motion from down below—past the deep water berth, the dingy little marina that consisted of a few slips and wharves—caught his eye.

Oh, it's my future husband, Ezra thought, his hand rising to his chest as his heart squeezed.

The man crouching by his boat had been Ezra's eye

candy ever since he'd spotted the new guy lurking around the docks a couple of weeks ago.

He had strong shoulders, the kind that could lift beams... or Ezras. His hair was short and ruffled by salty sea spray, his faded T-shirt and jeans clinging to him. Best of all, he was currently stripping out of waterproof overalls. Even those unforgiving materials did great things for an ass that could best be described as miraculous.

Unfortunately, he was wearing clothes underneath. A sigh of disappointment slipped from Ezra's lips.

Oh, this man was so handsome he should be fighting off the boys... but sadly, he wasn't Ezra's date. Only in his fantasies.

The closest Ezra had ever gotten was twice passing him in the parking lot between the art gallery and the harbor. Ezra had smiled and fled for his car before they could actually exchange words.

Ezra was never going to find the courage to walk down the dock and ask this guy out. He'd have to keep his future husband to his daydreams.

The best Ezra could do was "Paul" from Grindr, who was due to meet him—and no doubt disappoint him—any moment now.

Ezra tore his eyes away and strolled down the street toward the bar, resisting the urge to stare over his shoulder at the marina for as long as he could.

He ought to praise his luck that he'd been online at just the right time to score a same-day date. Paul was driving up from California along the coast highway, between work meetings. He'd agreed to meet for a drink here, and then...

Fun. Ezra was getting tired of the word. Only part of the time was it true. Even then, there were practical matters, like making sure your sweetheart-for-the-night didn't keep an axe behind his bedroom door.

Ah, romance wasn't dead while Grindr was alive.

Ezra swallowed his trepidation as he headed into the familiar bar. He'd lowered his standards a lot since moving here, an hour or more away from any decently-sized cities with more than a handful of prospective boyfriends.

"Evening, Cher," he greeted the proprietor of Cher's End Table, a tiny dive bar that served as the town's only watering hole.

No sign of his date. It was six on the dot. But then, Paul might need to find parking first anyway.

Ezra's mind wandered back to the guy at the harbor. He'd only caught glimpses here and there over the last couple of weeks. Enough to know that he was new to town.

Maybe he was starting life afresh like Ezra was—young, single, and ready to mingle. He could only hope so.

Paul was nothing to daydream about yet. He'd only seen one blurry photo of the guy, complete with a filter that made it look like a J.C. Penney's photo shoot from the '80s. His profile was almost blank.

Ezra held out hope that Paul didn't know how to come across on social media but was more interesting in person. He fidgeted his way through drinking one Sprite, and then a second.

By quarter past, he was pretty sure he'd been stood up. It was impossible to park more than fifteen minutes in any direction from the bar.

Cher was busy talking to Gregory, the Irishman who was always at a corner table with a pint glass. So Ezra fidgeted with his phone, browsing the news headlines for interesting topics of conversation.

Just as he was about to give up and buy himself a consolation sandwich from the grocery store across the road, the door swung open.

A full twenty minutes past their arranged meeting time, a man who vaguely resembled Paul's profile picture walked in. His searching gaze sweeping across the bar confirmed to Ezra that this was his date.

Ezra rose slightly and waved to attract his attention, his heart doing that familiar first-date beat skip. This was the moment to make a first impression.

"Hi," he greeted, taking in the man. Paul looked like his picture, at least. He had a wide, square jaw and dull eyes. When he reached the table, he cast his gaze around as if searching for something more interesting than Ezra to focus on.

"Hey." Paul pulled out his phone and fiddled with it. "I'm getting a drink."

"Cool, sure." Ezra folded his hands and waited. He watched Paul head to the bar and back, his gaze fixed on his phone the whole time.

Paul put the phone down on the table when he got back and finally looked at Ezra, scanning him up and down as if assessing him. "So you're Ezra."

Already, Ezra's hope was fading into disappointment. But everyone deserved a chance to make a good impression. "Hi. You must be Paul. I hope so, anyway," he joked, offering a smile.

Paul didn't smile back. "Good." He sipped his beer and looked around the place again. "Never been here."

"It's a cute little town." Ezra had only moved to Hart's Bay a few months ago, and he was full of stories about it already. Despite the tragic consequences for his love life, the move had opened up new doors for him.

Paul's disbelieving grunt stopped his enthusiasm in its

tracks. "Sure." He picked up his phone again and started thumbing through it.

Okay, maybe he needed to be more interesting. Ezra fidgeted with his hair, twirling the straight red strands around one thumb. "Did you have a good day at work?"

"No." There was no elaboration—Paul spoke abruptly, his tone short.

Okay, shit. Maybe he'd had a bad day. Ezra tried once more. "Oh, I'm sorry. Anything fun planned, at least?"

"You." Paul finally looked up at him, sipping his beer. "Just wait till I finish this beer first. Need to unwind."

"Stressful day, then," Ezra offered, his stomach tight. He wasn't sure he wanted to take Paul up on this offer of fun after all. But what would it hurt? He might turn out to be great in bed.

"Yeah. My client couldn't give a rat's ass about me, you know?" It was the first full sentence Paul had spoken, and it encouraged Ezra. He nodded to show he was listening as Paul kept talking. "My boss doesn't, either. They all just expect perfection. All the time. All the time," he repeated, gesturing with his beer. "It's so shitty."

"Ugh. I've had some pretty crappy jobs—" Ezra started.

"No kidding. It's just for the paychecks, you know?" Paul chugged at his beer, his eyes narrowing. "You do something creative, don't you? Media kid?"

Close, but not at all. "I'm a painter."

"Ha." Paul's laugh was short, and it didn't reach his eyes. He looked back at his phone, thumbing and tapping at the screen without saying anything.

The silence stretched between them as Ezra fidgeted with his Sprite and tried to decide what to do. He deserved better than this, he knew. But there wasn't anything better available, so...

"Do you like art or anything?" Ezra asked.

Paul drained his beer in a few long gulps, tipping his head back. Even Ezra's interest in his bobbing Adam's apple and pursed lips around the neck of the bottle was more... artistic than anything else.

He imagined painting this moment, but without showing Paul's face. Just the man's lips to his collarbones, his lips around the bottle, the angry twist to the corner of his mouth.

Paul sighed and burped as he finished the beer. He set down the bottle with a sharp *clink* on the tabletop. "Are you always this annoying?" His tone a few minutes ago had been positively warm and glowing compared to this brusque attitude. "I don't have all night. Let's get this over with."

Ezra's cheeks flushed, but before he could say anything, he spotted Paul's screen. He had Grindr open—and not just the nearby screen, but a message chain with someone else.

No strings attached with this guy, then, he thought ruefully. Paul really was just searching for a quick fuck. If not Ezra, it would be someone else nearby.

And Ezra hadn't even had a good hookup since he moved from the city almost six months ago. He was starving, and it showed in his muse.

His art wasn't coming as readily to him now. The dissatisfaction that crept through his spirit made his paintings bleaker. They'd lost that edge of charm and whimsy with which he always tried to imbue his work. Just blowing off steam might loosen up the screws.

Ezra stared at his lap for a few moments, his self-esteem and righteous anger stopping his tongue. But he didn't have to love it. All he had to do was go along with it.

"Excuse me." The voice that interrupted them wasn't Paul's. It was crisp and just as brusque, though.

When Ezra looked up, his whole body lit up like a thousand-megawatt lamp flooding the nooks and crannies of his heart.

It was him: the guy from the marina.

The scent of the man—sea water, oil, and sweat mingled with clean soap—imprinted itself on him instantly. From here, he could make out every fleck of his blue eyes. His tousled blond hair looked soft.

"You, man." He was frowning at Paul, his arms folded. They looked even more muscled from here. He looked like an avenging angel—just a wall of muscle and fury. "If you can't treat this guy nicely, you might as well fuck off."

Paul sneered up at him. "What's it to you?" He reached across the table, making a grab for Ezra's hand.

Ezra flinched away, his gut roiling. Suddenly, the thought of even letting Paul *look* at him made his whole body shiver, head to toe. "No, he's right. You don't have to be a dick to get dick."

Paul shrugged and stood up. "Fine," he spat, the dismissive word making Ezra flinch. "Sluts like you are a dime a dozen anyway."

The man from the marina unfolded his arms, but Ezra touched his arm to stop him from going after Paul. "No," he whispered.

Electricity crackled between them. Not the static kind, but the kind that made his head spin for no discernible reason.

Instantly, the man softened and looked over at Ezra, listening to him. "You sure? I bet I could throw his ass into the square from here."

The thought made Ezra smile. He let his finger trail down his arm, across those strong biceps. "Yeah, I bet you could."

Was this the wrong moment to flirt? He wasn't sure he'd

get a *right* moment, so he was seizing the moment with both hands.

There was something else he'd like to seize with both hands.

Ezra's cock throbbed with heat, his energy shifting in response to this man's. He'd barely said ten words to protect Ezra, but already, Ezra *wanted* him.

"How can I thank you?" Ezra continued, batting his lashes.

The guy grinned and pulled away from his touch, but it was gentle rather than the abrupt wall that Paul had thrown between them. He sat where Paul had been moments ago. "No need. I'm just glad I wasn't screwing anything up for you. He wasn't your type, was he? I'm just some dumbass straight guy. I didn't want to mess with some gay mating ritual I don't know shit about."

Nooooo. Ezra didn't even have to fake his pout as he propped his chin on his fist. "You only screwed up my chances of *getting* screwed."

Damn it, this man had won himself bonus blowjobs, and he didn't even want to redeem them?

Not that Ezra would have spat out his dick *before* this encounter, but now Ezra had extra motivation to want to repay him.

Damn it, why does he have to be straight?

"But I was pretty turned off by him," Ezra added, feeling the need to clarify. "He's not at all my type."

"What is, then?"

"Dumbass straight guys." Ezra winked. "Especially when I know their names. I'm Ezra."

The other guy laughed again and then reached over the table to take Ezra's hand in a firm shake. "Rusty," he introduced himself. "I'm flattered, but I think you'd have a better chance with another dumbass gay guy. There must be better fish in the sea."

"I just tried one," Ezra nodded toward the door. "They're either taken, already like a brother to me, or an asshole like him who's only after one thing."

Rusty gave him a frown. "Okay, let me buy you a drink and you can vent at me. Least I can do for scaring off your, uh..."

"Fuck buddy?" Ezra tested the waters to see if he could embarrass Rusty. "He's not a date if he didn't buy me a drink."

Sure enough, Rusty's ears went red when Ezra said those words, and Ezra beamed. Okay, he could kind of understand Aaron. Making straight guys blush was adorable.

Rusty grinned. "So what can I get you?"

"A mojito, please," Ezra said, his heart fluttering unreasonably. There was no point in getting invested in this guy. He was nice and all, but he'd just emphasized how straight he was.

Which made it all the more mystifying that he'd jumped in to help Ezra, without expecting anything in return. Maybe he was playing a long game. Lots of straight guys didn't mind a blowjob as long as they didn't have to do anything in return.

That was totally Ezra's wishful thinking, wasn't it?

Just one little lick, he imagined himself pleading later—down on his knees, staring up the length of his hard body to meet Rusty's pretty blue eyes.

Fuuuck, he was getting hard. Ezra shifted and crossed his knees, digging his nails into his thigh as he tried to forget that image. Or at least save it for later, when he was alone.

Rusty came back a minute later with a beer and a mojito, sliding the latter toward Ezra.

"Thank you. That's really too kind of you," Ezra said. He was still glowing with a stupid smile.

Rusty had swept in, not caring that he was interrupting Paul. And better still, he hadn't caused a scene. He'd stood up quickly, quietly, and effectively to a bully.

It was enough to make Ezra swoon. He'd never had a guy stand up for him like that before.

"No problem," Rusty said, leaning in and holding out his beer to clink. "Even I can tell that you're way too cute for him. I'll handpick candidates for you if I have to, but don't give in to assholes like that who only want to tear you down. You're worth more than that."

Rusty sounded fiercely certain, and Ezra took a breath to deal with the intensity. It was dizzying, having Rusty's gaze focused on him. "How do you know?"

"I've been in the gallery and seen your work," Rusty said, offering him a smile. "It's really neat."

Ezra's jaw dropped. None of the other guys—his roommates and coworkers at the artists' co-op—had told him that *this* man had visited. He was going to kick their asses later. "Oh!"

"You're the painter, right?" Rusty asked. "The guy I talked to said so."

"Yeah, I am!"

Wait, he noticed me before my paintings? Ezra could have died happy on the spot. He'd been sneaking glances at the guy down at the marina, eating his lunch outside on sunny days, but he hadn't caught him looking back before.

Which raised questions that Ezra didn't want to entertain, like *would a straight guy really come ask about me?*

That would open up five hundred hours' worth of fantasies. Ezra's heart didn't need the ache that was bound to lie at the end of that road.

"And you... go out on the water?" Ezra offered. It was a little less weird to admit that he'd seen him around, if the interest had been mutual. "I've seen you hanging around the docks. Not a sentence I usually say to straight men." He couldn't help pushing the boundary, seeing how Rusty would react.

Rusty wasn't offended. In fact, he tipped his head back and laughed. His teeth flashed, and he was even *more* unreasonably beautiful. Damn it, who had allowed that?

Ezra's chest loosened and he could breathe again, relief flooding him. He hadn't wanted to make Rusty uncomfortable.

"Yeah, I've been down there a lot lately," Rusty agreed. He thought for a moment, an adorable little line appearing between his brows. Then, he set down his beer. "In fact, before I finish this, do you want to take a spin around the harbor?"

"In your boat?" Ezra perked up. "I've never been on the ocean."

"Seriously?"

Ezra laughed. "I grew up in Seattle. I've dipped my toes in the ocean. But I never took the ferry or anything. And I'm not really an outdoorsy fisherman. Never had the chance."

"Well, let's fix that." Rusty grinned. "It's just an excuse to show off, really."

Ezra giggled, not even bothering trying to keep his composure. *Oh, he already did that when he saved me,* he thought. *Now I just have to keep myself from jumping him.*

The sun had already set, and the night was closing in quickly. The first stars were probably out by now, but it wasn't pitch-black.

Ezra hadn't expected an offer of a romantic evening

cruise from a straight man. But it was also exactly what might cheer him up.

"I'd love to," Ezra answered. The wall he'd hoped to keep between himself and his fantasies crumbled into dust as he followed Rusty to the door.

Maybe what his spirit needed more than sex was one night of giving in to his daydreams. Just the opposite of what he'd nearly gone and done, but it was still one night.

What could one night hurt?

2

RUSTY

A long day on the water didn't dampen Rusty's enthusiasm to get back out there for a quick spin—and this time, introduce his new friend to pleasure boating.

Sure, he might not be interested in Ezra *that* way, but who wouldn't step in after overhearing what he had? Rusty's blood still boiled at the little he'd seen from that asshole.

He'd only seen Ezra's sunny smile a few times before, but it was back now. "Thank you again," Ezra said in a soft voice. He twisted his hands together as he looked over at Rusty.

Rusty waved it off, a blush creeping to his cheeks. He hadn't stepped in for the praise—it had clearly been the right thing to do. "My pleasure. Really."

But he couldn't shake the thought. Ezra's face now was a far cry from the way he'd sat across from Paul at Cher's, his shoulders slumped and gaze on the table, clearly weighing up what he felt he deserved.

God, no. That was just wrong.

It made Rusty happy to see Ezra's light steps, the ends of

his long, straight red hair fluttering in the breeze. He bounced on his toes as he walked, and he gestured with his fingers every time he talked.

He reminded Rusty of a sea sprite, or a merman. Hearing he'd never been on the water had taken him by surprise. That was within his power to fix—and it would cheer him up even further, too.

From the first moment he'd spotted the man watching him from the art gallery doorway, Rusty had taken an immediate shine to him. He'd caught glimpses of him laughing with friends and engaging with customers.

Something about him had caught Rusty's curiosity, and he still wasn't sure what it was.

Rusty led Ezra past the now-familiar construction site near the harbor. An old warehouse was being converted into boutique shops. Even in the few weeks Rusty had been back home, they'd made tons of progress. The sign on the fence said the grand opening was scheduled in a few weeks' time. Unlike every construction project ever, they seemed to be on track.

"You know anything about this place?" Rusty asked Ezra to make conversation as they passed by.

"Oh, yes!" Ezra followed Rusty to the arch that framed the top of the docks. "I'm painting murals in each of the stores. A bunch of my friends are involved with it."

Rusty smiled at the news. "That's awesome." Already, it was a far cry from the town he'd left behind five years ago. He couldn't remember the last time anything new had opened.

"Yeah, I'm glad the developers asked me to work on it. I'm doing a different harbor scene on the back wall of each place." Ezra rubbed his chin. "Though I'm a little bit behind. I'll catch up, though."

"I'm sure you will." Rusty stepped onto the ramp that led down to the wooden dock. The metal was punctured with holes, the edges sticking up to provide more traction. "Watch out, it's slippery."

Ezra nodded, strode forward, and slipped immediately.

Rusty's chest lurched with adrenaline as Ezra's arms windmilled. The redhead was the slender and leggy type— all limbs, especially right now. He caught himself on the railing, his body twisting as he did so.

"Whoa!" On pure instinct, Rusty's arm looped around Ezra's waist, pulling him tight against his front. He grabbed the railing with his other hand, too, to steady them both.

Their bodies pressed together, Rusty straddling one of Ezra's thighs, Ezra's shoulder pressing into his chest. Rusty couldn't help noticing the way he instinctively reacted to having someone pressed so close to him. For a weird moment, he wished they weren't in their winter jackets.

God, he needed to get laid, but that was a whole different story of his sad love life.

Ezra blushed, still clutching the rail with one hand and Rusty's arm with the other. "Sorry. These shoes don't have any grip."

Rusty glanced down at the Converse on Ezra's feet and rolled his eyes playfully. Those things were totally flat. "City boys," he teased. "Am I going to have to lift you into the boat?"

He shifted his hips slightly and loosened his grip on Ezra. Nobody needed to get mixed signals from his body's natural reaction to closeness to another human after so long. That semi was taking its sweet time to fuck off, though.

Ezra batted his lashes outrageously. "You might need to, tragically," he breathed and then let go of Rusty. "I'm good."

Rusty kept a hand near Ezra anyway as they strode down the ramp to the flatter-but-no-less-slippery dock.

It was impossible not to notice the flirtation, and Rusty didn't mind one bit. He could recognize a compliment, even if he couldn't seem to get along romantically with anyone. Also, objectively, Ezra was gorgeous, which increased the compliment that much more.

The second time Ezra wobbled, he didn't quite slip, but his gaze flashed guiltily to Rusty. "I'm fine." Definitely a landlubber, then.

Rusty took Ezra's arm. "No, you're not," he said with a laugh. "I can't let you drown."

"Such a gentleman," Ezra purred, wrapping his hand around Rusty's arm. He smelled nice up close—kind of coconut and floral. "My night got so much better."

"Good," Rusty said with an approving nod. He was still indignant that anyone would treat someone like that, especially Ezra with his kind spirit and talented soul. Anything he could do to cheer Ezra up and remind him that he didn't need to settle for some asshole like Paul was good.

Plus, he might make a new friend. Most of his high school buddies had left town, just like he had. With just his family and his best friend Pascal in town, he could use more friends his own age.

After unzipping the boat canopy, Rusty stepped inside and held out his hands to help Ezra in. Ezra stepped toward him, balancing delicately with one foot on the edge of the boat.

No way. Rusty could all too easily picture him tripping and getting caught between the boat and the slip. He didn't know as much about water safety as his parents and the older generation here in Hart's Bay, but this was 101 stuff.

Instead of waiting to see him wobble, Rusty grabbed

Ezra by the waist and swung him into the boat. He already knew Ezra was light enough to do it easily.

"Whoa!" Ezra giggled and swayed on the spot when Rusty set him down. "Strong."

"Why, thank you." Rusty winked. "I'd hate all those bicep curls to go unappreciated."

"I can tell you they're appreciated. Maybe not by your target audience, but still…" Ezra pretended to fan himself.

Rusty grinned and pulled life jackets out of the lockbox at the back of the boat. It wasn't much—a twenty-foot outboard power boat—but more importantly, it had come free. His best friend had bought it a few years ago and it hadn't seen much use. Now that it was fixed up, it would do for their purposes for now.

"Put this on before we go anywhere," Rusty told Ezra and tossed him an orange vest.

Ezra fumbled but caught it. "Look! I did sports." He held the jacket aloft like a prize before sliding it over his head and taking a bow.

Rusty burst out laughing. When he'd offered a boat ride, he hadn't thought he'd be cheered up too. But he was, buoyed by the good company, the moonlight, and the prospect of a gentle boat cruise. He already liked Ezra's high spirits.

All his stress about work and his lack of friends had already melted away. Pascal was great, but they rarely saw each other these days.

He slid on his jacket and clipped it into place, then tried not to laugh as Ezra poked at the buckles and craned his neck to see what he was doing. "Let me help."

Ezra puffed his lips out in a sigh. For a moment, they looked unreasonably soft and pouty. Nothing like Rusty's chapped lips from salt and sea air. "Is my city boy showing?"

Rusty shook off the moment of fascination and nodded. "Absolutely." He took one strap at a time and tightened it, glancing up to make sure he wasn't squeezing Ezra too hard.

For a few moments, there was a pressure in the air between them that Rusty didn't quite understand. He wasn't used to putting his hands all over his guy friends before he even got to know them, but he had a feeling Ezra didn't mind.

"This orange does nothing for my hair," Ezra complained when Rusty reached the other side and tightened the final strap. That broke the moment, and Rusty could suddenly breathe again.

"Oh, no. My heart weeps for you," Rusty teased, which made Ezra burst out laughing. "I'll get you a designer print."

"Thank you. Anything but animal print."

Rusty smirked and started the boat with a few hard pulls, then slid into the driver's seat. "Orange camo it is."

Ezra settled onto the slippery, ripped seat and crossed his knees primly. "Not orange. I'd look great in regular old camo, though. Greens go well with red hair."

It was hard to resist a glance at the long, straight locks as Ezra ran his fingers through his sleek hair, tucking the ends into the collar of his life jacket. It looked ridiculously touchable. Was it crazy to ask to pet Ezra's hair? Yes, Rusty decided and bit his tongue.

He untethered the boat from its moorings and coiled the ropes, then headed back to the wheel and steered them away from the slip.

"Ooh. That's rocky." Ezra's fingers curled tightly around the edge of the boat, his eyes wide.

"You all right?" Rusty put his plans for speed on ice for now and glanced sideways at Ezra. Now was when they'd find out if he got seasick easily.

"Yeah, yeah," Ezra assured him with a laugh. "It's just different than I expected." His voice was light and curious, not filled with fear.

"Can you swim?" Rusty asked.

Ezra stared at him, his skin pale. "Yeah. Why?" He glanced back to the shore as if assessing the distance.

Rusty burst out laughing and clapped Ezra's shoulder, one hand on top of the steering wheel. "Don't worry. I'm teasing." Plus, it was good to know in case of emergencies. Life jackets were good, but swimming lessons were still a must.

"Oh! You jerk," Ezra gasped, his shock melting into a laugh. "If you tip us over and I get salt water in my hair, I might not talk to you for at *least* ten minutes."

Rusty snorted. "I'll do my best to stay upright."

So far, the glide of the boat was nothing to Rusty as he navigated to the breakwater. It was a still night, so at least it wouldn't be much choppier out there. But it was the ocean, and conditions could change in a moment.

"Here we are," he announced as they entered the soft chop of the surf. It was a gorgeous day for late November, so the boat wasn't bobbing much more now.

"Eek!" Ezra held on tightly to the side of the boat, but he was smiling.

"Weirdly, I like it when I'm going faster and the waves are higher. Feels steadier somehow. At this speed, you feel every little tip and bob, you know?" Rusty aimed along the shoreline, planning to do a gentle loop.

"Can I stand up?" Ezra asked from behind him and to his left.

"Go for it," Rusty encouraged him with a smile, keeping the steering straight as they meandered along the coastline.

Ezra wobbled like a baby deer but kept his footing,

moving toward the center of the boat on instinct and gripping the edge of the hard top that covered the front half, where Rusty sat. "Oh. Oh, this is... kind of cool."

"Not so bad, the outdoors?" Rusty asked.

Ezra beamed. "Not at all." He turned his face into the wind for a minute, his hair slipping out from the collar of his life jacket and flowing behind him.

It took all Rusty had to keep his eyes ahead for logs, seals, rocks, and other obstacles instead of staring at Ezra. He looked unreasonably pretty, like a catalog model.

Was that envy? Rusty couldn't work out the emotion that knotted his chest, and he tried to let it go and relax.

Out here at night, it was even more peaceful than the daytime. He'd live on the water if he could. As it was, working from the boat gave him an excuse to spend all day out here.

Ezra eventually wobbled his way to the front and sat in the left-hand seat under the canopy, gazing ahead through the window and at Rusty in turns. As if reading his mind, he asked, "What do you do for work?"

"Oh, um." A blush crept up Rusty's cheeks as he winced. It was a too-familiar setup, with him as the punchline.

The last girl he'd tried to date—the latest in a long string of failed two-week relationships—had laughed in his face and dumped him on the spot for telling her what he was moving back to Oregon to do. Just as well. A long-distance relationship between Oregon and Maine wasn't a great idea.

"It's... kind of... a thing. A sea thing. In the boat."

Ezra wasn't letting him out of it. He grinned, folding his arms and turning sideways on the seat. "Now you have me curious. Boat porn?"

"What?" Rusty yelped, the boat jerking slightly as his hands slipped on the wheel. "No. Oh, God. Is that a thing?"

"Everything is, on the internet," Ezra sagely advised him. "Boat-based porn could be hot. Not up here, though. Chilly and rainy here."

"It's nothing pornographic," Rusty said hastily, trying to steer the conversation back to something that wouldn't make the heat build up under his skin in this strangely unfamiliar fizzing way.

Ezra propped his elbows on his knees and leaned forward, chin on his fists. "Mmhmm?" He was the picture of curiosity, and the attention only made Rusty more flustered. He turned the wheel to start them looping back toward the harbor, in case the conversation got awkward.

"Um," Rusty finally said when it became obvious there was no way out, and gulped. Here went nothing. "I'm starting a seaweed farm."

But instead of bursting out laughing, Ezra lit up. "What? Really?" For a moment, Rusty didn't know how to react. Ezra's exclamation was excited, not mocking.

"Yeah... it's a pioneering project." Rusty shot him a sideways glance. "Most cultivation out here is done in tanks, but they're looking at renting out underwater acreage along the coast if this goes well and the industry grows."

"That's so cool. I love sushi," Ezra said, grinning at him.

That was a common reaction. Rusty laughed. "I'm not growing that species yet, but it's a future goal."

"How'd you get into it?" Ezra asked, paying more attention to Rusty than the shadowy coastline he navigated.

The lap of water, the ruffle of wind along the canopy, and the taste of salty sea air were almost hypnotic, especially on a perfectly clear, still night like this.

Rusty slowed the boat, not wanting to call this trip quits just yet. "I moved out to Maine to work as a guide. That wasn't paying the bills, but I heard about a job gathering wild seaweed. Turned out to be a lucrative business. I learned all I could, then moved back home to try it here."

"In Hart's Bay? That's such a great idea." Ezra looked excited even from a few glances through the gloom. "There's already so much knowledge about the ocean from old-timers here. And warehouses and buildings to store the harvest. And it's close to Portland, hippie central, to sell it..."

"Exactly. You just quoted my business plan. If only everyone was so optimistic." Rusty smiled, but it was a bittersweet thought.

"Who's not? They're crazy," Ezra said firmly. "Ignore them."

Rusty's lips twitched, and then he couldn't hold back a laugh. "My parents."

"Oh, shit." Ezra covered his mouth with both hands, then flapped his wrists in Rusty's direction. "I mean, ignore me."

"That would be hard." Rusty snuck him a sideways glance and grinned as the truth slipped out without him really meaning it to.

He didn't know how to interpret his fascination with Ezra, but at least he knew he hadn't been steered wrong by it. He'd found a firm friend already.

"But no, you're right. I'm going to make it work and show them they're wrong." Rusty shrugged, angling the boat toward the harbor at last. "And I can get why they're reluctant to trust the sea for a living again."

Ezra sucked in a quick breath. "Were they caught up in the... collapse?"

Rusty nodded. "Dad worked on one of the Harts' boats. Mom worked in the office of the shipping plant. I keep telling them it's different and there's gold in these waves again, but... I can't blame them."

Ezra quietly nodded and laid a hand on his knee. "Still, I think you're really brave."

Suddenly the windshield was blurry. Rusty blinked a few times as he pulled the throttle back to coast toward the marina.

He couldn't risk a look at Ezra or he might embarrass himself. He loved that Ezra laid his feelings out there without hesitation, but it was also disconcerting.

"Thank you," Rusty finally managed and nodded ahead of them. "Can you grab a rope and stand by the side of the boat without falling in?"

Ezra laughed. "Sure." He bounced to his feet and shuffled to the back of the boat. "Do you want me to jump?"

"No!" Rusty nearly twisted in his seat as he shouted the word. The idea made him panic. He'd have to shut off the engine and dive in after Ezra and hope they didn't get caught under the boat...

It was Ezra's turn to giggle. "Kidding. I wouldn't even try," he assured Rusty. He was beaming. "Thank you for keeping a dumb city boy safe, though."

Rusty waved it off and focused on pulling the boat in for a smooth approach. On a clear day like today, it was easy to glide within inches of the wharf so that all Ezra had to do was reach out and grip the cleat. Then Rusty reversed before shutting off the engine.

He brushed past Ezra as he hopped up onto the dock, took the rope, and wound it around the cleat. He repeated with the bowline and then climbed back down to shrug off his life jacket.

"That was great," Ezra breathed out once he was free of the life jacket. He passed it over and waited for Rusty's hand to climb out.

Okay, Rusty wasn't imagining the tingle that coursed

through him as he took Ezra's waist to boost him out of the boat. That was a new one to him.

Was this... a *crush?*

Rusty's jaw dropped. He nearly dropped Ezra into the water, but instinct saved him. His hold on Ezra was so tight that the redhead squeaked and swatted his hands away as soon as he had his footing on the wharf.

"Sorry," Rusty chuckled, trying to brush off the moment's thought.

No way could it be a crush. But on the other hand, he'd never actually slept with a woman, so... it could explain why he couldn't stay with a woman long enough to go to bed.

"What's up?" Ezra cast him a curious glance.

Shit. Duck and cover, Rusty told himself. He smiled instead, searching for a topic that wasn't *my dick is doing weird things when you smile.* "You like painting nature?"

"Yeah, I sure do."

"I'll take you out to see the area in the daytime, if you want. Hiking, kayaking, that kind of stuff. I do a lot of camping, too." Rusty hardly knew what he was saying. All he knew was that he wanted to see Ezra again.

Maybe it was just a combination of loneliness and responding well to a compliment. Ezra clearly thought he was hot, and who wouldn't be flattered?

Rusty needed to figure these thoughts out, and he couldn't do that from sitting around thinking about it.

"That would be awesome!" Ezra lit up. "Thanks. I really need a different perspective to refresh me right now."

Yeah, Rusty knew the feeling. "My pleasure."

He took Ezra's arm again to walk him up the dock, but this time he was acutely aware of how Ezra's hand on his arm made him feel.

Like he was a big, strong protector and Ezra was the delicate flower he wanted to sweep off his feet and keep safe from the big, bad elements out there.

Maybe it was a platonic, friendship crush. Like when he'd met his favorite coworkers on the job in Maine and gotten to know them and wanted to spend all the time ever around them.

Yeah, Rusty tried to convince himself as they reached the top of the ramp and dry land again. That was probably it.

Still, turning to say goodbye to Ezra made him feel like he was parting ways after a great date.

"Thanks for everything," Ezra told him, smiling. "Let's swap numbers so we can hang out."

Yep. Hang out. Definitely.

After Rusty waved goodbye to Ezra and they climbed into their respective cars, he didn't start his truck up yet. Instead, he sat in the darkness listening to the hum of Ezra's car disappearing around the corner.

The autumn evening had closed in around them while they were on the water. Why did it feel like a bright summer morning, shrouds of long-settled mist finally burning away?

3

EZRA

The bubble popped when Ezra stepped onto the *Welcome All* mat on his front porch.

He was home—and now tonight would be just like any other evening. Supper with his roommates, TV, maybe a board game with lots of shouting and a bottle or two of wine shared amongst them all.

It wasn't *bad*. By all accounts, he and his artist friends were happier sharing this big old house and saving money than they had been struggling to make rent in one-bedroom apartments scattered across Portland. Their new roommate, Benji, was settled in. He'd just taken Jesse's room, since Jesse had moved in with their hunky neighbor.

But now, Ezra had to go back to the real world. No moonlight cruise with his dreamboat glancing at him sideways while their boat cut a clean line through the glassy water.

Ezra's knees went weak again just *thinking* of how romantic that had been. He wanted to squeal and burst through the door and tell his friends every detail.

But he also didn't want to face the reality: that Rusty was just a nice straight guy who'd seen a chance to cheer him up.

Ezra wasn't young and dumb. Well, young but not *that* dumb, anyway. The first rule in gay world was "don't crush on straight guys" for good reason.

The first thing everyone would tell him was not to get his hopes up. Actually, first there'd be a round of teasing, telling Ezra to go get him. And it would only be worse knowing that they were all joking, that the unspoken truth they were dancing around was that it was a fantasy.

So he quietly let himself inside and slipped his shoes off, then bypassed the living room and headed upstairs before anyone could notice him.

A shower would serve a twofold purpose. He could scrub his forearms of the ever-present paint flecks and rub his dick to the memory of Rusty lifting him around effortlessly.

Ezra grabbed two towels and a facecloth from the closet and wrestled his clothes off in the bedroom, wishing with everything that it was Rusty doing just that.

A whimper escaped as he sat on the bed to get his jeans off. He was definitely crushing fast and hard.

You'll forget him by tomorrow, he tried to tell himself. It happened all the time: seeing a hot guy around town, being super into him, and then letting it go.

But Rusty's number was burning a hole in his phone, and he had the promise of future nature expeditions with him. And they'd gotten on so well. Even if it was their first meeting, it had felt like seeing an old friend.

Vibrant voices and laughter trailed up the staircase as he wrapped the towel around his waist and headed for the upstairs bathroom. Their constant presence around each other had only annoyed him for the first week or two. It took getting used to after a reclusive life in his studio loft. But after settling in here, establishing his life and finding his place in the town, Ezra loved this routine.

Now, he found himself biting back a frown of annoyance as he closed the bathroom door and locked it. Ezra sighed as he hung up the towel and turned on the shower water.

They were all unattached so far as he knew. When they'd moved here, they'd all promised each other it was a fresh start. No more complicated romantic entanglements of finding out you were sleeping with your first boyfriend's ex–best friend's one-night stand from last week.

Jesse had broken that rule right away. He'd claimed Finn before they'd even unpacked the pots and pans. But the two of them worked together so well that Ezra couldn't blame him.

Ezra's dream guy wasn't gay, available, and living next door. Didn't mean his imagination couldn't run wild. Life wasn't fair, so he was going to damn well indulge his fantasies.

And with nobody paying attention or banging on the door to get in the shower before work, he could take his time. Maybe with a good pipe-cleaning out of the way, he could look more rationally at Rusty next time he saw him.

Ezra stepped into the hot shower and tipped his head back to let the water run over his face, through his hair and down his body.

Once he was soaked, he pushed his hair behind his shoulders and turned back-on to the stream, gliding his hands down his chest and stomach.

He'd felt Rusty's strong fingers around his waist more than once today. It was all too easy to picture them gliding down from his waist and over his hips, skimming his thighs.

How would he touch Ezra? Gently, conscious of the strength in his hands? Or hard, rough, trusting Ezra to take everything Rusty gave him? Would he be shy, having never been with a man before? Or confident, inexperienced with men but certain of what he wanted from him?

Fuck, Ezra was gone already. His cock was hardening, rising between his legs, thick and hungry now.

He leaned against the shower wall, turning side-on to the stream and closing his fingers around himself. Ezra resisted the urge to start jerking himself fast and hard, trying to draw out the moment even more.

What if they shut the boat off and drifted together under the moonlight? Could he crawl into Rusty's lap, squeeze himself between the wheel and Rusty's body until their cocks lined up and ground together?

Ezra's grip tightened as he imagined stretching his fingers to accommodate a second cock alongside his own. He'd grind himself along the length of Rusty's shaft, the sensitive lengths sparking nerves deep inside each other's bellies.

Rusty would hold him around the waist, one hard arm keeping their bodies crushed together as he grabbed Ezra's hair in a tangle at the back of his head.

He wanted Rusty to haul him in for a kiss, desperate and openmouthed. And he wanted Rusty to fuck him.

God, did he ever.

Ezra's whole body throbbed and thrummed with heat at the visual of himself riding the bigger man's lap, throwing his all into rising and falling on the cock stretching him open.

Rusty pinning him to the wheel, an iron grip on each of Ezra's arms as he rose from his seat so he could hammer into Ezra, hard and fast and unrelenting.

Ezra's cries of pleasure drifting into the night across the ocean, instead of stifled in his throat here in the shower. And Rusty gasping Ezra's name against his mouth, his nails digging into Ezra's skin as he lost control and blew his load deep inside Ezra's hungry, tight little hole.

He bit his lip hard as his body throbbed uncontrollably. He was tipping over the edge now, unable to stop himself.

Ezra's strokes slowed just a bit to milk the sensitive nerve endings, and then he gasped, rolling his head back against the tiles. He spilled his load across the shower floor, squeezing his eyes shut.

Fuck, the heat flooding his cheeks made his whole body burn. It was different jerking off to some imaginary stranger instead of having an actual face and name and *person* to imagine.

As he rinsed himself and the shower, Ezra's knees wobbled for a different reason altogether. But that hadn't broken the connection between them. Quite the opposite, he wanted to see him all the more.

Ezra's mood dropped fast. By the time he made it back to his bedroom, a towel around his waist and another around his hair, he was kicking himself.

There was no way crushing on a straight man ended well. Throwing himself at the nearest man to be nice to him was no better than sacrificing his self-esteem to get laid.

As he blow-dried his hair, someone knocked on the door. It sounded like Beau, judging by the voice. He clicked the blow-dryer off so he could hear them. "Hey, Ez. You comin' downstairs? Dinner's ready."

"Yeah, maybe in a bit," Ezra answered, rubbing a hand down his face. "Pretty tired."

"All right, man. We'll leave leftovers. Take it easy."

"Yeah." Ezra smiled slightly to himself as he listened to Beau's footsteps retreat downstairs. His broad-shouldered, smiling roommate was nothing if not easygoing. He always just wanted everyone to get along.

If Ezra brought his mood downstairs, it would only bring everyone else down. The last thing they needed was to counsel him through his dumb, unrealistic crush.

So he wouldn't tell them about Rusty.

No. Secrecy didn't sit right with Ezra. And it would make it seem like there was something there—a spark of something, a reason they were keeping secrets.

Fine, Ezra decided as he changed into sweatpants. He'd tell them about Rusty but let them know that he was straight. Just so they didn't tease him or get their own hopes up. He could do that. He could have a straight guy friend, right?

Ezra grabbed a T-shirt and shrugged it on, then padded downstairs in bare feet to join the others. No need to dress to impress those who saw him before 9:00 a.m., without coffee in his hand.

Speaking of which, he could grab a drink before he joined the others.

"Hey, it's Ez!" Jesse beamed at him as he reached the kitchen. He was there pouring a glass of wine for himself.

Although their former roommate lived next door with Finn, he came and went from here like a second home. He probably hung out more here than his own living room, unless he and Finn were doing gross couple-y cuddling and movies type stuff.

Ezra smiled back and pulled him in for a hug. "Hey, babe, how's it going?"

"Great. You like your new roommate? He's pretty neat." Jesse pulled back and examined him.

Ezra had been friends with him for long enough that Jesse could tell when something was up, so he made himself smile and shrug off all his thoughts from minutes ago.

"He's great. Yeah, we'll keep Benji," Ezra said with a smile, nodding over his shoulder as the man they spoke about came in. The stained glass artist who had just joined their little art gallery and housing co-op was small, about Jesse's build. He had bright pink dyed hair and a septum piercing. Next into the kitchen was Ross, wearing all black as usual.

"Oh, phew." Benji pretended to faint with relief. "I've passed the trials."

"We'll see how dinner is," Aaron added. He clutched his chest when he saw Ezra, then checked his watch. "The date went that well, huh?"

"He didn't last five minutes. And *not* in bed," Ezra added as Aaron started to grin. He shook a finger at Aaron and twirled to grab himself a wineglass. "He was a dick."

"Oh, babe." Aaron came up for a hug, hovering in place behind him until Ezra's hands were a safe distance away from all the wineglass stems. Then his arms swooped in and he grabbed Ezra.

Ezra laughed. "Nah, it's okay," he assured his roommate as the others filed in and took their seats at the long kitchen table. "It's a good thing."

"No wasted time," Aaron nodded.

"And I made a friend out of it. Not him, someone else. A newcomer to town. Well, he's moved back here."

"*He,*" Aaron repeated meaningfully, raising his brows and looking at the others. A few *oohs* sounded from around the table.

Ezra snorted and pushed his hand back through his still slightly damp hair. He'd prepared himself carefully for this reaction. "Nope. He's straight, and he's *so* not my type. Outdoorsy and everything. He runs a seaweed farm."

"Oh, wow." Finn looked curious, but before he could ask anything, he was interrupted by far more important questions.

"Is he a beardy lumbersexual?" Benji wanted to know.

He came to the kitchen counter to retrieve the tray of enchiladas in the oven.

That made Ezra laugh. "About the opposite, actually." He took his glass of wine to the kitchen table and settled down on the bench.

Beau plopped into a chair, too. "Smelly hipster?"

"Boy next door," Ezra told Beau with a laugh. "Need I remind you he's straight? Can I get to the important part?"

"I guess," Aaron drawled.

Finn saw his chance to ask. "What's his name?"

"Rusty Campbell." He'd put his surname into Ezra's phone, a considerate modern gesture that signaled he was looking for more than one night of fun.

"Oh!" Finn sat up straight. "I think I went to school with him. He was in the grade below me. He's back home now?"

"Apparently. And growing seaweed. I thought that was really cool, and we want to be friends with people that are cool." His friends all nodded. "Entrepreneurs gotta stick together."

"Damn right. Maybe we can sell his seaweed in our gallery!" Jesse exclaimed, sitting up straight.

"Maybe we should ask him before we make business plans for him," Ross reminded Jesse, deadpan as always. "He might not have capacity."

"Oh, yeah." Jesse looked over at him. "Still, that's great. I'm sure we can find a way to support him."

"When my shop opens, if he's selling retail, we can stock it as a snack," Aaron offered.

"Oooh, *my shop*," Ezra teased Aaron again. "Are you opening a new shop? I hadn't heard. Go on."

Aaron flipped him off as the others laughed. He was opening his own coffee place in the new waterfront boutiques in just a few weeks' time. Right now, he spent most of his time either there or using the back workshop of the art gallery to paint furniture or make phone calls.

"How about we host a dinner party?" Ezra suggested, brightening up as the idea occurred to him. That way Rusty could meet his friends, and he was sure they'd all like each other.

Beau was the first to clap in approval. "Yeah, have him over! And Rain and Colt, and Dash..." He was already making a guest list.

Ezra counted spaces at the table. "Yeah, we can just about fit everyone if a few people eat standing up."

It was an excuse to see Rusty again, and to make sure he was fine hanging around a bunch of gay guys. It was one thing being around Ezra, but quite another being part of his everyday life.

It feels like auditioning a new boyfriend, Ezra caught himself thinking before he could stop it.

"This weekend?" Beau suggested. "Like tomorrow night? Is everyone here free?"

Phones came out as people started to text those not sitting at the table.

That left the responsibility of texting Rusty to Ezra. He gulped as he opened a new text message thread. For a wild second, he wondered what would happen if Rusty had given him a fake number.

But no, as he typed out the message in WhatsApp, a profile picture of Rusty appeared. He stopped typing and tapped it to have a look.

Also unreasonably gorgeous. He was wind-ruffled, dressed in a bright jacket and giving the camera a big grin and thumbs-up. It was a goofy, light-hearted photo that just made Ezra's crush-o-meter spin wildly.

Hey. My roommates and I are having a dinner party tomorrow. Are you free?

Ezra pocketed the phone and helped pass plates of enchiladas down the table until they all had enough.

"Hopefully this works," Benji said nervously as he fidgeted with his hair. "I haven't doubled the recipe before."

"Shush, darling. It looks incredible," Ezra assured Benji. "Also, if it fails, we have backup food. Grapes, made better." They all laughed at that one, and Ezra lifted his wineglass in a toast to the chef. "To new beginnings."

Benji beamed back at them, and Ezra's heart jolted as he thought about the other meanings of what he'd said.

To new friendships, he could have said. But he hadn't. He'd said *beginnings*.

Ezra was on a collision course with heartbreak, and he couldn't pull the throttle back. All he could do was close his eyes and brace for impact.

4

RUSTY

Rusty's destination wasn't too hard to find. Nobody used street addresses if you were around here. It was just *the yellow house by the corner with the elm tree*, or, in the case of this shared house, *the place with all the art outside.*

Obviously nobody had given Ezra the memo about skipping addresses, so he'd texted Rusty that morning—12 Oak Lane.

This house really did look a far cry from the aging home that he vaguely remembered along this street. Now, there was stained glass hanging in the front living room window, the roof was cleared of leaves and debris, and the front lawn was trimmed.

There were little glass ornaments and solar lights along the few steps from sidewalk to front porch.

Gorgeous, painted pots sat on the steps with flowers inside—and, on looking around, Rusty spotted the same style of pots on the steps of the place next door.

The number plate hanging next to the doorbell confirmed that this was indeed number twelve, so he raised his hand to knock. It was more polite to try first than a potentially aggressive old doorbell chime hardwired into the ceiling.

No need. The door flew open and Ezra stood there looking radiant in a simple white T-shirt and jeans. His hair was pulled back in a ponytail with strands framing his face on either side.

"Hey!" Ezra beamed at him. "You're here!"

"I'm here," Rusty echoed, raising his hand in a wave. He carried a wine bottle in his other hand. "Uh, I hope you like red."

Ezra laughed in that free-spirited, high giggle that already had the power to make Rusty's spirits lift instantly. "Hon, no wine goes to waste around here. I've never met a bottle I didn't like."

Fuck, he looked nice even in simple clothes, and Rusty suddenly grew self-conscious of his choice. Dark, well-fitted jeans and a collared shirt and tie. He'd figured it was a safe bet in case this was a *dress up* dinner party.

"Never?" Rusty stepped inside and glanced around, instantly relaxing. There were a couple other guys around—nobody in ties, but some in pretty tops or button-down shirts. He didn't feel like as much of a pretentious jerk.

"Well, there's a few bottles in the grocery store I wouldn't talk to unless the place was empty," Ezra conceded, grinning, taking the bottle. "But not this one. Thanks very much. You didn't have to."

"He brought wine!" Someone bounded up and grinned. "We like him already. You must be Rusty?" He shook hands enthusiastically.

"Yeah." Rusty laughed.

"Don't mind my boyfriend." That was Finn Hart—years later, he was still easy to pick out of a crowd. Rusty hadn't seen him since he'd graduated high school. "Rusty! Good to see you again," he greeted, grinning.

Finn had been popular at school, the kind of guy who got along with everyone without even trying. Now he was looking really good as he wrapped an arm around the bouncy, shorter guy's shoulders and grinned. Love suited him, apparently.

"Oh, and I'm Jesse."

"Great to see you, too," Rusty answered, smiling at them both. "Hi, Jesse."

Others approached him and he did his best to remember them—Ross, with black nail polish; Benji, in a shirt as loud as his dyed hair; Aaron, wearing a shirt with *ABC Coffee* embroidered on the breast; Beau, broad-shouldered and enthusiastic as a golden retriever puppy.

Then he stumbled on another familiar face: Rain, Finn's cousin. In the same house as Finn. As far as Rusty knew, the cousins had never been on speaking terms.

Lots of bad blood still ran through the town after the fishery shutdown, and a split in the Hart family was one of those side effects.

Rusty blinked a few times and glanced between them, not sure how to address the situation, or if he should.

Rain just chuckled. "We get that a lot these days. Hi." He reached out for a handshake. "You're looking great. Happy to be home?"

"I am," Rusty admitted, then shook hands with Colt, who sat next to Rain with a possessive hand on his shoulder.

Rain smiled. "Me too. Town's gone through lots of changes."

The Hart family's reunion was one such change, apparently. Good. Life was too short to carry that shit around with you. And Rusty should know; his parents still wouldn't speak any positive things about Floyd, Rain and Finn's grandfather.

They'd forgotten to mention how many gay people were suddenly living here. If Rusty wasn't mistaken, he was the token straight guy in the room, and it was strangely refreshing.

Rusty had never been in a gay space apart from a leather bar in the other Portland—Maine—that he'd accidentally wandered into, thinking it was a hole-in-the-wall restaurant. One glimpse at the bar had set him straight.

"It sure has. You guys started Seaglass Gallery, didn't you?" Rusty settled into the dining room chair that Ezra steered him to, which turned out to be next to Ezra.

Good. He had one friend here already, then, and several guys who had known him before. He was already more relaxed.

"We did!" Jesse waved with a wooden spoon from the kitchen. "Pass this along, baby," he told Finn, passing him some bread as he stirred a pot. "We heard you're a seaweed maestro?"

Rusty's cheeks flushed as he looked at Ezra, who gave him a guilty grin. "Maestro?" He laughed. "Far from it."

"Oh, don't be shy. We don't bite." Aaron fluttered his lashes. "Much. Unless you ask us to."

Ezra cleared his throat and looked over at Rusty. Worry was written over his face.

Rusty shot him an amused glance and grin to try to tell him it was fine. "Okay, well... I moved back here a month ago to start a trial underwater farm. Right now, they don't harvest wild seaweed here like they do in Maine, where I went to work for a few years. I'm trying to bring that here. It could boost the economy, create jobs, and give us tasty sustainable food all at once."

That was his elevator pitch. It needed work, he'd be the first to admit.

"That's so cool!" Finn reached out for a high five. "I love seeing people coming home."

"Did you stay here?" Most people their age fled the town quickly, but Finn had a special attachment to the place.

"Yeah." Finn passed him the salad bowl as they started to serve themselves. "Not a lot has happened up until... well, a few months before you arrived. Things are changing fast now."

Other conversations started up, too, while Finn caught him up on the recent town news.

Before long, Rusty lapsed into silence so he could just watch and listen while he ate. The creamy sweet potato casserole was delicious and the company even better.

"Can you believe that customer today?" A few of them shook their heads at each other.

"What happened?" Rusty asked. That opened the door for stories of terrible customers—but they quickly switched to talking about their favorite customers and sales, which segued into discussing their crafts.

It was cool to hear about so many arts. They all seemed to respect each other's crafts, too. There was no *it's easier to do that than what I do* stuff going on.

"Oh, you know the people who came in for wedding favors?" Ross spoke up. "They asked me if I'm a wedding photographer." He rolled his eyes. "I've done a few, but I wanted to leave that behind."

"But man, it pays so well." Benji leaned in. "Money helps, right?"

"It does. And it's a wedding here in Hart's Bay, so I don't actually mind." Ross played with the rubber bracelets around one wrist. "They're getting married in the square."

"No way," Finn gasped. "Why?"

"Apparently they met at Cher's."

A chorus of *awwws* went around the table, and Jesse clasped his hands, his eyes sparkling.

It was impossible to miss the rings on his and Finn's fingers. "Hey, are you guys...?" Rusty gestured between them.

"Just engaged," Finn answered, grinning. "So far. We're waiting until the perfect moment for a wedding."

"Shotgun, or planned?"

"We'll see." Finn winked. "Hey, we met in there, didn't we, babe? We should do it in Hart Square, too."

Aaron giggled. "He said, *We should do it in Hart Square.*"

"Oh, shut up, perv." Jesse pretended to throw a napkin at Aaron, who ducked and laughed even louder. Still, there was a sheepish grin on his face as he looked over at Finn.

It was hard to miss, and Beau gasped. "Did you...?"

Rain cleared his throat. "I don't want to know," he announced. "My cousin, guys."

That made them laugh and drop the line of questioning. Instead, Ezra encouraged Beau to describe his latest jewelry piece. Beau was being modest, but Ezra was cheerleading for him. "It's so good, hon! Seriously. You're getting better every year, and you were already stellar!"

Being around a bunch of open, proud gay men in his own hometown for the first time ever was a strangely mind-blowing experience. But at the same time, Rusty found himself intensely jealous as conversation ranged from hot male pop stars to their work days.

He couldn't figure it out. Was it because they were getting to experience this town without the baggage? But

Finn and Rain each had plenty of baggage of their own, and they were contented enough now.

Maybe he was just wishing he could be one of them. They all seemed to have a great household here, and he was living by himself, rattling around a cottage that could easily fit two.

That must be it, Rusty figured. He was lonely and looking for friends.

Friends like Ezra. The redhead was sparkling when he was around all these people, nothing like the desperate, lonely man he'd caught a glimpse of in the bar. But they *were* the same person, separated by just one day.

What was the difference? The question captivated Rusty. Here, he was facilitating others' happiness, confident but sweet, making sure people felt included. Rusty had already noticed him use pet names three or four times in this conversation.

"So, how'd you like the casserole?" Benji was sitting on Rusty's other side, and he spoke up to catch Rusty's attention. They'd finished their meals and cleared the plates, and now they were drinking—most of them wine, a few drinking beer.

"It was great. Was it yours?" Rusty answered. He had really liked it; it wasn't just a polite white lie.

"No, but I'll take the credit." Benji smirked. "Nice and creamy, just the way I like it."

Rusty had expected this—and then wondered if he was egotistical to expect someone in the room to flirt with him. But it still meant he was prepared to smile and nod, pretending it flew over his head. "Nothing like a good casserole."

Not satisfied with this, Benji touched Rusty's arm. Maybe he thought Rusty needed a stronger hint. "Seaweed farming is really cool, though. I like guys who can handle their rope."

Rusty's cheeks flushed. He couldn't pretend he didn't understand that hint. "Yeah?" He laughed. "Sorry, it's a two-man business, and my best friend's straight, too."

"Damn," Benji pouted. "Not even with exceptions?"

Rusty heard Ezra put down his wineglass particularly firmly. He'd tuned into the conversation, then. Rusty just smiled at Benji and nodded.

"You never know. With a few glasses of wine, miracles might happen." Benji winked as he sipped his third glass of wine. He leaned around to look at Ezra. "Spaghetti's straight 'til it's hot. Right?"

"And some people *are* straight, and we shouldn't pester them," Ezra answered, his tone curt.

There was a momentary lull in the conversation, but Beau spoke up loudly. "Should we move to the living room? Start a movie?"

As they all meandered from the open-plan dining room and kitchen to the living room in their own time, standing in gaggles and talking, Rusty checked his phone and pretended to be dismayed by the time. "I might have to duck out early."

"Aw, no," Ezra pouted, and for a moment, Rusty felt guilty.

The last thing he wanted was to cause tension with wine flowing and conversations going. Ezra was annoyed that Benji was trying his luck, but it didn't bother Rusty. In fact, he gave him props for trying. It wasn't Benji's fault that he was so not Rusty's type—in more ways than just being a guy.

Ezra, on the other hand...

Okay, it wasn't just about Benji. He needed to get home before the wine made him do something he regretted. And he really did have an early morning on the water, checking on the lines at low tide.

Rusty shook his head and smiled. "I'm sorry. It's been a great evening. But the tide waits for no man."

"I don't want you half-asleep—or hungover—on the water," Ezra said immediately, nodding. "I get it. Let me walk you to the door."

Rusty ducked into the living room to wish them all good-bye, smiling at them. He'd had such a good time this evening that he already hoped he'd be invited back.

"You'll come around again, right?" Beau piped up hopefully.

"Yeah." Aaron nodded. "We can always fit another at the table. Just like I can always fit another—"

"*Anyway*," Ezra spoke up loudly as the others laughed, cutting Aaron off. He grabbed Rusty by the arm. "I'll rescue you from my so-called friend here."

Aaron pouted but waved, settling into conversation with the others over what movie to choose.

As they stepped outside onto the porch, Rusty smiled at Ezra. "Thank you for inviting me over. I had such a good time."

Ezra was in his socks on the porch, shifting from foot to foot. But he wasn't rushing back inside or anything. "Yeah? I'm glad. I was worried. Thank you for coming."

"Oh, it was my pleasure." Rusty wasn't sure if he should go in for a hug, a handshake, or what. "My weekends are usually pretty boring."

"Well, next time you want to liven one up..." Ezra offered a grin. "You know where to come."

"That or I'll steal you away," Rusty offered.

Oh, God, his mouth was doing that thing again. The

thing where it moved and made words before he thought through the implications of them.

Like being in the wilderness, all alone, with this man who had worked his way under Rusty's skin so quickly.

Sure, he'd enjoyed being around the others, despite the strange jealousy he felt. But he hadn't reacted to their every move all night the way he had Ezra's.

It had been easier when they'd sat next to each other at the table because everyone was around, and conversation was distracting. But out here on the porch, just the two of them, Rusty's heart did that crazy little *flipping* thing again. It was harder to ignore now.

"If you still want to. I hope we didn't scare you off early," Ezra added with a tentative smile. "I didn't get as much of a chance to talk to you as I wanted."

Oh, man. Far from it. Rusty shook his head. "Oh, no! Not at all. I can't blame him for trying," he said with a wink. He still wanted to spend more time around just Ezra, though. "How about we go on a hike tomorrow when I'm back from checking the lines? If you're off work. It's a little quieter, as far as... you know, talking. Tonight was pretty crazy."

Right answer. Ezra bounced up onto his toes, his grin back. "Yes! I can make that work."

"That's great. Yeah, that'll be fun." Rusty reached out for a handshake to seal the deal, but Ezra had already surged toward him to fling his arms around his neck for a solid hug and cheek kiss.

It doesn't mean anything, Rusty had to remind himself as his body surged with heat. *He's a guy. You're straight. Don't take your loneliness out on him.* Taking advantage of Ezra would make him feel rotten.

So he peeled himself away with a grin and a wave, and

strode for his truck before he could do anything really dumb like kiss Ezra on the cheek in return.

Tonight's dinner had left him with far more questions than answers. But at least he had more friends now, so as long as he kept showing up, maybe his loneliness would subside.

Then, he could find a nice person to date—a girl, like he'd been dating since high school—and avoid hurting anybody in this equation.

Yes. That was a good plan.

5

EZRA

If it was dumb to crush on a straight guy, it was epically dumb to snap at his new roommate for teasingly flirting with him. Roommate harmony didn't lie that way.

The jokes were no worse than he and his friends made all the time. But something about the teasing had rankled, and Ezra knew exactly what it was.

Jealousy.

But Rusty had offered up the perfect solution last night when he'd offered to go out for a hike after work. They'd get to see each other for the third time in three days.

This time, Ezra and Rusty would be alone again. Plenty of time to solidify that friendship bond until nobody could get between them. And Ezra would get to experience something Rusty loved.

More importantly, a little exposure to the outdoorsy lifestyle would probably kill Ezra's crush.

He already knew he was no match for Rusty. He tripped over cracks in the sidewalk, let alone tree roots. He owned five pairs of Converse and no hiking boots. Most of his shirts were cotton, not special magical sweat-wicking stuff.

As he waited for Rusty to swing by and pick him up, Ezra chewed his lip. He stared at his feet again. He'd chosen his pair of Docs, which at least had some ankle support, but were his heaviest shoes by far. His thighs were going to feel this later.

Too late to doubt himself, though. There was a honk outside, summoning him from the house.

Ezra had packed a sandwich, apples, and chips along with a bottle of water into a little backpack. That made him feel prepared, even if he was hopelessly dreading the exercise part of this outdoor stuff.

The pickup truck pulling up outside the house made Ezra beam. He scurried down the path, doing his level best to look excited for the walk, rather than for the chance to see Rusty again. He levered himself into the truck.

Oh, God. There went his heart, all pitter-patter at the sight of Rusty in a clingy gray T-shirt. A V-neck shirt at that, which just led Ezra's eyes down to the muscles the shirt clung to.

And he looked *hot* in trail pants, the loose canvas kind that made most people look like tents.

This is not fair.

"Hey! All ready to go?"

Ezra didn't miss the dubious look Rusty cast at his outfit. He'd ditched jeans, at least, and chosen long pants. He had a few plaid long-sleeved shirts for painting, so he'd layered the cleanest one over an old T-shirt.

It wasn't trail gear, but it would have to do. He was painfully aware that he looked more like an artist about to head to the harbor than a hiker.

"You didn't have to drive," Ezra assured him with a

smile. He could have been down at Cher's bar in a five-minute walk.

"We'll see if you say that on the return trip." Rusty winked as he steered the truck for the waterfront. "How was your night?"

"Pretty good," Ezra said. "We watched a bunch of stuff on Netflix. Nothing good was on, so we just skipped between channels every time someone got bored and put together our own storyline. It's avant-garde TV."

"Sounds exciting," Rusty teased. "An art statement?"

Ezra chuckled. "Yeah. About the impermanence of broadcast media... or something."

Rusty parked in the big lot between the art gallery and the boutiques, and the two of them climbed out.

"I see you brought food? Water?" Rusty checked with him, circling around the truck hood.

"Yep!" Ezra beamed, wiping his damp palms against his legs.

Oh, man. He couldn't shake the feeling that this was a bad idea. His last time going on a hike had ended in tears at age twelve because he'd tripped over roots. His parents had decided that being outdoorsy was a good solution for an introverted child who hid in his room making art instead of socializing. That hadn't lasted long.

They walked in front of the gallery toward the start of the coastal path, which lay between the other end of the building housing the gallery and Cher's End Table.

You get to spend time with Rusty, Ezra reminded himself. And that had been lots of fun in the boat. It would be even more fun on the trail, where Rusty didn't have to worry about navigating big rocks that could smash up the boat. Right?

"How were the lines today?" Ezra asked as they

mounted the path to the coast. It was a sharp climb from harbor level to the cliffs that lay to the northwest of the town.

He'd managed this much, but he'd never gone beyond the rocky beach below where the town sometimes held barbecues. Not even to the sandy beach they'd pass along this hike, where the surfers hung out. No point in going there until the surfer boys arrived in the spring.

Rusty chatted about seaweed spores and all kinds of things Ezra didn't understand, but sounded like promising signs. From what he gleaned, the seaweed was growing well.

"How fast does it grow, anyway? Are we talking harvest in the spring?"

"Early spring," Rusty nodded. "Or late spring. And then we see how the harvest is."

"And you find out if you get to do it again next year?" Farming was a rough business, no matter whether on land or sea. Ezra offered a smile.

Rusty chuckled. "Yep. Hopefully I at least make enough to cover my living costs and business startup. Then I can start scaling up. If it's a bust... well." He sighed. "There's always a job waiting for me in Maine."

That was a jolt to Ezra's system.

Right. Not everyone arrived here and just *stayed*. The business could well crash, based on a hundred factors nobody could control. And if it did, Rusty couldn't just hang out here because it was a nice place.

They weren't even past the cliffs before Ezra started to sweat. His boots felt too heavy already, and he was out of breath trying to keep up with Rusty's pace. But he was damned if he was going to complain about it.

"The wild harvest is a great business in Maine, but the permits just aren't in place yet here." Rusty was chatting blithely, seemingly happy to share all the details. Ezra took in about half of them, when he wasn't trying to catch his breath.

Ezra nodded, smiled, and sweated as the burn in his lungs grew worse, and his thighs shouted at him for missing leg day every week this decade.

Oh, God. He was actually dying.

No, Ezra told himself, biting his lip. He wasn't going to be overdramatic about it. He could survive this, one minute at a time, and impress Rusty. And that mattered to him, for some reason that probably had more to do with his heart than his ego.

"Oh, here's a nice view—oh! Are you okay?" Rusty finally slowed as he reached a nice, scenic lookout place and looked over at him.

Ezra braced his hands on his thighs after waving him off. Okay, his lungs were seriously burning and he hadn't said a word in fifteen minutes, but he could keep up.

He dabbed at his forehead with his sleeve.

"Oh, no. Let me know if I'm going too fast." Rusty's face crumpled as he reached for Ezra's shoulder. "Let's stop for a breather."

"Yeah." Ezra wiped the sweat away and tried for a cheerful smile. Disappointment already prickled at him, though.

He'd known *logically* that he couldn't keep up with Rusty, and that alone made them a bad match—apart from the pesky incompatible sexualities. But experiencing it himself was a bitter pill to swallow.

I bet Benji could keep up. Ezra's brain chose the worst possible time to remember that he'd talked about going on hikes with his college friends.

"Sit down for a minute and enjoy the view." Rusty still sounded concerned, and it only made Ezra feel more guilty.

"Yeah." Ezra sat, taking the water bottle that Rusty passed him. Even his hands were tingly and flushed, like his body was desperately pushing sweat out of every available surface. Oh, man. Before long he was going to be a smelly mess.

This was why nature was a terrible idea. Much better on canvas than in person. At arm's length, where it wasn't full of biting insects and hills and other enemies.

"It's okay. We can take it at your speed," Rusty said with a friendly smile, but it only drove the knife in Ezra's gut home. "Don't stress."

I want to be a better match for him. And he wasn't that guy, and he couldn't be. None of the things that were different between them were things he could change.

He wasn't going to magically *like* dragging himself up hills and through woods, no matter the company. And he wasn't going to magically become whatever kind of woman Rusty went for.

Probably outdoorsy, Lycra-clad, and perky.

Tears sprung to Ezra's eyes. He gulped water and passed the bottle back. Even his hand was shaking with exertion. "You know, I think I should turn back and... go have a breather. I've seen this view."

He waved at it, even though he couldn't describe it for his life. He'd spent this whole rest break sweating and guilty.

"I want to get it down on paper before I forget."

"I get that. I could go back with you." Rusty smiled cheerfully. He wasn't even a little bit mad at him. Even though he was ruining a perfectly nice plan for a day out.

Damn it, why was he so *nice*?

Ezra waved Rusty off. "No, don't let me hold you back. You wanted to go hiking. You keep going. It's only a few minutes back."

"Yeah?" Rusty eyed him like he wasn't sure if he'd fall off the cliffs without supervision.

Ezra laughed, the sound forced to his own ear. "We're practically spitting distance from home." He grabbed his backpack and shouldered it, wincing as his lower back protested. Even his heels hurt from his damn boots.

"Still, let me walk you to the door, so to speak." Rusty leapt to his feet, his expression eager.

But that only made Ezra feel worse. Little did Rusty know how much he wished this were a date—and how glad he was that it wasn't. At least this way he was disappointing himself more than Rusty.

He wanted Rusty to leave him alone so he could wallow, damn it. He swallowed the heat of anger at himself for not being a good enough hiker to even go on one stupid little trip. "No, no. Seriously. I'll see you later."

Rusty slowly sat down, now frowning. He was gazing at him with those sweet, earnest eyes. "If you're sure..." He hesitated. He clearly wanted to walk him back, but Ezra didn't want Rusty to see him getting so mad at himself.

Ezra offered a smile, hoping the water building in the corners of his eyes didn't show. "Yeah, it's cool. Catch you later."

He headed back the way they came, emotion choking his throat.

Damn it, why did he have to be such a pain in the ass? Ezra was normally proud of who he was—high-maintenance moments and all—but right now, he hated it.

And he hated his own temper, which had held him back more than his own exhaustion.

For that matter, he hated this stupid path and its stupid tree roots and rocks and steps.

He kicked a root on the way by. At least his Docs

shielded him from that. Actually, that felt kind of nice, taking the pressure off the spot of his heel that was rubbing the boot.

As he walked, he kicked random objects—a boulder here, a tree trunk there—to give himself a moment's relief. It already felt like it was forming a blister. He limped by the time the final grassy slope was in sight.

Ezra burst through the side door of the art gallery, but nobody was back there to witness the dramatic entrance. Stupid Sunday and most of his roommates taking the day off work.

Beau poked his head through the door that separated the gallery and workshop. He took one look at Ezra and gasped. "Ez?"

"I don't want to talk about it."

If he did, Ezra might spill things he didn't want to say to anyone. It was bad enough he was letting them take over his own fantasies. He didn't need his friends knowing about his weakness for straight men with muscles and sweet smiles.

"Okay," Beau said softly. "Want a hug, or want me to leave you alone?"

Ezra pouted for a few moments and shook his head. "I'm pissed off. I might bite."

Beau backed off and raised his hands. "Fair enough. Let me know." He retreated and let the door swing closed behind himself as he went.

"Will do, babe." Ezra let his breath rush out in a sigh once that door closed, too, leaving him alone in the big, concrete-floored, empty space.

Thank God. Ezra was a sweaty, grumpy, pissed-off mess.

On the bright side, that gave him raw emotion to fuel into work. Pouring his emotions onto canvas was the ultimate drama queen move, but it was all he could think to do with them.

Ezra swiped at his eyes with the side of his hand and grabbed a small canvas so he didn't waste too many supplies if this was an incoherent mess.

Grays, blues, and purples. The palette was obvious.

The subject, though, wasn't the coastal view he'd told Rusty about. It was the ultimate in melodrama, but Ezra pulled his phone out, switched to selfie mode, and snapped.

Ouch. He *was* a fucking mess right now.

He fought the instinct to delete the photo, to self-edit and present himself in a better light. No, that wouldn't be cathartic. What he needed was to own up to himself.

He was owning his messy, gritty emotions: jealousy and bitterness dragging down his self-esteem.

Ezra set his phone down on the chair nearby and started working in broad brushstrokes. This wasn't going to be a detailed picture. Messy strokes to capture his jaw, the twist of his mouth, the furrow of his brow, the clenched lines near his eyes holding back tears.

The man who took shape on the canvas was a side of Ezra he hadn't fully acknowledged before Rusty had rescued him at the bar. It didn't even look like him, but it was.

This was the guy who would throw himself at an unavailable man, make a pain in the ass of himself, and run away from the mess.

That was it. More than anything, Ezra was worried he'd tanked the friendship. Or, worse, that it would just slowly dwindle into nothingness now that Rusty knew that he wasn't lying about being a hopeless city boy.

Rusty had looked at him with such admiration in the boat when he'd walked around without fear. But that had been different.

There was a quiet knock on the door. Ezra barely budged, mumbling, "Yeah?" He let a few more strokes of color fill in the dark, swirling background.

"Hey." The voice wasn't Beau's. It was Rusty.

Ezra spun on his heel, suddenly conscious of the paint streaking his cheeks and hands. Painting wasn't a neat and clean business. Especially this kind, pressing the brush hard against the canvas to let tiny droplets spatter across the surface.

With his back facing the door, so was the canvas. Rusty's gaze fell on it, and he froze in place, looking between it and Ezra.

Ezra cringed.

Oh, God. Could a hole in the floor open up and swallow him now? This had to be more self-indulgent than running to Twitter to post quotes of sad lyrics after a tiny thing went wrong in life.

But Rusty didn't laugh or roll his eyes or even sigh. Instead, he tilted his head. "Oh, wow. Can I...?"

It took Ezra a moment to realize he was asking permission to come into his workspace. He swallowed hard and nodded, setting the palette aside and trying to wipe his hands clean on his shirt. "Yeah. Um. Come in."

"Oh. That's you. Wow."

"Yeah." It was impossible to deny it. Ezra made a grab for his phone, locking and pocketing it before Rusty could get a look at the original photo. He sank onto the now-vacated chair and checked his palms, then rubbed his face.

Rusty shook his head slightly, but it wasn't judgmental. He actually had that expression of wonder on his face again. "That's so cool. Even if... um, it looks a little upset."

The strokes were still broad and messy, so Ezra could have argued the point, but the colors, the mood, the unfiltered emotion… was impossible to ignore. "A bit. Sorry. I can be a drama queen."

Rusty grinned. "No, it's fair. I came to apologize. I dragged you on a vigorous hike for a first-timer, and I didn't even think about slowing down. That was dumb of me. That's why I'm a terrible guide."

At least that made Ezra's nervousness subside. He smiled back. "You are?"

"Yeah. Why do you think I had to get into my business?" Rusty chuckled. "No tourists to lose track of. Just yourself, the sea, and the boat."

Ezra smiled, rising to his feet to approach Rusty. With the air between them clearing, his mood started to rise. "I'm sorry I was such a city boy. And that I ran away to come, uh… paint and cry about it."

Rusty just shook his head. "It's a healthier way of coping than drinking over at Cher's. And you make something out of it. I just go grumpily drive the boat around until I calm down."

"Really?" Ezra laughed, picturing Rusty scowling through the windshield and doing donuts on the water. "I mean, I guess so."

Rusty put his hand on Ezra's shoulder, and the weight was solid and distracting. "How about we try something else? Like kayaking? You liked being on the water." He bit his lip. "If not, I'll just take you out in the boat more."

Oh, yeah. Take me in your boat. Ezra blushed. Damn it, he was turning into Aaron, seeing innuendo at every opportunity. He managed not to say it out loud. "Yeah? You wouldn't mind?"

"Not at all. That'd be fun." Rusty looked relieved. "So, we're good? I haven't killed you? Or pissed you off?"

"No!" Ezra exclaimed. He breathlessly laughed. "I thought I'd pissed *you* off."

Rusty shook his head and opened his arms. "Hug it out?"

Ezra gladly stepped into his arms and squeezed him back, pressing his face into Rusty's shoulder.

Pressed so close to Rusty, all the tension rushed out of Ezra's body. It was like exhaling after holding his breath underwater.

And it was addictive. One breath only made him want more, so he clung to Rusty, wondering how long he could hold on before it got weird.

He wanted to tuck himself against Rusty's body and fit into every curve and crevice until they fit together like a salt-and-pepper shaker set.

Damn it, why hadn't he just stopped to talk to Rusty? He'd been so desperate to impress him that he hadn't wanted to risk seeing his reaction.

Well, no more. He was noticing that side of himself now—it was impossible not to when it was painted on canvas right there for all to see.

Ezra pulled away and smiled. "Kayaking," he promised with a nod. "We'll try that."

"It's a date." Rusty seemed oblivious to his word choice and the way it made Ezra's knees go weak and the blood rush to his ears.

Damn it. This man was going to be the death of him, one way or another. If not from nature, from embarrassment.

It was official: crushes sucked giant octopus balls.

6

RUSTY

This was more like it. As Rusty breathed in the sea air, he smiled at the figure in the front of the two-man kayak. Ezra swayed from side to side on the waves, but so far, he'd kept his balance.

Rusty's week had dragged on almost painfully after the failed Sunday date.

Not *date*-date. Friend-date. Right?

A few days of stormy weather had kept him from bringing Ezra back to the water. In the meantime, he'd texted Ezra every day, making sure his new friend knew that he didn't blame him for not being the hiking type.

In exchange, Ezra was starting to tell him about his roommates' latest antics. It sounded like there was always something interesting going on at the house.

Rusty might drop by that weekend with something special to eat. He wanted to take them up on their offer of an open door.

It was nice to have friends. Even though he and Pascal were starting this business together, his best friend worked as an accountant, so he didn't have much time to spend on the water. The friends he'd made while Rusty was away were fellow accountants—nice, but kind of boring.

Rusty didn't want to crash that friendship group. Weirdly, he had more in common with Ezra's friends than he did with Pascal's. Maybe more in common with Ezra than Pascal.

Ezra wasn't an outdoorsman, but neither was Pascal. When Pascal did come out onto the water with him, he was clearly putting up with the elements for the side income, not because he loved the salt spray on his face.

"This is so cool!" Ezra exclaimed. He stopped paddling, resting it in front of himself as he looked around.

He still tired easily, but that was fine. That was why Rusty had put him in the front of the two-man kayak he'd borrowed from his dad's friend, so that Rusty could steer while Ezra rested. That, and he was lighter.

All Rusty could see of him was his hair sneaking out of the life jacket where he'd tried to trap it, flipping this way and that as he looked around. This time, he'd armed himself with a thick beanie, which was a smart choice.

"You like it?" Rusty was over the moon to share this with him.

It was a whole different way to experience nature—up close and personal, just skimming the surface of the water.

"I love it."

"Would you like to see the farm?"

"We can?" Ezra gasped and twisted to see him, which sent the kayak tipping from side to side. "Oh, shit. Sorry!" He grabbed the edge of the boat with one hand, nearly dropping the paddle.

Rusty burst out laughing. It was a good thing Ezra was so cute. Watching his enthusiasm about everything in life was invigorating. "You won't be able to see much, but if you squint, maybe."

"Okay." Ezra shook his shoulders and arms, then picked up his paddle. "Which way?"

Rusty glanced around for reference points and then steered them with a stroke of his paddle in the water. "There we go. This way."

Only the closest of the lines was within kayak distance. They'd need a boat for the others. But it was still cool to share this with Ezra while they were close by.

"At least it's a warm day," Ezra cheerfully offered, distinctly out of breath. "For almost December now. That'll be a good thing." He squirmed in his seat. "Ow. This seat."

"Yeah," Rusty agreed—the seats in this thing weren't great. He avoided moving too much, though, because that would definitely send them both in. "Why is it a good thing?"

"For when I inevitably—oop!" The boat rocked to the side as Ezra settled again. "Do that! Oh, God. Don't hate me when I send us both in."

"I'm waiting to take the plunge," Rusty assured him, grinning. He steadied them again before dipping his paddle in for another firm stroke. "You don't kayak without getting a cold shower now and then."

Ezra's breathing was heavy, but he seemed to be enjoying himself, unlike their Sunday misadventure. Just seeing him squeak with excitement when a seal popped its nose out of the water made the whole day worthwhile.

"I think that's Lucy!"

"Huh?" Rusty looked around, but there was definitely no other boat around. "The seal?"

"Yeah! Don't you know her? Oh. I guess she might have started coming after you moved away." Ezra reached out and wiggled his fingers at the seal, and all Rusty could imagine was trying to keep the kayak upright if a playful seal decided to buffet them. But the seal slipped under the waves again, and Ezra looked over his shoulder with a pout. "She hangs out at the docks, too."

"Oh!" Rusty wiped the ocean spray and sweat from his forehead and took a moment's break from paddling. Now that Ezra mentioned it, he'd seen a dark shape slipping from the dock into the water once or twice.

It took longer than Rusty had expected to get out to the lines. The two-man kayak was considerably heftier than his own single-man kayak, especially without an equally experienced paddler.

It was more fun, though, because he got to enjoy Ezra's running commentary. He wasn't too breathless today, apparently.

"I didn't know my arms had muscles there. I didn't even know I owned shoulders. Oh, I'm going to be a stacked beefcake after this. Look out for me on the cover of *Men's Health*." He flexed one arm over his head. "You like?"

Rusty grinned. "Yeah. I'll get you to spot me yet."

"I spotted you right away," Ezra countered, his tone light and playful. It was impossible for Ezra to look back at him while paddling, but Rusty could hear the joke in his voice instead. It reminded him not to take Ezra's flirtation seriously.

Part of him didn't want it to be a joke. But it was just fun. Acting on it would make it weird.

Rusty drew a breath of relief. "That orange buoy. Pull up alongside it." He did his level best to steer them as Ezra paddled the wrong way, got caught in a wave, and had to spin around again.

Eventually, with laughter on both their parts, they managed to paddle next to the line.

"Oh, there it is!" Ezra peered into the dark water below. Before Rusty could stop him, he leaned over to get a better look at the rope disappearing deep under the waves.

"Whoa...!" It was too late. Rusty couldn't counterbalance Ezra enough to save them.

In one elegant—if disastrous—flip, the kayak went bottoms-up, dumping them both into the water.

Ezra squealed as soon as he hit the cold water. He kept shrieking in short, breathy bursts as he trod water. "Cold! Water's cold! Freezing! Oooh-ahh-eeeek! My poor nuts!"

Rusty was laughing too hard to keep treading water. He let the life jacket keep him on the water's surface as he grabbed the kayak. "Get your paddle before it floats off."

"My unborn children just retreated deeper into my body than any man has ever gone," Ezra gasped. "Which is saying a lot."

Rusty nearly choked on salt water as he started laughing again. He managed to flip the kayak back over. Then, he calmly instructed Ezra and held it steady while Ezra slithered back in and stretched out to weigh it down.

It took some doing to get himself back in the boat without tipping it all over again, but eventually they managed it while Ezra clung to the buoy to help.

"Okay, I'm upright. You sit up, too," Rusty instructed, and they were back upright, both shivering. "Straight back home, I think. We'll save the farm tour for a steadier boat."

"Fr-fr-freeeezing," Ezra gasped, steadying his paddle across the bow. "That's motivation to paddle hard."

They set off together to head back home. Although Rusty had feared Ezra's mood dropping again after the dip, it only seemed to lift. He was giggling a lot, cold and wet though they both were. He seemed much less self-conscious today, and that was a big relief.

He's going to need warming up later, Rusty thought and then blushed. His house *was* a little closer to the truck. But inviting him inside for a hot shower... well, it sounded like an invitation, didn't it?

Even he gave an exhausted cry of relief once they made it into the calm waters of the harbor. But their task wasn't quite done yet.

They had to work together to get the kayak out of the water. Even though Rusty tried to take more of the weight, Ezra determinedly did his best. It made Rusty smile to see him stagger under the weight while acting casual.

Once the kayak was back on the rack in the bed of his truck, the paddles and life jackets stowed away, Rusty leaned on the side of the truck to catch his breath. "Great job."

"You think? I didn't totally fail by dunking us both?" Ezra laughed breathlessly. He'd knotted his wet hair up into a bun at the back of his head, and he draped along the side of the truck like he was boneless.

"Nah." Rusty offered a hug. "You did great for your first time."

Ezra's wet body made Rusty feel strangely warm. Their clothes clung to them and each other as he moved in to accept the hug. "Been a long time since I heard *that* sentence," Ezra quipped.

Rusty laughed and broke the hug, flicking Ezra's arm. "Oh, behave. In the truck with you. I better get your soaked ass home."

It was an easy, joking way to hide the way his whole body had stirred with interest.

"You wanna come in with me?" Ezra asked casually.

"Most of the guys are probably out, and I can show you my favorite art. The stuff that's not for sale."

Oh, wow. That was a hell of an offer. "Are you sure? I'd love to see what's important to you."

"Well, you just showed me your life." Ezra stood close enough to him that their toes bumped as he shifted his stance. He had his head tipped back to gaze up into Rusty's eyes. "I'd love to return the favor."

Was it Rusty's imagination, or was there innuendo there? *Ignore*, he advised himself again. His sex-starved brain was looking for an opportunity wherever it could get one.

"Thanks. That would be great. I've got a change of clothes in the truck."

"Oooh. Smart." Ezra pulled open the door and scrambled up into the passenger side, and Rusty circled around to get up into the driver's seat. It gave him a few moments to shake the thought and the semi that would be way too noticeable in soaked clothes. Thank God for the cold fabric dampening his responses.

When he climbed inside and looked over at Ezra, he instantly noticed his teeth chattering, his slender arms wrapped over his chest.

"Oh, shit. You're cold."

"I'll be fine," Ezra tried to wave it off, but Rusty shook his head and cranked up the heater in his truck. It was only a few minutes' drive, but it would start him warming up, at least.

He reached out and took one of Ezra's hands, pressing the cool skin between both his own, much warmer, hands. "Jesus. Not much insulation on you." The skin gradually warmed between his palms, and he took Ezra's other hand, too.

"A shower will help," Ezra assured him. His voice was faint, his gaze fixed on Rusty.

Wait, am I coming on to him? Or just helping him out? Rusty caught himself wondering as he let go of Ezra's hand to shift into gear. He'd never grabbed any of his straight guy friends' hands to warm them up after a long day at sea in the dinghy, that was for sure. But with Ezra, he hadn't hesitated.

Thankfully, the drive was so short he didn't have much time to get lost in thinking about that.

Rusty grabbed his bag of spare clothes after shutting off the truck and then followed Ezra onto the front porch as his friend unlocked the door.

"Brrr." Rusty was glad for the burst of warm air that met him in the doorway. Even the brief interlude of heat in the truck made the air outside feel nippy.

When they stepped into the house, Ezra squinted around, leaning to look into the living room. No sign of anyone. "Anyone home?" It was late afternoon now, around four o'clock.

Rusty held his breath and listened for a reply, but they got nothing back.

Ezra smiled and looked up at him. "Home alone. What luck."

"More chance of getting the shower to ourselves, then," Rusty joked. He tried his damnedest to ignore the thought *that* provoked. *Separately,* he wanted to add, but that wouldn't improve the situation. Better to pretend he missed all the implications.

"Come on. Shower's upstairs." Ezra kicked his shoes off. They both laughed when his shoes squelched. "Oh, those will never dry out."

"Sorry. I hope you weren't attached to them. Salt water fucks with shoes really fast." Rusty followed Ezra to the staircase, glancing up and trying to ignore the way Ezra's cotton pants clung to his ass.

"Nah. Those can be my watersports shoes." Ezra's lips twitched, like he was desperately holding back a grin as he looked back at Rusty. His face was the picture of innocence. "So to speak."

Rusty wagged a finger. "You're not going to make me blush, mister." Ezra was a handful, but he was starting to get a sense for him.

"Damn. I'll have to try harder." Ezra led him over to the door at the end of the hall. "I'm in this one. Towels are in the hallway closet. You can have first shower. Be quick, though."

Rusty shook his head. "Not a chance. I'm fine. You're the one freezing." He waved his hands at Ezra as he gingerly sat on the end of his bed.

Ezra shrugged. "Okay, thanks. I'll be fast, then," he promised. "Don't worry about sitting on my bed or wherever."

And then he grabbed a towel from the back of the door and reached to strip his shirt off.

Oh, God. He was getting naked here, in front of Rusty, without a second glance his way.

Of course he was. The laundry basket was in the corner of his room. It would be weird to bring wet clothes to the bathroom and back, wouldn't it?

Rusty sprang to his feet and turned his back on Ezra to make it obvious that he wasn't watching. As much as he kind of wanted to see the lean body highlighted by the drape of wet fabric...

That wasn't a very platonic thought.

Instead, Rusty studied the art on the wall next to his bed, arms folded. He could barely register what it *was*, his thoughts were so distracted by the sight he knew was behind his back.

"I'll tell you about the art in a minute," Ezra promised, and as much as he wanted to, Rusty didn't dare glance back.

"Yep." Rusty focused on it for the first time when he heard the door close behind Ezra.

It was a large landscape, much bigger than the piece he'd seen in the workshop. A couple of feet in each direction, taking up the middle of one wall. A meadow at the end of autumn, dots of color forming bright bursts of colorful flowers among dried grasses. The late-summer sun sank toward the horizon, oranges and yellows in the sky fading to pinks. Or was it rising? He couldn't tell.

Other pieces decorated the walls: portraits, landscapes, object studies. Not just paintings, either. There were sketches in pencil and charcoal, and what looked like a half-finished drawing of a cottage. Yet even though it was only half-drawn, the cottage not even fully on the page and no background at all, it was up on the wall. It must mean something to Ezra.

"Your turn."

The voice made him jump and glance around. Ezra was back, a towel wrapped around his waist, his hair sleek and all swept around to drape over one shoulder. And his chest was bare, water droplets trickling down to his abs.

He gave Rusty a grin. "Go on, shoo. Give me a minute to prepare my curator's notes about all this." He walked into the bedroom and over to the dresser, pulling open a drawer.

Go. Now. It was a sensible thought, and Rusty obeyed instantly. "Thanks," he said over his shoulder and shut the door behind himself.

As he found the hall closet, he shook his head. He'd left

his bag of clothes in there, but he could deal with that in a minute.

He needed to get out of these wet clothes and into a hot shower first. And away from a half-naked man who was doing things to him that he'd never expected from another man.

By the time he made it back to the bedroom, Rusty was thinking much clearer. It helped that he heard Ezra rattling around in the kitchen downstairs, so he was alone in Ezra's room to get dressed.

A minute later, as Rusty sat on the bed to pull his socks on, footsteps came up the stairs. "Are you decent?"

"Not bad, I've been told," Rusty raised his voice to answer, grinning at the closed door. It wasn't strictly true—he'd never tested it out with anyone—but he wasn't about to admit that and have Ezra laugh at him. *With* him was much better.

Ezra laughed. "Well, you'll need to give me a hand."

"Oh." Rusty scrambled to his feet and pulled open the door. Ezra stood there with two mugs of coffee clutched in one hand, a plate of cookies balanced on the other.

"Snack delivery." Ezra flourished his hands.

"Oh my God." Rusty stood aside so Ezra could get by and left the door open. "I'm getting the VIP treatment."

"I always spoil my gallery visitors," Ezra joked. He set everything down on the dresser, where Rusty carefully took a mug of coffee and a cookie from the plate.

"Okay, so this one..." Ezra waved his mug at the large landscape that had first caught Rusty's eye. "It's a place near my grandparents' old house. It was a little ways inland.

There was this pretty field nearby. I used to go there at sunrise and pick berries."

That explained the berry bushes, thick and dark in the foreground. "Oh. I wasn't sure if it was sunrise or sunset." Now that he studied it, sunrise made more sense.

"Which did you think first?" Ezra asked. He dunked a cookie into his coffee mug.

"Sunset. Is this like a glass half-full or half-empty test?" Rusty smiled sheepishly.

Ezra chuckled. "I wasn't sure myself, after I'd painted it. I'd like to think every sunset brings a sunrise in the end, too."

Rusty stood there as the meaning of Ezra's words sank in, his gaze wandering over the details of every little brush stroke. "Yeah. I think so, too."

One piece at a time, Ezra talked about people he'd known in the portraits, or the feelings he'd been trying to capture. He didn't talk about every piece, but Rusty hadn't expected that.

And then he reached the half-finished cottage piece. Ezra hesitated, his gaze fixed on the page. When he finally looked at Rusty, his lips were downturned. "And then there's this one."

Rusty sank onto the bed and put his coffee mug on the bedside table. "Yeah?" He hoped he sounded encouraging. Who lived in that cottage? What was the story?

Ezra sat next to him, twisting his hands in his lap. "I wanted to show my idea of Heaven. But it hurts too much to finish yet. I always mean to, and I can't do it when I try."

"Oh." Rusty sucked his breath in. The piece was sketchy, like it was taking shape. But now that he looked at it afresh, it could be that the artist's mind wasn't sure what to put on the page.

"My little brother, Jon, died in a hit-and-run car accident

fifteen years ago." Ezra's voice was quiet. "I got into art therapy afterward to deal with it, and then... I fell in love with art and just kept going."

Rusty's jaw dropped. His whole heart squeezed in an ironclad fist. He simultaneously wanted to hug Ezra and hurt whatever asshole had torn apart his family. "Fuck. Oh, man. I'm sorry, Ezra."

Ezra scooted closer, until their thighs touched. "No, it's okay."

His body language didn't match his words. Rusty followed his heart instead of his head and slid an arm around Ezra. He'd had no idea about the tragedy in his past, but then, how could he? Ezra seemed so sweet and easygoing.

It was the right choice. The breath rushed from Ezra, and he melted into Rusty's hold. He slid his arms low around Rusty's hips, resting his forehead on Rusty's shoulder.

A moment later, he pulled away and smiled up at him.

Something crackled between them—a kind of intimacy that Rusty had never experienced before.

Could this be platonic? Or was it shaping into something more? Rusty wasn't sure what to think at all.

Rusty and Pascal had never had the kind of heart-to-heart moments he'd already shared with Ezra. But maybe it was like the way Ezra used pet names for people. Maybe it was an Ezra thing, not a *them* thing.

The door banged downstairs, and both of them jumped and laughed. Rusty's sounded nervous to his own ear, and he stood up quickly.

"Thanks, man. That was really sweet of you to share. Hug it out?"

"Yeah." Ezra smiled back at him and stood up to squeeze him back. This hug was a little more forceful, like any buddies sharing a moment together. "Let's head downstairs and see who that is."

Rusty nodded, but as they left Ezra's room, he couldn't help sneaking one more look at those two pieces—the landscape, full of promise for a new day, and the cottage, looking like one of those promises half-fulfilled.

Ezra was much happier today than he had been last weekend. If only Rusty could say the same. If he could just get a handle on what *this* was, he'd be a hell of a lot happier.

But the more time they spent together, the more boundaries seemed to be blurring. Every conversation brought them together in a whole new way, like a row of dominoes. So where the hell did it lead?

And where did he want it to lead?

7

EZRA

"More seagulls than that. Splatter the wall with little white streaks, like my Saturday night."

Aaron sailed past Ezra, on his way to the stockroom with enough rolls of paper towels balanced in his arms to make a nose-high stack.

"I'll consider your request," Ezra answered, rolling his eyes at Aaron's retreating laugh.

He put down his paintbrush and stepped back for another look at the landscape unfolding across the wall.

Walls were a very different surface to work on than canvas. It had taken some trial and error to figure out the best way to paint local scenes in the backs of each unit of the new boutiques.

He'd saved Aaron's until last, but each mural had taken a little longer than he'd expected. He was pushing his timing now. With nine days until the grand opening, there was barely time for the paint to dry and all the fixtures below that wall to be put in place.

The mural was only half-done. Right now, the right half

of the landscape extended in faint pencil outlines, not yet filled in with the first wash of colors, much less finished.

But Ezra's hand was cramping, so he took a minute to shake it out. He rubbed his thumb into the muscles near his pinky, strolling around the shop.

Having already needed some hasty paint thinner application earlier that day, Ezra was careful not to lean on anything. His smock got the worst of it, but there were always flecks, and Aaron had nearly cried when blue paint smudged on the black countertop.

The atmosphere was tense. He could hear hammering and drilling from the other units as all the owners got their shops ready to go for the last weekend of November.

Movement in the harbor caught Ezra's eye as he approached the front door.

The view from here was wonderful now that they'd added a patio in front of the boutiques. The gates and docks had been cleaned up just enough to make them rustic, rather than decrepit.

The powerboat approaching looked familiar. There was just one guy driving it—and it didn't take him long to confirm that it was Rusty.

As Rusty moored, Ezra followed a whim and took out his phone for a few snapshots of him getting out of the boat, crouching next to it to moor up. That would make a hell of an atmospheric subject for a piece.

A strange part of him didn't want to share, like Rusty was his alone to watch. But the artistic merits were hard to argue. With a lower perspective, silhouetting him against the sky...

Ezra's knees went weak at the thought of Rusty silhouetted above the frame. He brought his fingers together to alter the framing in his imagination. Maybe cut out the other boats, just a hint of the cleats poking up from the bottom of the frame.

"Dude, really?"

Aaron's joking tone turned strained all too fast these days. He was standing at the stockroom door, his arms folded as he glared at Ezra.

"What?" Ezra defended himself, pocketing his phone and mirroring him.

Aaron scoffed and shook his head, moving to the boxes piled on the other side of the coffee shop. His latest supply delivery had to get packed away so they could keep laying flooring. "It's nine days to go."

"I know. You told me that today, four times. This makes five." Ezra strode back to the painting, narrowly missing Aaron's arm as he flung it out in a gesture toward the window.

"And yet you're taking creep shots of hot unavailable guys for your spank bank?"

"Whoa." Ezra whirled to frown at Aaron. That was not okay. "I'm not creeping on him. It's an art reference."

"Yeah, sure." Aaron rolled his eyes. He brushed past him and grabbed a box, then spun on his heel to bring it to the stockroom, still talking. "That's why you leap down Benji's throat every time he talks to Rusty."

"So? You ogle every guy who comes within a hundred feet," Ezra snapped. Aaron telling anyone off for paying attention to men instead of work was rich.

"Yeah, and you don't see me down there on my knees right now," Aaron called from the stockroom.

Ezra rolled his eyes and picked up his brush, shaking out his wrist. "Yeah? Maybe you should be. Get some stress out of your system."

"Stress? I can't imagine *why* I'm stressed." Aaron glided

past again with a dramatic flourish. "Only opening the first shop I've ever owned, nooo biggie..."

Ezra drew a deep breath and let it out, resisting the urge to poke Aaron with the paintbrush. It wouldn't help matters.

Aaron wasn't himself, and he *was* under a ton of pressure, so he wouldn't hold it against him. But he needed to lay off. "I promised I'd get it done on time. Hey. Come here, hon," he gestured.

"Don't have time to talk, or breathe, or sleep..." Aaron grumbled in a nonstop stream, mostly to himself, but he did put down his box and approach.

Ezra tilted his head and waited for Aaron to stop talking. Then, he opened his arms for a hug.

Aaron groaned, but he surged forward to grab Ezra in a hug, swaying back and forth with him. "I'm sorry," he moaned. "I don't want to be a dick. But I am."

"You, not wanting dick? Unheard of," Ezra teased, and that got a little laugh out of him, at least. He rubbed Aaron's back. "You'll open on time. You've got tons of people to help in the last few days if need be."

"I know." Aaron squeezed him tightly. His voice was already more level, his breathing less frantic. "Sorry. I trust you to get things done on time. It's just... the what-ifs going around my head." He wiped his eyes and pulled back to dig a tissue out of his pocket. "Ugh, I'm a hot mess."

Ezra nodded and kept a hand on Aaron's shoulder. "Least you're a hot mess. Instead of an ugly-crying mess like me. How dare you pretty-cry? I go all splotchy."

Aaron laughed again, dabbing at his eyes with the tissue. "Everything I do is pretty. Even douching."

"*Dude!*" Ezra shoved Aaron's chest, and his friend laughed—a full, real laugh—for the first time all day. "I didn't need to... oh, God. Now I want to wear shower sandals."

"I didn't say I do it in *our* house," Aaron snickered. "That's what portable kits are for."

Ezra whined and pressed the heel of his hand into his forehead. "I regret this conversation already."

"Delicious regret. Just what I live for." Aaron's steps were lighter as he grabbed a box. "Speaking of which, I'm sorry I brought Rusty into it."

That was an unexpected apology. Ezra stopped just as he balanced his palette on his hand again and looked over. "Oh? I mean... thanks?"

Aaron caught his eyes for a moment in passing and just nodded, not saying anything more.

Ezra's gut tightened, and he turned back to the wall to start dabbing more seagulls across the sky in tiny, swishing strokes. Had the others noticed the way he reacted to Rusty?

God, it made him feel like a loser. He was *that* guy, crushing on someone who'd never really want him. But then, was that true?

He wasn't imagining the moments they'd shared. The way Rusty looked at him sometimes, starry-eyed and curious. He hadn't seen Rusty look at any of his roommates that way.

And the moment walking back into the bedroom after the shower.

Fuck, any more chemistry and they could have burned down the house in those few seconds before Rusty left the room. Ezra was positive he'd seen Rusty's eyes skim his body, like he was evaluating. Figuring out if he liked what he saw.

Ezra gulped and shook his head, dabbing blue aggressively on the sky to finish filling it in.

At least his friends all knew Rusty was straight and had stopped hitting on him. Even Benji had behaved himself when Ezra had brought Rusty downstairs after the shower.

Ezra was feeling a weird amount of pressure. It was

Jesse's room to rent out, Benji's job to settle in harmoniously, Aaron's shop to open, and Rusty's business to find success. But he took on board others' emotions all too easily. He always had.

It was good, sometimes, being sensitive. Not all the time. When others were struggling, Ezra could veer wildly off course.

At least his muse seemed to be back. Art had come easily today—both commercial pieces and one for himself. He was continuing that self-portrait from last weekend. He wanted to keep filling in details, even if it brought up strange emotions within himself to work on. Maybe *especially* because it did.

It would be easier to just get laid, Ezra thought and then rolled his eyes. His stupid heart. When it was set on someone, he didn't like other people. It felt weirdly dishonest to pick up some other guy.

"You wanna talk about it?" Aaron's voice came from behind him.

"Um..." Ezra focused on the sound of footsteps back and forth, listening to Aaron carry the last few boxes into the stockroom. "I'm stupid. You're gonna tell me that right off the bat."

"No, I won't." When Ezra looked back at Aaron, his friend paused. He leaned his box on the counter, picking at the flap. "You're lots of things, Ez, but stupid isn't one."

"I feel stupid, then." Ezra frowned at his palette, dipping his brush in water and dabbing it in a different shade of blue. Focusing on spreading the color across the wall was a distraction that let him talk.

"Why?"

Ezra filled in a cloud, shifting from foot to foot. He didn't quite answer—not the way Aaron would expect him to, anyway. "I started a new self-portrait the other day."

"I saw. Is it the one in blue and purple?" Aaron asked after a moment.

Ezra nodded and then glanced back to make sure Aaron had seen his silent response.

Aaron was watching Ezra work. He met his eyes and smiled gently when Ezra looked at him. "I like it. It's powerful."

"Is that how you knew something was up?"

"That, and Beau said you were a mess the other day. Then Rusty came in and you two seemed to be on good terms again. You're all floaty after you see him. But then you get moody, too. It's not like you. And I'm a little bit jealous, but not so jealous I'm gonna harsh your mellow."

Ezra blew out a sigh through his lips. Damn it.

Ever since the dinner party, he'd been coasting along through his normal life, not really thinking about how he was coming off to everyone else. Of course they'd noticed.

"You don't have to hide it, you know," Aaron offered. "We all get our heart involved sometimes when we shouldn't. We're not going to judge you. And whatever you are, it's not stupid."

"No romance." Ezra turned back to the wall and smeared blue across it, working efficiently to finish the last corner of the sky. "That was the rule, you know."

Aaron laughed. "Babe, is *that* all that's worrying you? That wasn't a life-and-death promise. And some of us have already broken it."

"Yeah, when we moved in next to a hot, single, interested, and most importantly *gay* guy." Ezra rolled his eyes.

"Is it?"

"Is it what?" Ezra rinsed his brush. That was the first

tone done, at least. He could get it at least three-quarters finished today. By tomorrow, the rest would be done.

"Is being gay the most important thing?" Aaron leaned back against the counter, thumbs hooked into his waistband.

Ezra frowned. "What? Of course. I can't date someone in the closet, Aaron. You know me." Keeping a relationship a secret would kill him. He'd never tried, and he never would.

"We put a lot of labels onto ourselves. Bear, leatherman, twink, straight-acting..." Aaron gestured. "Slut," he added, pointing to himself with his thumb and grinning. "Labels aren't a bad thing, not at all. But they make other people look past the other pieces of ourselves. Sometimes if you think of someone too rigidly, you don't leave room for who they really are. I'm not saying keep secrets. I'm just saying... be open."

Ezra wasn't sure where this was going. His heart beat a little faster. Was Aaron saying that he thought Rusty wasn't straight after all?

"Sometimes we use labels because we're afraid that someone will see those missing parts. If you call yourself a slut, nobody sees how easy it is to break your heart." Aaron's smile was small and sad.

Ezra's heart squeezed. He set down his palette quietly and turned to Aaron. This was definitely a moment, and it sounded like Aaron needed to talk as much as Ezra did.

His friend had sworn off dating last New Year's Eve, after breaking up with yet another "future husband" and moving out of his apartment in a rush.

They'd all assumed he was going through a phase of working the casual sex out of his system and he didn't want a boyfriend again. What if he did? What if he was lonely?

"Oh, don't give me the doe eyes," Aaron scoffed, waving a hand at Ezra as he approached.

Ezra still reached out to take Aaron's hand. "No, I think I

hear you." Maybe there was more to Rusty than met the eye. "I don't want to get my hopes up, that's all."

Aaron shook his hand free and pulled Ezra in for a half-hug instead. "I know. But sometimes you gotta take the chance and see where it goes. I like seeing you look happier. Chase that. Let the labels come later." He looked around, and Ezra followed his gaze to the walls of the coffee shop and the chairs stacked in the corner, waiting to be arranged just so. "God knows where this whole coffee shop business will go. It just feels right, you know?"

"Yeah." Ezra *did* know just what he meant, and it made him smile.

"And you know what the right thing for you is. Deep down." Aaron poked Ezra in the gut, making him squeak. "I know you do."

Ezra sighed and nodded. "I'm just scared of what might happen."

"Ez..." Aaron laughed and swept his arm around to indicate the coffee shop. "Preaching to the choir."

"I know." Ezra had to crack a grin. Telling Rusty that he liked him was nothing in comparison to opening a damn coffee shop. But at the same time, it was a hundred times harder, because the risk of rejection was right there and in his face.

He tried to follow his heart no matter where it led. And already, the path looked so different than he'd first imagined. Why not follow it a little longer and see what happened?

"Anyway," Ezra said, squeezing Aaron around the shoulders. "Thanks for listening."

Aaron kissed his cheek and patted his chest. "Anytime. But if you end up sleeping with him, I'm going to be jealous forever."

"Huh?" Ezra laughed. "You get a lot more action than me."

"Are you calling me a slut?" Aaron pretended to gasp, clutching his chest with both hands.

"Yeah." Ezra grinned and poked Aaron in the cheek.

Aaron burst out laughing and swatted his hand. "Asshole. Yeah, but. A straight guy! That's, like, a third of the porn on my hard drive. I can share some, you know. If you need inspiration for how to woo them." Aaron gave him an exaggerated wink, then scooped up the box, pirouetted, and headed for the stockroom.

Ezra grinned as he headed back to the back wall to fill in more clouds. "I think I'll cope without the tutorials. Thanks for the offer."

"You can't say I didn't try. Sharing is caring." Aaron disappeared into the stockroom, and moments later, a box ripped open while Aaron started singing some new pop song under his breath.

Ezra shook his head fondly as he gazed at the wall. He had a lot more questions on his mind now, though.

Which of them was using Rusty's labels as an excuse? Could they both be doing it, really? An excuse to want him, or to *not* pursue him?

God, this whole crush thing was complicated. Couldn't he just go back to silently ogling him from the art gallery doorway and jerking off to the memory later?

Nope. He was in too deep now. Everyone around him was noticing his crush. It wasn't like he could hide it, and it would only start to hurt sooner or later.

Just having one of his best friends on his side—and knowing the rest would have his back, too—made so much difference. He felt less guilty about his heart wanting whom it wanted.

There was only one way out: actually tell Rusty how he felt. Have a conversation, heart-to-heart, like they'd had several times now. Only this time, address the elephant in the room: Ezra's great big gay crush.

Before he could second-guess himself, he whipped out his phone and sent a text to suggest dinner on Friday night at Millie's, the local restaurant.

He'd let his crush drag him along this far. Time to take the bull by the horns and ride it.

Heat flushed Ezra's cheeks, and he shifted from foot to foot, resisting the urge to adjust himself and probably smear paint across his crotch.

Maybe in more ways than one, if I'm very, very lucky.

And that was fantasy material enough to keep him painting furiously for the rest of the afternoon.

8

RUSTY

Why did it feel like a date as Rusty pulled up in front of Ezra's house?

Maybe because it was Friday, he was wearing a collared shirt and tie, and they were heading to Millie's—the local traditional spot for date night.

Also, he and Ezra had been texting at least a few times a day all week. Rusty had missed seeing that smiling face on days when he didn't pop into the gallery to say hi on his way home.

Before he could honk, the door opened and Ezra hurried out. It didn't close behind him—a couple of his roommates were in the doorway. They leaned out and waved, so Rusty leaned down and waved back, through the truck window.

It was great to have a friend who would come with him to Millie's on a Friday. Oh, man. It was so close to a date that the only things between him and kissing Ezra good night were his own assumptions about himself. And that thought really shouldn't have been so hot.

"Hey." Once Ezra was in the truck, he stroked his hair,

tucking it all in front of his shoulder and playing with the ends. It was a cute nervous habit Rusty had noticed. "How's it going?"

The air was tense, nervous. Exactly like a first date. What the heck was going on?

"Good. All the better for seeing you," Rusty answered with a smile. He took off the parking brake and cruised down the street toward Millie's. "You?"

"Phew. Glad to get a break. It's been all painting, all the time."

"In a good way? Inspiration struck?"

Ezra snorted and folded his hands in his lap. "My bills struck. That's the same thing, right? I got it all done, but now I want to sleep for a week."

That made Rusty laugh. He glanced over with a nod. "Yeah, I bet. You're still in as my date next weekend, right? For the grand opening? Don't make me show up on my own."

Throwing the *d*-word out there wasn't as scary as he'd expected. As long as he played it casual and smiled, like there was no hidden meaning, it didn't have to change anything.

"Of course I am. Wouldn't dream of it." Ezra's giggle sounded nervous, and Rusty cast him a quick glance. It was hard to read the smile Ezra directed at him and drive safely, so he focused on the latter.

"Good. I even got a new tie for the occasion," Rusty told Ezra.

"Is it also a plain, dark color?" Ezra was teasing, wasn't he? Sure enough, when Rusty glanced over, he was grinning. "Like the rest of your wardrobe? This straight guy could use a queer eye, you know."

Rusty played along. "Okay. I could use a good makeover.

What would you suggest?" He was genuinely curious. All he'd ever done when clothes shopping was look for things that fit him and worked well together. That meant sticking to safe, plain colors that he couldn't go wrong with.

"More bright colors. You can pull them off. Don't be afraid of them," Ezra said. He drummed his fingernails on the ledge under the window.

"Pink shirt, yellow jacket, and an orange tie. Gotcha."

"Arrrgh!" Ezra covered his face. "I regret suggesting this already."

"My tie will match my life jacket."

Ezra snorted. "You're ridiculous," he told Rusty, but there was a note of something in his voice that gave Rusty pause.

Fondness? Yeah. That had to be it. Rusty couldn't figure out if that was what he *wanted* it to be.

"Here we go," Rusty said as he pulled into the parking lot and glided into a spot. His voice sounded loud in the sudden silence between them.

"Thanks for the ride. One of these days I'll have to return the favor. If you want." Ezra grinned at him.

Rusty deadpanned, "I could be into that."

Normally Ezra was the one trying to make Rusty blush, but it was Ezra's turn to gasp. "Rusty Campbell! I do believe you've got a dirty mind hidden away there after all."

Not that hidden away, Rusty thought. It took every ounce of willpower Rusty possessed not to say that out loud.

If he started flirting tonight, he wasn't sure he could pull back. The clear box he'd tried to place the relationship into was growing fuzzy.

Instead, he just grinned and climbed out of the truck, strolling for the door of Millie's. Ezra caught up with him and shadowed him inside.

"Oh, hello! Ezra—and Rusty."

That was Kathy, one of Millie's daughters. Her mom had founded the restaurant, but now Kathy and her sister ran the place, and their kids worked here during summer breaks. But the co-owners still took turns as the restaurant hostess, seating people and making conversation.

Her question was implied. Rusty did all he could not to react to it. "Evening," he answered, sticking his hands in his pockets. "Table for two, please?"

"Sure thing." Kathy grabbed two menus, cast them one more look, and led them over to the windows overlooking the coast.

The ones with the best views, and the tea lights on them, and sometimes flower vases in the summer. The *date* tables, as the high schoolers in town called them.

Rusty had no idea whether he should steer them past that section or not. Maybe she was seeing something that he couldn't.

Or didn't want to let himself.

"Here you are." Her voice had a slight uptick as she looked at them both, but mainly Rusty.

Rusty nodded firmly and slid into one seat. He wasn't going to chicken out of this. "Thanks," he told Kathy and took the menu he was handed. It was laminated and the font was tacky, but every dish had some special resonance with him. "I don't know if I'll need this, though," he joked.

"Baked mac and cheese?" She propped her fists on her hips. "Still?"

Rusty laughed. For someone who had broadened his palate to include wild edibles like seaweed, there was still no replacing Millie's mac and cheese. "You got it."

"Then I'll have the same thing." Ezra smiled over the table. "I trust your recommendation."

"Okay!" Kathy laughed and collected the menus from them both. "And to drink?"

They both asked for Coke, and once she'd walked off, Rusty expected the awkward moment to settle between them.

It didn't. Instead, Ezra just smiled at him. "So, how about your week?"

"The growth this week is fantastic. I'm not as worried about the shoots not taking hold of the ropes anymore. They're all firmly anchored."

"But it's practically winter." Ezra shook his head. "I can't get my head around that. Things growing underwater in the winter. The water should be super cold, right?"

"That's why it's such a good crop," Rusty told him, straightening up as he smiled. "It can grow when not much else does. Even up in Alaska, it's prime season right now."

Ezra shivered. "Way too cold for me."

"You get cold easily." Rusty remembered the aftermath of their cold dip. How could he forget the shower he'd been so tempted to share?

"I do." Ezra pouted and fidgeted with the ends of his hair, twirling it around his pointer finger. "Drawbacks of being a beanpole."

"You? No," Rusty said, shaking his head. Ezra was stronger than he gave himself credit for. Maybe he wasn't broad and solid as a house, but he'd seen him shirtless. There was muscle there, however much Ezra joked about himself. "You're good the way you are, man. Takes all kinds to make the world go around."

He was rewarded with another of Ezra's bright, sunny smiles. "That's what I always think. That, and *be nice, life's too short.*"

"It's a good philosophy." Rusty's heart kept giving

nervous flutters. Was it time to admit that he was feeling a hell of a lot like this could be a date?

The more he pushed the fact away, the less he could escape the fact that he was here—not just willingly, but eagerly flirting. At least, Rusty wanted to make him smile. *Was* that flirting? "I admire anyone who brings sunshine into our world. Whether through paintings, or being a good friend, or... any little way."

"Oh, I'm glad to light up your life." Ezra pretended to fan away compliments, primping his hair. "Delighted, in fact."

Rusty gave him a slow smile. "You do."

Now that he was looking Ezra in the eye, he couldn't actually bring himself to look away. The dark gaze that burned into his own made his cock stir with interest in his pants, and that was another inescapable fact.

Thank God Kathy arrived with their drinks. As Rusty looked over quickly and thanked her, he couldn't help but feel like he'd been caught with his hand in the cookie jar.

It didn't help that she waited until Ezra wasn't watching her and then gave him a big wink.

The blush that swept across Rusty's cheeks took him aback. He cleared his throat and folded his arms as he asked Ezra more about his week at the artists' co-op and let him ramble about the goings-on of his friends.

It sounded like they were getting close to crunch time on the coffee shop. Ezra sounded tense as he talked about Aaron not being himself. Things had to be pretty crazy for Ezra by association.

"If they need any help with moving heavy stuff..." Rusty offered, lifting his shoulders in a shrug. "Let me know."

"Really?" Ezra blinked at him and then smiled. He

leaned over to brush Rusty's hand before he took his drink. "Thank you. That's so sweet."

"It's nothing," Rusty mumbled, waving off the praise. He hadn't even *done* anything. He didn't deserve the credit until he did. Even then, lifting some tables and chairs around was the least he could do for his new friends.

They settled into an easy conversation over supper. Ezra's voice sometimes wavered when he talked about growing up with his little brother. He had a brave smile, but he couldn't always meet Rusty's eyes when he joked about Jon and how they'd gotten along as kids. Rusty had to fight to hold back the sympathy for him.

It was hard, though. Knowing that Ezra's life had been brushed with tragedy so early made Rusty just want to wrap his arms around him and never let go. But Ezra didn't cry or mourn. He smiled, instead, as he celebrated the bond they'd had.

Then, Rusty wound up describing his disastrous start as a tour guide in Maine, which brought them both to laughter as they worked on their suppers.

It was exactly how he'd remembered it: crumbly bread topping, and so creamy that every bite melted in his mouth. Best of all was Millie's special ingredient—ketchup, just enough to add a new dimension to the flavor without drowning it.

"Do you miss it back there?" Ezra asked.

"No way." Rusty smiled. "I thought I would. I have buddies on Facebook that I want to stay in touch with. But I didn't make many friends outside work. I tried, and... yeah." He flushed with embarrassment. "Blind dates were the closest I got to dating."

"Oh?" Ezra grinned wickedly, and Rusty groaned. "Come on. You have to share."

"No, I don't." Rusty shook his head hard. "I'll save you the secondhand embarrassment."

Ezra fluttered his eyelashes, and damn it if something in Rusty's chest didn't just give way instantly under that look.

"Fine. I tried like, four or five blind dates. They were just awkward as hell." Rusty bit his lip. "I felt like it was my fault. Like I should have been able to single-handedly sweep them off their feet."

"Maybe you're dating the wrong people," Ezra said with a simple shrug.

Well, obviously. Even if he didn't mean it that way, Rusty couldn't fight the growing feeling that he was right. He nodded. "I was."

Kathy came to clear their plates, and when she asked about dessert, Rusty nodded. "I don't know if I can, but I want to try."

Metaphor for his life, really. And Ezra didn't miss it. "A good attitude," he said with a wink. "That hot fudge brownie volcano looks epic, but way too much for one. Split?" Ezra offered.

Rusty's whole chest felt warm. The idea of sharing dessert with Ezra made him tingle with happiness he hadn't expected. "Yeah. That'd be cool."

"Coming right up," Kathy said as she headed off to the kitchen. Conversation started again much more easily now, filled with flirting on Ezra's part and earnest curiosity on Rusty's.

Rusty even insisted that Ezra take the last spoonful of filling once they'd cleaned every crumb of the chocolate volcano from the plate. Time seemed to speed into a blur as they talked about growing up in the big city versus a small town. Neither of them were in a rush to leave.

"One bill, please," Rusty said when Kathy passed by at a natural lull in the conversation.

"Oh, are you sure?" Ezra was reaching for his pocket, but Rusty shook his head.

"Positive. I dragged you outdoors and you put up with it, so I get to pay now," Rusty told him with a wink, and Ezra didn't argue. It made Rusty feel good to treat him to more than nice words and a few boat trips.

But as they rose and made their way slowly to the truck, it suddenly hit Rusty that when he dropped Ezra off, their... date, or not-date, whatever this was... would be over.

Unless one of them went to the other's house afterward. And that was *definitely* firm date territory. Fuck, Rusty was just digging a deeper hole for himself with every passing day.

They pulled up outside Ezra's house much too soon, and Ezra unbuckled.

"Thank you for a great evening," Ezra said softly, lingering in the truck instead of jumping out. "I really enjoyed it."

"So did I." Rusty let go of the steering wheel and shifted, his body naturally turning toward Ezra's. It was like he didn't want to let him go, like a sunflower turning toward its sunshine.

Whatever signals Rusty couldn't keep contained, Ezra was picking them up. Every damn one. Because Ezra slid over toward him, and instead of going in for the hug, he rested a hand on Rusty's thigh and leaned in to press a kiss against his cheek.

The breath caught in Rusty's throat. Such a simple, warm brush of his lips, yet it seemed to light Rusty's whole face on fire. He turned his face quickly toward Ezra.

He didn't even know how to ask the question that hung

between them. He just met Ezra's gaze and reached out to touch his arm, and then Ezra was leaning in again.

Like the air had been sucked out of the truck cab, he struggled to breathe. But he didn't need to, because Ezra's breath ghosted against his parted lips, and then their lips pressed together.

They were kissing. Holy shit, Ezra was actually kissing him—right here, right now.

The kiss was warm, slow, and lingering, if all too brief. That was all Ezra's doing. Rusty barely moved—just frozen in shock and surprise.

Yes. That was the only word that seemed to resonate through his whole being, like someone had just unlocked a part of his brain he'd never bothered to pay attention to.

He was getting hard, and his brain supplied every damn fantasy he'd half-heartedly tried to conjure up with women before. It had worked, but dimly. Now? Every thought was Technicolor etched into his brain.

Just a couple seconds after the kiss began, Ezra must have noticed Rusty going still. He pulled back sharply, his eyes widening in alarm. "Are you... Was that... Shit."

Rusty didn't know what to say. Pleasant didn't even start to describe it. Earth-shattering was much closer. Good? Bad? Those words fell away in the face of the pull between them.

If he hadn't been seat belted in, he wasn't sure he wouldn't just push Ezra flat on the seat, straddle him, and make out with him until dawn right here on the truck seat.

Ezra started to slide away, grabbing for the door handle, and all Rusty knew was that he couldn't let Ezra leave again, upset and fragile and filled with pain that Rusty wanted nothing more than to take from him.

"Shit," Rusty breathed out again. He reached for Ezra's arm and caught it, tugging gently. "Stop. Don't go."

Ezra heard the plea in his voice. He did stop, turning his gaze toward Rusty. It was half-wild, like a deer deciding whether to risk danger for the sustenance being offered on outstretched hand.

"I'm sorry." Rusty's voice croaked, his mouth suddenly dry. "I've been leading you on."

"And you're not gay. I know." Rusty hadn't expected the pain in Ezra's voice—not at all. "I'm sorry. I thought you were coming on to me. It was just me hoping."

"No," Rusty said firmly. He didn't want Ezra believing it was his fault that he couldn't make his own damn mind up. "No, it's me. You've been making me think about everything differently."

"I have?"

Rusty just laughed. Of course Ezra had no idea of the nights Rusty had spent lying awake, one hand on his half-hard cock, trying to decide whether to indulge yet another fantasy about Ezra or call it quits.

Most nights, the fantasy won.

"Oh." Ezra quivered in Rusty's hold, his eyes widening. "But I... I don't want to risk this. Our friendship."

"Yeah." Rusty's shoulders sank in relief. Ezra understood why he hadn't said anything sooner.

How reckless would it be to throw away this amazing new friendship and rush into something totally new? Something he might screw up, without ever knowing it?

Rusty was slowly piecing it together, but in the bigger picture of his life, they'd moved so quickly and he wanted to be sure he could commit before he led Ezra on.

There was a difference between *I'm into you* and *I want you in my life forever*, and the last thing Rusty wanted was to hurt Ezra by mixing up the two.

He let go at last and rested his arm on the wheel. "I don't

know what was going through my mind, but I know I like you. And I like being around you. You're not shaking me yet."

"So I can't run away and live in the mountains and make brokenhearted paintings," Ezra joked, but his smile was shaky.

Rusty shook his head firmly. "Not unless you can kayak in and out. I've seen you hiking."

For a minute, his gut clenched. He'd meant it in a friendly, bantering way, but what if Ezra took it as a back-handed insult?

But Ezra just grinned. "You shady fucker." He pretended to slap Rusty's arm and then drew himself upright. Now, he looked more put together at least. Not upset and ready to hide from the world. Rusty wasn't making that mistake again of letting him do so.

Rusty grinned back at him. "So shady. But no, thank you for a great evening. It was a lot of fun."

"Even this bit?"

"Every bit," Rusty promised.

The smile Ezra gave him was worth it all. Ezra slid closer again, gave him a one-armed hug, and then scrambled out of the truck cab. "See you soon, huh?"

"Yeah. You too."

After he watched Ezra walk inside, it took Rusty a long minute to remember to start up his truck again. He was still in mild shock that any of this had just happened.

But more surprising than anything else was that he'd really liked that kiss. Ezra might have done all the kissing, but his biggest regret was not kissing him back.

What would that feel like?

Rusty had no idea what it meant about him that he really, really wanted to find out.

9

EZRA

"Hey, Ez is back!" Beau jumped Ezra at the door, half hugging him and craning his head to look out the door before Ezra could shut it. "Where's Rusty?"

"Oh, he couldn't... come in." Ezra tried to act normal. He'd just had the roller-coaster ride of his life, and his emotions were still lurching up and down in his chest.

The hurt of Rusty's near-rejection swept him away one moment, and then the excitement that he hadn't actually turned him down, and then nervousness about how long it would take Rusty to be ready for more.

They'd talked and laughed and even shared dessert so easily, though. It was the first date of his dreams, with the man of his dreams. That one inconvenient detail of his sexuality seemed less and less relevant, if Ezra just trusted his instincts.

"And why isn't he here, mister?" Benji folded his arms as he interjected from the couch. "Hogging him?"

Beau's laugh was quick and nervous, like he sensed potential tension. Which he didn't, because Ezra was definitely not jealous of Benji. There was no reason to be jealous over a guy who was *just friends* anyway.

Even if he was, impossibly, Ezra's dream guy.

Fuck.

He had kissed Rusty. However incredible he'd tasted, however soft and warm his lips and skin, he couldn't escape the fact that Rusty hadn't kissed him back.

He'd never felt such a one-sided kiss before, and it hurt worse than a slap in the face to feel Rusty stiff as a statue under him. Thank God Rusty hadn't let him run off but had insisted that this didn't change their friendship.

Ezra was starting to question his own mind. He'd been so sure there was chemistry between them, and then...

"He has to go home for work," he lied easily and headed for the kitchen so nobody could see the truth on his face. "And it's wine o'clock for me. You'll have to catch me up on the news in a sec."

These few moments he stole alone in the kitchen helped. Ezra put himself back together as he slowly fetched a wine-glass, set it on the counter with a clink, and found the open white wine in the fridge.

Damn it, Ezra should have talked to Rusty like he'd meant to. Actually admitted his feelings, terrifying though it was.

Before he left the kitchen, he set down the glass and sent Rusty a quick text.

Ezra: Thank you for a great night. My friends say hi and they miss you.

He only had to wait moments for a response.

Rusty: No, thank you! I'll come over in a few days. My turn to cook for all of you!

Ezra: That would be great!

That gave Ezra something to distract his friends, too. He

pocketed his phone and took his glass to the living room. As he entered, he announced, "I've guilted him into coming over soon. He's even bringing food for you jealous hos."

A cheer went through the guys in the living room—most of those who lived here.

"Jealous hos get fed," Aaron said, smirking as he pulled his legs up next to him. He scooted over, making room for Ezra. "Sausage dinner, and cream for dessert."

"If I weren't holding a full glass," Ezra threatened idly, pulling at the pillow behind Aaron as if he planned to smack him with it.

Aaron held up his own glass like a shield. "Red!" He pointed to the contents.

Defeat. Ezra sighed and stuck out his tongue, then settled back to look around. Thankfully, the conversation was already moving on, and Ezra ignored it.

From their reactions, Aaron had kept Ezra's secret. He kept casting perceptive glances in his direction, and when Ezra got up for a refill, Aaron shadowed him to the kitchen.

"So?" Aaron asked quietly when they got there.

Ezra fumbled with the fridge door. He pushed his hair behind his ear and tried not to fidget with it. "Huh?"

"Your eyeliner, outfit, and jeans all say *date*," Aaron pointed out. "Don't even try that with me."

Ezra chuckled and sighed, letting the door close once he'd grabbed the bottle. There was no point in trying to lie. "Fine," he sighed. "Yeah, things are changing between us. I think I pushed it too far, but... he's just giving me nothing to go on. Everything I do, he seems *fine* with."

Aaron folded his arms and set his glass aside, shaking his head when Ezra gestured toward it with the bottle. "I'm nervous for you. Don't let him take advantage of you that way, you know?"

Ezra raised his brow. He nearly spilled the wine. "What happened to *don't mind his labels, follow your heart?*"

Aaron laughed, his voice hushed. He looked tired tonight, more so than usual lately. "I'm not going to try to tell you what to do. You might unleash your redhead fury on my ass."

Ezra didn't even realize his brows were arching, lips narrowing into a pout, until it was too late. He huffed and rolled his eyes. "Your ass only wishes."

Aaron didn't let him distract him. "You look less bubbly and more... broody tonight. That's all. I'll be here to kick his ass if that's what you need. The offer's always open."

Ezra nodded slightly and reached out to trail his hand down Aaron's arm. "Thank you, babe."

Aaron smiled back and then put his glass in the sink. "I'm off to bed."

"That's not like you." Ezra checked his watch and gasped. It wasn't even ten at night. "Early morning at the shop?" Thankfully, his mural was done. He no longer had to fear holding Aaron back with some half-finished work at the opening day.

Aaron snorted. "Oh, save your pity. I'm being a very good, wholesome boy for a few nights. I'll treat myself to an orgy later to make up for it. In my new place. Those counters are divine, and also expensive. I should get the most out of them."

Ezra didn't doubt it. He grinned and waved Aaron off to bed. "Have fun planning that."

He headed back to the living room and slipped into his place, listening to his friends. But by the end of another couple glasses of wine, alcohol had fueled his courage.

It wasn't too late to tell Rusty how he felt. In fact, it

might be very important to do so if he was going to avoid making an ass of himself again and again.

He sent a quick text to start.

Ezra: Everything's good between us, right? Just thought I'd check since today was pretty wild.

Rusty: Yeah, totally! Except there is one thing on my mind. I was too nervous at the restaurant to bring it up and I guess I should have.

Ezra: What was that?

Rusty: "Us."

Ezra's chest tightened. *Us*, with quote marks? What did that mean? But before he could clarify, Rusty went on.

Rusty: I keep thinking about our relationship. I don't know why I'm so okay with everything between us. I can't promise you anything and I don't want to use you, you know? That would be a dick move.

Ezra gulped. Fuck, it made him tingle all over to think of Rusty using him, but he probably didn't mean *that* kind of use. Completely distracted, he tried desperately to think of anything else to say.

But he couldn't, and he had to say something. So he gulped back his trepidation and kept the flirting turned up.

Ezra: I don't mind being used by the right guy ;)

Rusty: :)

Just a smile emoji. That was it. Damn it, had Ezra overstepped at last? He rushed to answer.

Thank God for the wine flowing through his veins, making his head buzz and the room walls not stay exactly where he put them when he turned his head.

Ezra: Look, I should have been upfront, so here goes. You're so my type. And I never met a straight guy who was so okay with me casually flirting.

He licked his lips and pressed the Send button, then kept tapping.

Ezra: Are you uncomfortable by me flirting and calling you babe and hugging and all that stuff? Or me being so flamboyant?

Oh, the wait was excruciating. He tried to smile along as the guys laughed about cult classic movies, thankful that nobody was calling him out directly for being so distracted. Every few seconds, his eyes dipped to his phone to watch the dots bounce, which meant Rusty was typing.

Rusty: Thank you for telling me that! No, I like you being you. It's cute. I figured out pretty early that you're affectionate with everyone. It wasn't until now that I realized things were... you know, at this point. And I was too nervous to bring it up, but I find you cute a lot of the time. No damn idea what that means about me or what I'm going to do about it. But I want to be around you while I figure it out. And now I guess I hit send and try not to hyperventilate?

Ezra's heart lifted. Here was that most dangerous of feelings creeping in again: hope.

Rusty wasn't giving him a clear *no*, even when he gave him every chance to do so.

In fact, he was giving him a very strong *maybe*.

Which meant the answer might be yes, and all it would take was some patience. Well, Ezra had that in spades. A moment later, Ezra nearly snorted. Not really, but he could try. And poor Rusty was waiting on his reply, no doubt as anxious as Ezra felt right now.

Ezra: Yeah, no problem! No pressure. Things must be stressful. This stuff takes time to process.

Rusty: You're the best. Thanks, Ez.

Ezra: Welcome, babe!

A moment before he sent it, he looked at the last word

and wavered for a moment. No, Rusty had just said he was fine with pet names. Ezra took the plunge before he could change his mind.

He wasn't going to filter himself. Rusty hadn't yet been weirded out by any of Ezra's authentic self. If he needed someone who was less... well, *Ezra*... then that was his problem.

And Ezra was done with trying to fill whatever needs he thought other people had. Except, the little voice in the back of his conscience reminded him, he was conveniently offering to fill Rusty's needs. But that was different. That was a friend who needed help exploring labels and broadening his horizons.

Rusty: I gotta get to bed. But see you soon, OK?

Ezra swallowed the disappointment. He wanted to talk to Rusty into the small hours of the morning, let the conversation wander as easily as it had in person.

God, he had it bad. At least Rusty knew now so he could steer around those situations. Or... just maybe... Rusty might choose to lean into them.

To kiss him first.

That was a choice Rusty had to make for himself, and all Ezra could do was stand back and let the chips fall where they would. And hope that at the end of the day, they wound up with *some* kind of relationship.

That conversation had muddied the waters more than cleared anything up. Ezra sighed and went for another glass of wine. He'd need it, to deal with the restless night he was certain lay ahead.

And first, it was time to try pretending to the rest of his friends that he wasn't imagining Rusty shedding his labels as quickly as their clothes on his bedroom floor.

10

RUSTY

Rusty's heart had a mind of its own these days.

Last night, he'd fallen asleep to the memory of that kiss. In the morning, he'd woken with the taste of Ezra still on his lips. Making coffee, stumbling through his morning routine, driving to his parents' house... nothing was the same when he was trying to ignore an insistent ache within him.

Rusty rarely remembered his dreams, but he could swear that he'd been dreaming of Ezra a lot lately. He was never far from Rusty's thoughts, and they texted most days. Sometimes it was dumb little jokes, and other times it was sharing how their days had gone.

Everything had seemed so simple last night: hang out with Ezra, figure out his feelings, talk it out, and boom, boyfriend time. Or just friend, if his heart leaned that way.

Today, though? The clarity of a night's sleep had made it sink in. The only way this was simple between them was if Rusty ignored how he'd *noticed* Ezra now.

And maybe that wasn't new. Before they'd even met, Rusty had noticed Ezra in a way he didn't look at most people. It had only strengthened over the past few weeks, like Rusty was keyed to Ezra. He wanted to smile when Ezra smiled and sweep him off his feet and away from the pain when he hurt.

Did that make Rusty gay? Bi? Who the fuck knew or cared? If he *really* listened to his heart, it had been telling him loud and clear from day one that he was into Ezra.

"And how's the farm looking?"

After a lazy Saturday lunch with his parents, the talk inevitably turned to business, and Rusty sat up straighter. He couldn't just tune this out and nod and smile.

It wasn't like his parents hadn't supported him over these last few months. They'd helped him move back here, find a place to live, and even connected him with suppliers for the thick rope and buoys he needed. And by *suppliers*, that meant folks around town who still had sheds full of now-useless gear they were happy to offload.

But all the while, they'd been acting like they were indulging Rusty in a phase. It was the subtle gestures that spoke volumes. His dad had just spoken with an eyebrow raise while his mom frowned.

"Great," Rusty answered as succinctly as possible. He'd been out yesterday morning to check on it, so he described the progress. "A few more inches of growth. All the lines are secure. The hard work's done at this point—or still to come. This is when I get to relax. And find a market for the finished product."

"That doesn't sound relaxing," Mom said. She fretted at the buttons on her sweater, which was draped over the curled armrest of the couch. It was still the same couch as when Rusty had been a kid, but with a few more red wine stains. The nice pillows covered them when guests were over. "Do you know how much you'll harvest? You can't promise what you don't have."

"A lot, if all goes well." Rusty fidgeted with his glass of water, trying not to let the skepticism get to him. "I was thinking about boats, too. I don't know if Pascal's old rust bucket will carry much for the harvest. It's a nice pleasure boat, but it won't hold up to aquaculture."

Dad nodded. He was in the corner armchair, the newspaper still open in his lap. He folded it up with a lot of rustling and set it aside. "A deeper draft would be better. Cecilia, do you remember who was selling their old fishing boat?"

"I think Gregory is finally letting go of his," Mom said. She leaned back into the couch, casting Dad an anxious glance. "But don't you think it's better to wait and make sure he needs it? There aren't exactly a lot of buyers around."

Dad nodded, his voice authoritative. "Good point, dear. You can probably name your price. He bought it for pennies on the dollar at an auction back then anyway. Wait until you need it before you buy."

Which was yet another sign that they didn't trust his experience. Rusty hadn't just jumped into this business without spending summers cutting his palms to shreds scrambling over slippery rocks and balancing in a dinghy in choppy waters.

"Or I could invest now, make sure it's still seaworthy, and have time to find another. I don't want to risk missing a critical harvest day," Rusty said, struggling to keep the annoyance out of his voice.

Even if they weren't expecting much from the harvest, he had to be ready to dry and store a lot of the stuff. So far, every species he'd ordered and sown was growing well, and he'd expected one or two duds.

When his parents had flown to Maine to visit him, he'd shown them a little of what he did for work, but that was their only exposure to the industry. They probably thought he was going to bring in a couple hundred pounds of the stuff at best.

Little did they know that Rusty planned to make the sea work for him, come hell or high water.

This wasn't the old days, and it wasn't the fishing industry they'd once worked in. Aquaculture was a whole different ball game.

"Don't count your chickens 'til they're hatched," Dad said, shaking his head. "The sea gives and takes away, son."

Oh, God. Here they went. It was all Rusty could do not to roll his eyes. "Gregory's boat sounds like a good investment no matter what," he said, rubbing his chin. Dad was right—a deeper draft would help him stay steady on windy days, especially when hauling soaked lines into the boat. "I don't really need to get close to the shore, and I can keep Pascal's boat in case I do. Wharf space is dirt cheap. Is that the forty-foot boat?"

Mom and Dad exchanged looks, and Rusty suppressed his groan. He hadn't cut the lecture off in time.

"It is, but don't rush headlong into buying it. Only a fool trusts the sea's bounty." It was Mom saying it this time, but they'd both said it so often in Rusty's life that he could almost recite it along with them. "Or signing contracts with stores."

"I'm not counting any chickens," Rusty promised. "I'm just getting tentative interest from buyers. When I know how much inventory I have, I'll follow up with them. And next year will be easier, once I have some data."

"Data can't predict everything." Dad looked solemn. "Everything can go well until one year, it doesn't."

Rusty sighed. He hadn't expected to persuade them in a few short months, but they could at least *try* not to crush his dreams. "I know. But I can't live my life taking no risks."

"You need to make it a calculated risk. It's not like growing turnips. You can't just put seeds in the ocean and wait for them to sprout," Dad said.

"Now who isn't taking risks seriously?" Rusty shook his head. "Growing turnips isn't cut-and-dried, either. Drought, insects, slugs—a million things could go wrong. If you're going to poke holes in my business plan, it's a little late now."

Mom huffed and threw her hands in the air. "I told you, George. He's not going to listen."

"No, I won't," Rusty agreed, rising to his feet. He knew they were speaking from a place of concern, but it was a bit too late to be naysaying his crazy plans. All it could do now was make him feel like shit for being in up to his eyeballs. "If you're just going to tear me down, I'm going to go home and catch up on my chores."

"We're here to support you, not make you feel bad." Dad stood up, too. "We're just worried."

"And no matter what happens, you'll always have a warm meal to come home to." His mom's quiet words sent a knife twist of anxiety through Rusty's belly.

"Thanks," Rusty said, fighting back his pride. He might be facing an uphill battle to win their respect in his chosen career, but he was pretty lucky, all things considered. They didn't want him to go through the same thing they had. "But it won't come to that."

He remembered a little of what had happened when they'd both been suddenly fired by the Harts after the fishery collapse two decades ago. Rusty had been young, but even he had noticed life changing dramatically, almost overnight.

Mom had found another office job after a few months of

searching, but Dad had had to search for longer. They'd eaten an awful lot of mac and cheese in those years. Rusty felt guilty now that, as a kid not understanding what pinching pennies meant, he'd complained about always having the same thing for supper.

Unemployment mac and cheese wasn't the toasted, cheesy, delicious kind like Millie's, but the kind with not quite enough milk or butter, beefed up with processed meats and limp green beans from a can.

It made him appreciate the dish at Millie's all the more. And, in turn, that reminded him of sharing that taste with Ezra for the first time.

"I hope you're right," Mom said. "And I hope our warnings come to nothing. But old habits die hard."

"I know." Rusty reached out for a quick hug, wrapping his mom in his arms and resting his chin on her head. He'd shot up as a kid and then filled out in his shoulders and chest while living in Maine. Now, he could twirl her around the kitchen when he wanted to really annoy her.

They let go and his dad clapped him on the back as they exchanged silent nods.

It was only then, when Rusty eyed the door, that the *other* reason he'd visited came to mind. Thinking of Ezra had reminded him.

Shit. He didn't exactly want to sit back down now and ruin his firm line in the sand. There were only so many skeptical and worried glances he could watch them exchange without starting to doubt himself.

He stumbled to a halt for a moment and looked back before shaking his head. No, he didn't need to complicate this conversation any more.

"We'll see you this week, right?"

"I'll drop by for dinner," Rusty promised and smiled. His

calendar was getting awfully full. There were already trips to see his parents, and phone calls to fill Pascal in on the business since he seemed too busy to come out with Rusty much. Now, he was adding Ezra-dates and visits to his big, crazy house to see Ezra's friends.

It was nice, though. Better than rattling around his house by himself, overthinking everything, like he'd been doing all morning.

"Is there anything else?" Mom was too perceptive as always, her eyes sharpening as she came to the doorway to see him off. From the living room, Dad looked over too, expectantly.

Rusty's palms went damp. He could climb into a boat and ride two-foot waves or coil lines until his arms ached without breaking a sweat. But saying these few little words? Impossible.

He tried to find them.

Mom, Dad, I'm into guys. Well, not just guys. A guy.

Was he bi? Gay? Having a quarter-life identity crisis? Would they think this was just a phase, like seaweed farming?

Rusty wanted them to know from him first, not from gossip around town. Even if he didn't know his relationship status with Ezra yet, as soon as he figured it out, the rest of Hart's Bay would quickly find out. He couldn't date Ezra without telling them. It would feel like hiding, in a bad way.

But the words dried up in his mouth. He'd already spent the morning under attack from his parents, and he didn't want them turning that skepticism against Ezra.

I really like Ezra. Maybe you know him? He's an artist. Oh, man. That was an equally unpredictable career. Ezra seemed to make it work, but that was the kind of thing parents raised a brow about.

Hell, his parents wouldn't care that Ezra was a guy, but Rusty cared. If Dad said, *Is this a thing now?* or Mom asked, *Can I set you up with this coworker's son?* then Rusty wanted to have an answer ready.

So he shook his head. "I appreciate the advice. But I'm stuck on what I'm doing now. If it doesn't go well, I'll figure things out."

"I know." Mom sighed and patted his cheek. She had to crane her neck up to do it. "You're a grown man. But you'll always be my little boy."

"Am I?" Rusty grinned and threatened her with a bear hug while she laughed and pushed at his chest. He picked her up for a moment before setting her down.

From the living room, Dad laughed. "I don't know what was in all that milk he drank as a kid." Rusty had inherited Dad's frame, but he was even taller. "I told you it was a bad idea."

"Don't blame me," Mom retorted. "Popeye got it wrong—it's all that seaweed he ate when he was over in Maine." She patted his chest. "But come over this week so I can make sure you get your land-based greens."

He laughed and hugged her again on the way out the door, waving to his dad before he headed for his truck.

Only once he was behind the wheel did he let the smiles and laughter drop from his lips.

The warning hadn't gone unheeded. It was a cold, wet shock to the system to remember his childhood and realize how right they were.

Maybe he was avoiding some risks, but there were others he faced instead. One stray piece of lumber drifting free from the log booms just up the coast could take out an entire line. A raft of bull kelp could float by and tangle the seedlings, choking their light. One storm—and winter was full of them—could spell the end of the harvest.

In his old job, half the work had been foraging wild seaweeds from the coast. That harvest was much the same, it was just trickier or easier to get to it depending on the weather. But he wasn't yet allowed to do that out here, which tied his hands.

Nature was an unpredictable beast to tame, and he was trying to break ground—or make waves. Being the first to surf a changing current came with the same kind of risk as being the last to jump on board a dying wave. For all his big talk, he could easily end up falling on his face.

Exactly like he might wind up doing with Ezra.

"Ugh," Rusty groaned, eyeing the door as he backed out of the driveway. Why hadn't he just steeled his courage and said those few little words?

There's a guy I'm thinking about asking out. Are you okay with that?

If anything, his parents would have a bigger problem with Ezra being new to town than him being a guy.

They'd want to know who his parents were and what they did, what grades he'd gotten in school, whether he'd been a rebellious teen or the quiet, studious one... all the things even Rusty didn't know yet.

A lot of people who stayed in Hart's Bay wound up dating someone local just because of their proximity. Rusty had always figured he'd move home, eventually find a nice woman in town—probably one he'd known back in high school—and finally, it would all click.

Instead, it was like he'd fished the missing puzzle piece out from the corner of the box, and he didn't quite know what to do with it.

Ezra, bless him, was being incredibly patient. But at the

same time, he was pushing Rusty, not meekly sitting and waiting to be chosen at the prom.

The thought of Ezra being meek made Rusty snort. He was quiet sometimes, but only when he was thoughtful. He felt deeply and wasn't afraid to show it. Hell, he'd as good as told Rusty that he liked him, and that took balls. Now it was up to Rusty to decide what to do about this.

God, Rusty liked him. With that thought in mind, the answer came to him almost immediately.

Maybe it was time to fulfill one of his promises to Ezra: take him to the backwoods, show him a different view of the area, and talk, one-on-one, with nobody else around to pry or get between them.

It was the best weather for it. They were supposed to get a storm soon, so if they moved fast, they should be able to get an overnight trip in first.

Rusty could spill his heart safely to Ezra, and then they could figure things out together.

It was a perfectly sensible plan, when Rusty tried to ignore the nervous excitement that coursed through him at the thought of being alone in the woods with this soft, strong, unbearably kind man who had taken up residence in Rusty's brain.

Rusty's hands shook on the wheel, so he tightened the grip as he pulled into his driveway.

Anything could happen. Everything could change. And Rusty wanted that more than he could make sense of.

11

EZRA

It was hard not to linger at the window on the side of the art gallery that faced the marina.

For the last few months, Ezra and his friends had haunted this window so they could watch construction unfold on the waterfront warehouse that had turned into boutique shops—and cute construction workers.

Now, though, his gaze drifted down to the docks. After his own spin on the water, Ezra could almost feel the restrained power purring through the deck as Rusty pulled into the harbor and jumped onto the wharf to moor his boat.

He poked his head into the back room, where Beau was hard at work, his big hands surprisingly deft as he threaded tiny beads onto thin wire.

"Can I take off for a minute?" Ezra asked, not wanting to interrupt him at work.

Beau didn't look up. "Sure. I'll keep an ear on the front door," Beau mumbled in his concentrating voice.

"Thanks, sweetie." Ezra headed through the workshop

and out the side door, trotting through the parking lot to the little run-down marina.

Rusty looked up, shading his eyes from the late November sun, and smiled in his direction. "Hey, there," he called.

"Hi!" Ezra scurried down the ramp, keeping one hand on the railing and making sure to stay on the sharp metallic treads now that he knew how slippery this thing was.

When he reached Rusty, there was an awkward moment where Ezra wasn't sure how to greet him. A hug and kiss on the cheek would be normal for him, but after Friday night, was that okay? Would Rusty be comfortable with that?

Once again, he took on board others' feelings—in this case, Rusty's—and it made him doubt himself. Thankfully Rusty took the decision out of his hands by sweeping one strong arm around Ezra's shoulders. As their bodies pressed together, Rusty turned his head to an angle, his rough lips brushing past Ezra's cheek. It was a clumsy greeting, but one that Ezra recognized: it was the way he and his gay friends greeted each other, and most straight men refused to do it. Insecure dweebs.

Ezra's cheek instantly burned, the sparks cascading across his face until he knew he was blushing. He pulled away and shoved his hands in his pockets, his chest swelling with joy.

Sharing this little ritual of hellos and goodbyes with Rusty meant a lot to him, and he was glad he hadn't fucked that up.

"Hi," Ezra said again. He laughed, the nervousness disappearing. It was hard to stay anxious in the face of Rusty's calm smile. "How's it going?"

"Great. Checked the lines—it's all good today. I'm gonna be more paranoid from now on, though."

"Oh? I guess winter is stormier." Ezra glanced in the boat, not surprised to find that Rusty had been on the water alone.

"Yeah. I went to talk to my parents on Saturday, and they did a great job outlining all the ways this business could fail." Rusty's frustration bled through every word, and Ezra's heart went out to him right away.

"Oh, God." Ezra rested his hand on Rusty's shoulder. "That must be hard to listen to."

"It can be." Rusty pushed a hand through his hair and then turned back to the boat, casting an expert eye across the lines that moored it. Apparently satisfied it was all in order, he faced Ezra again, eyes sparkling as he unhitched one button on the shoulder of his waders.

Oh, shit. Ezra's brain just stopped short as he stood there —right in plain view from the grocery store, the art gallery, all the boutiques, and several houses besides—and watched Rusty step out of his overall-style water-protective gear.

He was wearing just his plaid boxers now, and his thighs were hairy, muscled, and just as strong as the rest of him. Little tree trunks that Ezra wanted so badly to run his tongue up, until he could taste his sap...

Wait, Rusty was saying something as he grinned. Ezra gulped and shook his head. "Uhh?"

"Pass me my pants?" Rusty gestured toward the box that sat on the dock. "It's too cold out here to impress anyone." But his tone was lighthearted, and... dare Ezra even think it? Flirty! He was flirting!

Oh, God. What the hell was he going to do about that?

Ezra barked a laugh that wasn't at all like his usual, trying his best not to take a peek and independently verify his modesty. "I bet it isn't."

He found the jeans easily and passed them over. Rusty

placed one hand on Ezra's shoulder to lean against him for support when he stepped into them.

"Phew." Rusty zipped up and bundled his outerwear into the box before closing it again, tossing it into the boat. "Thanks. That's better."

"So, um, the conversation." They'd been saying something about Rusty's family before Rusty casually stripped in public. He was shameless, seemingly unaware of the throbbing bulge that Ezra now had to hide by standing with one foot crossed in front of the other leg.

Or he knew and he liked it, which was a possibility that turned Ezra on even more.

Rusty nodded and tucked his hands in his jeans pockets. "Oh, yeah. So things didn't go great. Could be worse, but I'm still a rain cloud."

"I know what that's like." Ezra bit his lip, wondering if it would sound too much like a strong hint. But he was *not* going to filter himself now, so he said it. "I had that with my parents for a while after I came out. Things were tough before they grew to understand me."

"Ah." Rusty frowned at him with concern. "But they're okay now?"

Ezra smiled, a lump in his throat. "Oh, yes. A lot better."

He was much closer to his parents these days. Even though he couldn't make it back for Thanksgiving this year, they'd no doubt exchange phone calls. After his brother's accident, his parents had realized that whatever their fears for him, it couldn't be worse than losing another child. It was a bittersweet silver lining that had come from the worst moments of their lives.

That sense of loss still threaded through Ezra's life at odd moments. It had held him back for years. Sure, he could love his friends wholeheartedly, but romantic relationships? That was somehow different.

It was asking a lot to believe that he wouldn't be abandoned again, with no warning and no chance to say goodbye. Ezra blinked a few times, trying to pull his mind out of that familiar pit.

At least it worked perfectly in whatever this was between him and Rusty so far. It gave Ezra time to believe in Rusty's sincerity while Rusty figured out what labels he wanted to use.

Rusty nodded. "I can only hope that once they have some evidence that I'm not going to end up living on my boat and selling shells to mermaids to make a living, things get better."

"As fun as that would be, I hope so, too," Ezra laughed. "Is there any way I can help?"

Rusty lit up. "Funny you should mention that. There's clear weather the next few days. We could take an overnight trip away from town. Leave in the afternoon, about this time of day. Get back in time for Thanksgiving. Escape town and all the stress for a little bit. I can check out the native seaweed species, give you some time to sketch or paint whatever you need to, and we can both call it a work trip."

"Oh!" This was so much better than Ezra had imagined. Not only was time together not off the table, but Rusty wanted *more* of it. He beamed. "That would be awesome. I haven't been camping in years."

He purposely left out how many years, or what had happened last time—enforced family hikes and all. It would be different with Rusty.

Rusty smiled back at him. "Great. We can take the kayak out on, like... tomorrow? Tuesday? What's your schedule here?"

Ezra laughed. Rusty had no idea how many mountains he'd move to make time alone happen. "I can make any day work. I guess your schedule is flexible, too, huh?"

"Right now, yeah. How about tomorrow night, then?" Rusty suggested, his voice matter-of-fact. But Rusty's body language was far from steady. He was fidgeting with his fingers nervously, his eyes bright and eager.

It made the chemistry between them spark and flare to life again—not that it was ever really dormant. It didn't feel like they should stand facing each other. Every time Ezra stood this close to Rusty, part of him wanted to just lean into him and wrap an arm around his waist.

That could be his touchy-feeliness talking, where he always acted that way around his friends and it seemed weird to stand too far apart. Or it could be his gigantic, inconvenient, impolite, and intoxicating crush on Rusty.

One of those two things for sure.

"Is this a date?" Ezra asked, barely daring to voice his question. His stomach was tight, and suddenly breath seemed harder to find. Not speaking up had led them into trouble not long ago. That didn't make asking this face-to-face any easier. "Or strictly buddies being bros? Or do you want to leave off the label? That's okay, too. I just need to know what this is so I can shave appropriately."

Rusty burst out laughing at that last comment, just as Ezra had hoped. "Can we go with that last one? No labels for now?" He looked even more nervous, shifting from foot to foot.

Whoa. It wasn't strictly platonic. That was a big step for Rusty—so big that Ezra's spirits lifted with pride in him. "Of course."

The relief was intense. Ezra hadn't been misreading the text conversation at all. In fact, he'd been underestimating how committed to exploring this new side of himself Rusty was.

Fuck, a part of him released tension he hadn't even known he was holding. He'd been worried about just being an experiment. Who wouldn't be, in Ezra's shoes?

Because Rusty was taking his hand now, his grip uncertain at first. Ezra's palm tingled where it lay in Rusty's, and he squeezed gently to encourage him.

"Feel free to tell me to fuck off, and find... you know, someone who knows what he wants and needs." Rusty's voice was quiet. "We can keep on going like this, but if someone else will make you happier... I don't want to hold you back."

Ezra snorted, trying to hide his wobbly knees. Rusty was *still* being every inch a gentleman. "Oh, humbug. You're not proposing to me," he said with a coy bat of his lashes, making Rusty laugh again. "You're not holding me back. You're steadying my keel."

He hoped the nautical metaphor made sense.

It was the right thing to say, because Rusty gave him a broad grin and squeezed his hand before gently letting go. "Mine, too." He looked happier about it all now, the nervousness dissipating. "Awesome. Okay, that's great. I'll need to get the right tent. And sleeping bags. Do I have two? I'm pretty sure I do."

As he talked, Rusty set off at a brisk stride up the dock for a few paces before he paused and offered Ezra his arm, squinting down at his feet.

Oh, fuck, Ezra *did* giggle now. Could a man be more perfect? He'd remembered Ezra's terrible city-boy shoes.

Ezra took the proffered arm, not about to pass up that opportunity. "We can share," he teased Rusty, only half-joking. "That'll help you figure a lot out in a hurry."

Rusty's glance at him was surprisingly sensual, his eyes hooded as his tongue darted out to run across his rough lips. How much Ezra wanted to kiss them until they were smooth.

After a moment, Rusty murmured, "I'm pretty sure accidentally fucking would only complicate things."

"But deliberately fucking would straighten them out. Or... un-straighten." Ezra smirked. "We're already dating. May as well get laid. Sex has a way of clarifying the situation."

"What?" Rusty stared at him, making Ezra stop and giggle at the bottom of the ramp. "We're dating?"

"Oh, sweetheart," Ezra said with another giggle. "We're going to the date restaurant on date night, sitting at the date table and splitting dessert." Then he felt bad that he might be pressuring Rusty, so he hurried to add, "That doesn't mean anything about your identity, if you don't want it to. But we're totally going on dates."

Rusty tilted his head as if he was processing it. "Oh." Then he kept going, leading Ezra up the ramp. "I kinda wondered, but I wasn't sure how to ask."

"You can always just ask me," Ezra rushed to assure him, squeezing his arm. "Anything at all, if it helps you figure things out."

He didn't miss the expression of gratitude and relief that crossed Rusty's face. "Cool. Thanks. I don't have any friends like that. Or... I didn't, before meeting you and your friends. No wonder it took me so long to start thinking about all of this."

Ezra ached for Rusty, going through life trying to figure out what was missing and without anyone to suggest the stunningly obvious possibility. "Oh, hon."

"I'm fine," Rusty chuckled, patting Ezra's hand as they

reached the top of the ramp. He let go of Ezra's arm and put his hands in his pockets again. "More than fine. I'm glad you're the first guy I've talked to about any of this. It's exciting, in a weird way. You know?"

Ezra nearly bounced on his toes, smiling up at Rusty. "It is!" He pushed his hair back and played with the ends. "I'm happy for you."

"Thanks, hon." The pet name was clumsy, and it made them both laugh. "Maybe not," Rusty added ruefully. "I can't pull that off like you."

Ezra was almost giddy, though. "I like it." He spoke candidly without even thinking.

Rusty smiled and reached out tentatively toward him. For a moment, Ezra wasn't sure where that hand was going, but it wound up on his shoulder—affectionate, but not as tender as a touch on the cheek.

Crap. Ezra spotted a small group heading into the art gallery, and he didn't want Beau to have to put down his work when Ezra was supposed to be in charge of the shop. "I'd better go. Sorry."

"No, I'm glad you came to say hi. See you Monday, then," Rusty murmured. "Or sooner, maybe." He leaned in, less awkward this time as he kissed Ezra's cheek.

"See you," Ezra echoed and strode away toward the art gallery, his whole body vibrating as if Rusty still touched him.

He wasn't entirely sure that he was walking. He might be floating, propelled by the high that this entire conversation had left him with.

When he approached the gallery, though, he realized that the group he'd spotted hadn't been customers at all. If he'd looked closer, he might have noticed, except that looking anywhere but at Rusty when Rusty was around was damn near impossible. It was his friends, carpooling from the house to work.

Ross, Aaron, and Jesse all stood next to the side entrance, and the door was open, Beau leaning in the doorway.

Why did it feel like coming home after curfew and meeting his parents? But Ezra had nothing to be guilty over. He straightened up and smiled at his friends as he waved casually.

"Hey, everyone."

"Ez," Jesse breathed out. His eyes flickered over Ezra's shoulder, no doubt toward Rusty. "Are you two...?"

Ezra gave him a stern look. "Now, now. You need to lubricate me with high-quality spirits if you want the juicy T."

He winked and sailed past the group, hoping his casual words covered up the way his heart pounded. It didn't, because when he turned to face them, they were all watching him still.

"He's... he's straight, though." Jesse's tone was tentative, but his expression was concerned.

Suddenly, Ezra knew exactly how Rusty had felt just days ago, fending off well-meaning concern.

How could he explain these fragile, tentative steps of exploration that Rusty had taken? To anyone else, they might come off as taking advantage.

Ezra could see the sincere confusion and excitement in Rusty's eyes and hear the shake in his voice when he talked about keeping the labels off for now. That was intimate, sacred to just the two of them, and he wasn't sharing it as cheap gossip.

The worst part was the sympathy in all of their expressions. Appreciated, but *so* unnecessary.

"It's fine," Ezra brushed them off and strode for the door toward the front of the gallery.

"No, but... if he's telling everyone that he's straight..." Ross murmured.

"Darling, you can't date a closeted man." Beau folded his arms. "It'd kill you. You aren't trying to do that, are you?"

Ezra laughed, and it was a genuine sound of surprise. "No!" They might be accidentally dating, but Rusty wasn't the kind of guy to seek favors in private while making Ezra feel like he was a shameful secret.

Far from it.

"Okay, leave off him," Aaron waved. "If he wants to make a straight friend, or suck his dick, or heaven forbid, *marry* him, it's his business alone."

For a moment, Ezra's spirits lifted. He shared a smile with Aaron, grateful that he was standing up for him while not revealing what he knew.

"Aaron just wants more sex in the world," Jesse giggled while the others laughed. "Perv. Ignore his advice."

"You can't ignore something this hot," Aaron rebutted instantly, waving a limp wrist up and down himself. "Anyway, I need to drag one of you over to help put together this machine thingy. I have a lot to do today. I need to exploit your tender feelings for me to extract unpaid labor ASAP."

Ezra rolled his eyes at the rest of them. "I'll help, if someone else takes the cash register."

When they agreed to do so, Ezra made his escape. Much to his surprise, Aaron said nothing at all about what they'd witnessed on their way over to the shop, or even inside when they worked together to assemble the grinder from shitty instructions and shiny parts.

Whatever he'd thought about Aaron before, he appreciated the hell out of him for sensing what he needed and giving him this space to think. Because right now, Ezra had no answers to his friends' inevitable questions.

"I'm going camping with him tomorrow," Ezra finally spoke up when they'd finished the machine. He was about ready to turn tail and flee at Aaron's inevitable comments, but all he got was a warm smile.

"Good for you."

Ezra pretended to gasp. "No lewd suggestions? Who the hell are you, and what have you done with my friend?"

Aaron's smile grew wicked in an instant. "Okay, if you're looking for suggestions: bullet vibes and cock rings. Great luggage-space-to-orgasm ratio."

Ezra fled to the sound of Aaron's laugh, but he was grinning as the sea breeze whipped through his hair again. Maybe things were falling into place, whatever his friends thought.

He didn't need an intervention. He needed to keep his hand on the wheel and muster all his patience. This was the test of his life. But the rewards? They might just last for a whole lifetime.

For a minute, Ezra stopped to look over the flat horizon where sky met sea while he let himself daydream. Tomorrow couldn't come soon enough.

12

———

RUSTY

Deep lavender and orange gold streaked the pale blue sunset sky, but these clouds weren't a sign of rain. They felt higher from down here in a kayak, strangely enough.

"We're heading there," Rusty told Ezra, who twisted about to try to see where Rusty pointed.

This time, Ezra managed not to wobble the kayak so much. Even so, Rusty found himself breathing in sharply and bracing for cold water, just in case.

Ezra heard the gasp and laughed. "I'm not *that* unstable. Only emotionally. Hashtag: Millennial problems."

It was Rusty's turn to laugh abruptly when he understood what Ezra was saying, and he couldn't keep the boat from wobbling slightly.

"Whoa. Come on, let's land before I break out my sparkling wit. And sparkling wine."

"Is that why your bag's so heavy?" Rusty exclaimed. The kayak had barely held up to the camping gear, food, and Ezra's pack, so he'd grabbed just the essentials from his own bag and left the rest in his truck.

Even from behind, Ezra looked guilty. He tossed his hair and gripped his paddle again to help turn the kayak toward shore. "No comment. But you can't expect a bit of wilderness to interrupt sparkling wine night!"

"Lord," Rusty muttered with a laugh. The kayak nose bumped the sandy beach and stopped dead. Even when Rusty threw his weight forward to scoot forward, they didn't gain much ground. That meant wet feet for at least one of them.

"I'll get out," he offered, even though he was farther back.

"What a gentleman," Ezra teased as Rusty carefully extracted his legs from the boat, rolled up his pants legs, and stepped out. "I'll dry you off later. With my tongue."

Rusty nearly fell out of the kayak with surprise. He laughed and flicked Ezra's ear on the way past, then grabbed the nose of the kayak to haul it in.

He held out a hand to help Ezra daintily step out and then grinned. "Let's pitch our tent first of all."

Ezra pretended to fan himself and Rusty blushed, ignoring him as he grabbed the bags to haul up the shore.

Ezra helped stow the kayak where the tide wouldn't wash it out to sea, and they unpacked the tent. Rusty had chosen the simplest tent he owned, which claimed to be a three-man tent.

"Three men?" Ezra said skeptically, holding up a collapsible rod and rotating it as he stared at the tent on the ground. "Only if two of them are locked together like were-wolves mating." He nearly took Rusty's eye out with the other end. "Oops!"

Rusty disarmed him and pointed to the log nearby. "Sit there and look pretty."

Ezra pouted but went, tucking his hair behind his ears

and kicking his feet against the sand. "Sorry. I'm useless at these things."

"Like everything, it just takes practice." Rusty didn't want Ezra beating himself up for not being good at tent assembly, so he relented under that pout. "Go grab the jug of water," he instructed. "We'll get supper cooking."

"Ooh!" That got Ezra's attention, and he jogged down to the water, his steps light and bouncy.

Rusty grinned as he watched, distracted for several long seconds by the sight of Ezra's ass wrapped in tight jeans. How the hell he'd been able to comfortably kayak, he had no idea.

Oh, right. Tent. And not the one in my pants, he thought. He gulped and shook his head to focus, then swiftly pushed poles into slots and bent the supports up. In a flash, the tent was assembled while Ezra went through the contents of the food bags.

"Holy crap, you brought a real supper. I thought we were going to be eating out of foil packets." Ezra raised his hands to the heavens and flopped onto his butt in the sand. "I won't even need wine to deal with this!"

"But we'd better drink it anyway. I'm not carrying that weight back to town if we don't have to," Rusty said.

"I thought you'd never ask!" Ezra scrambled for his bag and pulled out two portable plastic wineglasses, plus a bottle. The bag hadn't seemed that large, either.

"Did you even bring any clothes?"

"Probably. Maybe not." Ezra peeked in it. "Apparently not. Just my sexy underwear. Is the tent put together? I want to change into them and get comfy. I have my practical, anti-nut-twisting underwear on right now."

Rusty's head spun. That was a lot more information than he'd expected. He just dropped the sleeping bags, pillows, and mats in the tent and then gestured. "Be my guest."

"Thank you." Ezra sashayed past, but it was hard to elegantly swoop into a tent while stooping over and crawling. He wiggled his butt, though.

Rusty let the flap fall closed and shook his head, laughing. "I'm not even sure what to do with you." He moved over to the wine bottle, cracked it open, and poured two glasses.

"Oh, I have plenty of ideas." The tent walls were so thin that they could easily carry on a conversation while Ezra was... well... mostly naked. And Ezra's voice was dripping with suggestion.

Rusty caught his breath. He swigged several large gulps of wine, refilled it from the bottle, and wiped his lips before grabbing the fire lighters. "It'll take a bit to heat up the water. I was gonna go for a swim."

Naked. Because he didn't have his bag, which meant he didn't have swim shorts. The water was calm and the day clear, so they might as well take advantage.

He loved a cold dip—it clarified his thoughts and challenged him to push himself. Rusty didn't so much love the shrinkage it was going to cause, but he might just need it to keep himself in check right now.

"Oh, there's an idea!" Ezra sounded out of breath. "Saves me wrestling these jeans back on before I have to."

The tent unzipped, and it took every ounce of Rusty's willpower not to stare back at him. He kept stacking dry driftwood into a log house around the fire starter.

Ezra wasn't shy, though. He sauntered straight through his field of vision—lean, nude, and utterly captivating—on his way down to the water.

His red hair hung loose around his shoulders, to the middle of his back. Rusty's gaze wandered down from his shoulder blades to the small of his back and then the delicious, rounded curve of his ass.

Fuck. Rusty might not have labels for himself, but he liked that vision a little too much. "Okay, now I need a cold swim," he said. Even to his own ear, he sounded rattled and breathless.

Or maybe just excited. Way too excited.

"Come and get me, then," Ezra teased, glancing back over his shoulder with a wicked grin as he trotted to the water's edge.

"Just let me get the fire on first." Rusty's hands shook, and he cursed his matches. They kept going out without landing in quite the right spot. Perhaps it was because Rusty was so distracted.

Definitely something to do with the boner straining at his hiking trousers.

Finally, thank fuck, the fire lighter caught, and flames started licking their way up the dry wood. When he was satisfied it had enough fuel, Ezra's voice attracted Rusty's attention, and he glanced toward the water.

"Ooh, ooh, ah! Ahh!"

Ezra was dancing along the water's edge, only in as far as his ankles. He kept prancing, pulling his feet up out of the water.

"You can't slow-play it," Rusty laughed. "Just dive."

"Dive? And ruin *this* hair? Tsch," Ezra exclaimed, clicking his tongue. "I think not, sir."

Rusty tried to preserve his modesty a moment longer by ducking into the tent, but Ezra wolf-whistled when he presented his ass to the shore.

Rusty snorted and flipped him off, but his heart was pounding with excitement as he quickly stripped inside the tent. There wasn't much room to work—and certainly not room for a third man, despite the tent manufacturers' claims. Thinking about tent manufacturing standards helped resolve the pants situation—or perhaps it was the cool air.

When Rusty was naked, he drew a breath and squared his shoulders. He shrugged his way out of the tent, strolling down to the water's edge like he was walking to the mailbox at the end of his driveway. His mail flag was down—for now.

Ever since Ezra had informed him that they were actually dating, he'd been nervously excited. He didn't have to formally invite Ezra into a contract or sort out every label that applied to him.

That opened the door for them to just *be* together, in the most natural versions of themselves.

As Rusty waded into the water, he bit back the yelp of his own. His toes instantly tingled with the winter water temperature, but at least he was used to it.

Before he knew it, he was in up to the knees. When he got to mid-thigh, he lunged forward to take the rest in one breathtaking gasp.

Cold penetrated every inch of him, and his body burned strangely.

"Aiiii-yi-yi!" Ezra exclaimed, his hands over his mouth. "Don't die!"

Rusty gasped as the shock cleared his system. He bobbed, toes grazing the rocks against the bottom. "It's fine."

Ezra squealed his way into the water, but to give him credit, he *was* brave enough to join Rusty—even when the ends of his hair trailed in the water around his shoulders.

"There. I've done a nature thing. Can I get out now?" Ezra gasped, treading water.

Rusty gave him a grin. "You were very brave," he teased. "You can go warm up by the fire. It should be putting out some heat now—" He broke off and laughed.

So much for a romantic evening swim. Ezra was already lunging for the shore, walking in awkward bobs as his feet moved slowly through the water while he propelled himself as fast as possible, arms windmilling.

"Oh no, the air's even colder now," Ezra lamented, one hand going to his crotch.

"Towels on top of the sleeping bags," Rusty called after him. He bobbed in place as he watched Ezra sprint for the tent, all freckled limbs.

The evening *was* beautiful, but it was already chilly with the sun sinking below the horizon and the moon peeking through the trees. No sense in catching a cold in the water, then.

Rusty followed Ezra up the beach at a more leisurely pace, giving Ezra time to get some clothes on. He paused to stir the fire and encourage it. By the time he made it to the tent, Ezra was fighting his way out, his clothes sticking to his body.

"I feel so alive I might just be dead," Ezra declared, poking his head out of the tent flap. "I need fire."

Rusty chuckled. "Help yourself," he teased.

But his whole body vibrated like a fishing line when he realized that Ezra was on his hands and knees, his face right about at crotch level, and Ezra's eyes weren't staying down.

And Rusty liked it. Loved it, even.

For a moment, all he could think about was letting go of that tightly held self-control. Letting Ezra show him what it was like, and letting his instincts take over.

But no—they had to talk first. So Rusty stepped back and smiled, well aware that he was blushing, and then ducked into the tent and wrapped himself in the other thin microfiber towel.

It was awkward to get dressed in the tiny space, but it

made a big difference. By the time Rusty joined Ezra at the fireside, the kettle was boiling and the metal grate he'd set up over it was ready to cook.

"I can see why you like it," Ezra said abruptly. He was holding his palms to the fire, wiggling his fingers. "It's romantic, in the old-fashioned sense. And I guess the lovey-dovey sense, too. If you were to find someone who's... you know... good at this."

There was a note in his voice that made Rusty pause and turn to take him in. Ezra wouldn't quite meet his gaze.

Was he rejecting him subtly, suggesting someone else would be better for him? A moment later, Rusty shook his head to himself. No way. Ezra was rejecting himself right now.

"I've been single for way too long to test that theory," Rusty said instead, smiling casually. He gathered packages of food from the bags. "What about you? Any more misadventures lately?"

"Oh, I deleted my Grindr profile," Ezra said with a quick, enthusiastic smile. "It's been nice, not feeling like I'll miss Mr. Right if I'm not online."

"That must be nice," Rusty murmured, but he was selfishly glad, too. He couldn't stake a claim on Ezra, but he sure as hell didn't want some other loser trying to twist his self-esteem to suit their own ends.

"It is." Ezra was watching Rusty and not looking away, smiling slightly.

There was much more hanging unsaid between them than the words they actually exchanged. Rusty wasn't sure he was brave enough to fill in those gaps, though.

His heart thudded as he unzipped the bag of veggies, arranged them on the grill, and added foil-wrapped chicken breasts. While those cooked, Ezra clinked glasses and they started working through the bottle of wine.

Rusty's head was already spinning by the time they'd finished off dinner, and it wasn't from drinking. The way Ezra complimented his cooking made him blush, and the way Ezra asked about his business plans made him swell with pride.

Every damn thing Ezra did, he couldn't take his eyes off him. That in itself was a huge clue. But Rusty knew their relationship wouldn't survive if he led Ezra on and then backed off a second time.

Problem was, he might not be able to avoid it. They were sharing the tent tonight, and they might not be sharing a sleeping bag, but there was no way they could sleep on opposite sides, carefully not-touching.

There was no way he wanted to do that, either.

"This is a good way to spend a night," Ezra murmured, rejoining him at the campfire after a pit stop in the trees. Instead of sitting across the fire from him, Ezra sat in the sand next to him.

"It is." Rusty didn't hesitate. He'd been ready for this moment for days. He put his arm around Ezra, sighing at the way his nerves steadied and the crackle of anxiety subsided. "And I'm glad you joined me."

Ezra hummed quietly. "I'm really glad you invited me, even if I suck at hiking."

Rusty chuckled quietly. "Nobody's good at everything. And you're a natural in the water."

"That means a lot to hear from you." Ezra's voice was quiet, but Rusty could hear him perfectly.

The faint wash of the tide on the shore and the wind through the trees were the only sounds that interrupted them. The stars were rising over the sea, and the cool breeze made Ezra shiver and draw closer.

Rusty wrapped his arm tighter, and he shoved aside his fears. *Live in the moment,* he told himself and turned his head to look at Ezra.

Ezra shifted and met his gaze, eager but restrained. It was Rusty's job to make the first move this time. No—not his job, his *pleasure.*

He leaned in and kissed Ezra, his lips clumsy at first compared to Ezra's. But as he relaxed, it clicked, and it felt goddamn perfect.

The barest acknowledgement of his desire had made it explode within him. He'd never known he was missing it, but now? He needed Ezra, and he didn't know what to do about it.

This wasn't the awkward fumbling goodnight kiss of his failed dates, or the kisses he'd given while desperate to find a reason to be attracted. He wasn't bi—or at least, not attracted to women.

Holy fuck. I'm gay.

The moment of clarity was like the cartoons where someone got hit on the head with a rubber mallet. It made him want to beam with joy. The biggest answer to the question he'd never thought to ask, and it was so simple it had stared him in the face all along.

Rusty pulled Ezra into him sharply, his lips parting as he closed his eyes. Open-mouthed, wet, hot kisses followed, and Ezra's body melted into Rusty's.

Every touch of bare skin on skin made Rusty fizz like fresh pop.

Finally, they pulled back, and Rusty tried to get a hold of his heavy breathing. He took stock of himself and blushed. He was halfway to crawling over Ezra right here in the sand, one leg flung over his lap, his hands tangled in the back of Ezra's hair, one palm caressing his cheek.

"We can call that the first kiss," Ezra managed, his voice rough with unmistakable arousal.

Rusty blinked as he tried to wake his brain up and then nodded. "Agreed."

"And this is the second." Ezra's brush of lips against Rusty's was soft and playful, making Rusty grin. "And the third." He went naughtier this time, coaxing one of Rusty's lips between his teeth and nipping.

Oh, man, that made Rusty's whole body just twang and go all tight and hard in the right places.

"You can keep doing that all night," he breathed out hoarsely. "I have a lot to learn, apparently."

Ezra giggled softly, swaying into him and resting the side of his head on his shoulder. "And I'd love to teach you. But the fire's going out."

"Huh?" Rusty glanced over and realized he was right. "Damn. We need more wood."

Ezra burst out laughing. "I think we're well stocked, babe."

Rusty grinned, a shiver of delight tracing down his spine. The idea of sharing a tent while exploring this whole new kind of arousal thrilled him to the core. "Let's wash up the dishes first."

They kicked sand over the fire and carried the dishes down to the water's edge, and Rusty showed Ezra how he washed them and tossed them into a net bag to dry overnight.

By the time that was done, the exhaustion of a long day had set in, and they were both stifling yawns. It didn't stop them taking a minute together to stand on the shore, side by side. Arms around each other's waist, they gazed toward the star-studded blackness where the sky met the horizon.

"Perfect," Ezra murmured, and Rusty didn't have to ask. He knew exactly what he meant.

Everything *was* perfect right now. Who knew what would happen tonight, or tomorrow, or for the years to come? And who cared?

What mattered was the here and now. Always.

13

EZRA

It took Ezra several long moments to realize why he couldn't successfully cuddle with the warm body next to his.

Camping. Separate sleeping bags. Damn it, I didn't think that one through, Ezra thought. As he stretched, he froze and stifled his squeak of surprise. His muscles were stiff all over in a way he hadn't experienced in years—since his last workout at a gym.

He opened his eyes to peek at Rusty and then smiled when he saw him still asleep.

Wait, last night, did we...?

He'd only shared a bottle of light sparkling wine with Rusty. Definitely not blackout drunk. Why couldn't he remember?

Then, the answer to all his questions came at once.

No, he hadn't done anything with Rusty. They'd stumbled into the tent together, in silent agreement that sleep was their top priority. It had seemed like so much effort to get into the tent, and then changed, and then into their sleeping bags, before their eyes shut. Ezra had fallen asleep like a ton of logs and slept better than he had in years. Apparently this exercise stuff wasn't the *worst*.

Except for the soreness today—that could gladly fuck off.

He wriggled closer to Rusty, feeling like a video he'd seen on the internet of a bat swaddled in a washcloth. Once he managed it, Ezra pressed his face into the broad wall of sleeping bag that he presumed stretched across his back. At least he could catch a few more moments' rest, since Rusty wasn't up yet.

This trip is good, Ezra thought, smiling to himself as he snuck a hand down to fondle his morning wood. Even if he couldn't properly spoon with Rusty, it was probably just as well. It was rude to wake him up with a pressing need until they'd agreed that it was okay.

He bit his lip, pressing his palm into the hard length and swallowing the gasp. Falling asleep had cut off the conversation he desperately wanted to have, but there was still plenty of time this morning.

It was hard to banish the visions of all the things he wanted to do to Rusty in this tent, but his eyes were still heavy, and closing them seemed like a good idea.

Moments later, when he opened them, Rusty was gone. The light outside was considerably brighter.

Crap, he'd actually fallen asleep again.

Ezra slowly pushed himself upright, wincing as every muscle in his arms protested. He unzipped the tent and then smiled at the sight. He could just leave the tent flap open and enjoy it.

Rusty was bobbing in the water, splashing around like he was born to it. He was naked, which took up the majority of Ezra's attention. The scenery was pretty and all, but... he was naked, and suddenly, Ezra wasn't half-asleep anymore. And neither was his cock.

He gulped, shivering in the fresh breeze as it swept into the tent. Oh, that would help preserve a bit of his modesty. He didn't want to stride up to Rusty with a big, throbbing boner. That might scare him off.

Ezra giggled under his breath, grabbing his phone to check the time. While he was at it, he snapped a photo of Rusty, who had stood up so the water lapped around his thighs. Water droplets trickled down the rivulets in his back, and Ezra wanted to lick them all off him. That would make a hell of a painting.

If Rusty could bathe in the cold water in the morning, so could Ezra.

Ezra stripped out of his pajamas, then combed back his hair, tossed aside his phone, and ducked out of the tent. Instantly, he covered his sensitive bits with one hand against the chill. "I can do this, I can do this, I can do this," he muttered, his volume and pitch steadily increasing as he trotted over the sand.

"Well, good morning," Rusty laughed when he approached.

Ezra danced from foot to foot in the surf as soon as his feet touched it. It was cool but somehow warmer than the air around them. Not by much, though. He was shivering all over. "Oh, God, I can't do this!"

"I can toss you in," Rusty offered cheerily. Ezra glared at him, but it only made Rusty laugh. "You're adorable when you glare at me."

Ezra huffed and pushed his hair back again, dropping his hand to embrace the chill. "I'm actually dying," he announced, clutching his chest. "Of cold and exercise. Kill me now, before I have to paddle back. Why did I think camping was a good idea?"

Rusty laughed again, the unsympathetic bastard. "You'll live."

"You know, ten seconds ago I thought you were my new muse," Ezra grumbled. He squeaked as he stepped into the surf. "And now—eeek!—I'm sure of it. My muse is a real asshole."

God, Rusty's laugh was unreasonably beautiful. It rolled from him like a wave of thunder, like a bow vibrating a string in Ezra's soul.

Then Rusty reached out toward him, both palms outstretched. His smile was gentle and enthusiastic. He watched Ezra with an adoring expression like a goddamn golden retriever, and it made Ezra blush. "Come on. You can do it. It's better once you're in."

With that confidence in him, Ezra knew he *had* to. Whether he *could* was another matter.

He took a deep breath and ran toward Rusty. The cold water shock working its way up his thighs and numbing him instantly made him scream softly, flailing at Rusty's chest as he stumbled into him.

"This is the worst idea in the history of the planet, and if I get pneumonia you're personally responsible for making me chicken soup," Ezra whimpered, dancing from foot to foot.

His legs were ice blocks now, but he was afraid to writhe more than this. After all, they were mostly up to the *really* sensitive bits, and he still had a vivid memory of that unpleasant kayak dunking.

But Rusty didn't indulge his complaints. "You're a star," he breathed out, his arm wrapping around Ezra's waist as he pulled him against him.

Oh, fuck. Ezra's whole brain screeched to a halt at the

only possible distraction from the intense chill. They were naked, bodies pressed together skin to skin in the cold surf.

Ezra looped his arms around Rusty's waist gently, in case he wanted to pull back. But Rusty wasn't shying away. In fact, his grip tightened on Ezra as Ezra's thighs slotted between Rusty's, and heat shot through him. The contrast in chilly water and the sudden heat that burned through his cheeks was a wild ride.

"Well, hello there." Rusty's voice was soft. He looped his other arm around Ezra's waist, too, and then reached up to brush Ezra's hair out of his face. He tucked it gently behind his ear, his finger trailing down Ezra's neck to his shoulder again.

Ezra suddenly couldn't breathe, the air between them was so thick. "Hi," he whispered back, his body vibrating with the tension. The pain in his muscles nearly forgotten, he pressed a kiss against Rusty's shoulder and then gazed at him, chest tight with worry. Was that okay?

More than okay, apparently. Rusty only smiled at him, those gorgeous dimples appearing. "I like the idea of being your muse, even if I am an asshole."

Ezra swallowed hard. "Cool," he breathed out. It was such an inadequate response, but suddenly all his words seemed to fail him. There was no clever flirting left. All he wanted to do was show Rusty how he felt.

Ezra couldn't resist loosening his grip, letting one hand run slowly up Rusty's back. He didn't dare go down yet and cup that delicious ass, as much as he wanted to.

The touch made Rusty sigh, but the noise sounded pleased. In turn, he was running his fingers through the ends of Ezra's hair, playing with it against his upper back.

"Sleep well?" Rusty murmured.

"Really well. I barely remember going to bed," Ezra admitted with a laugh.

Rusty grinned. "Me neither." His gaze flickered between Ezra's eyes. "I think I wore you out, and I haven't even gotten you in bed yet."

The *yet* was about as subtle as a sledgehammer in the nervous, fragile excitement in the air between them.

Fuck, yes. That was a *go* if Ezra had ever heard one.

He grinned up at Rusty coyly, melting against his body as he tilted his face up for a kiss. "We can fix that."

"Mmm." Rusty didn't break Ezra's gaze, his eyes fixed on him like he was the prettiest scenery around here. He leaned down, meeting Ezra's unspoken cue and kissing him.

This kiss was slow and gentle at first, exploratory, but it didn't stay that way for long. Ezra pressed up into it, catching Rusty's lower lip and nipping it. As if to scold him, Rusty retaliated the same way, but he didn't let go of Ezra's lip for a long few seconds. Instead, he sucked on it, flicking his tongue along the sensitive skin.

Fuck, that made Ezra moan with pleasure. The sound only encouraged Rusty, though, and he grinned at him for a second before he returned to the kiss, wet and openmouthed and hungry.

Ezra wanted—*needed*—him. His nails dug into Rusty's back as he clutched tightly to him, his knees wobbly. The surf lapped around his thighs, but he hardly noticed now. If he was numb, that just meant more blood supply to other parts.

Rusty's breath was hot against his mouth, his kisses insistent and strong. One after another, they rained on Ezra's lips, and gradually on his cheek, tracing a line over toward his ear.

Ezra panted for breath, tilting his head to the side and holding on tight. "Fuck, that's good." Rusty's grip never loosened, though, as he found the spot behind Ezra's ear that made his whole body wobble.

Rusty's voice was hoarse as he pulled back. "That's an interesting effect. I'll have to remember it."

"Jerk," Ezra muttered, but he couldn't keep the dizzy smile from his lips. He kissed Rusty's chest, bending over to get at Rusty's nipples and exact revenge. One nipple at a time, Ezra kissed gently across the hard nubs of skin, flicking his tongue back and forth until Rusty gasped for breath.

As he'd hoped, Rusty's hands slid straight to Ezra's hips, his fingers lightly grazing Ezra's skin. "That's a nice view."

Ezra knew it, too. He was a couple inches shorter than Rusty anyway. When he bent to kiss his chest, it gave Rusty a view straight down his back, all the way to the top of the curve of his ass. He grinned and straightened up, licking a slow, sensual trail up Rusty's throat toward his lips. "Is it?"

"You tease," Rusty growled, his nails digging into Ezra's hips. He jerked him close, so close that Ezra was practically riding his thigh.

Cold or no, Ezra was getting hard. Judging by the pressure against his groin, he wasn't the only one. He glanced down and grinned. "Oh look, our dicks are staying clear of the water. How clever of them."

Rusty burst out laughing. He ground slowly against Ezra, his eyes going wide. "Oh, that's good."

"You know what would be better?" Ezra fluttered his lashes as he tilted his head back to meet Rusty's eyes again.

"What's that?"

"Getting our nuts out of ice bath danger."

Rusty finally pulled back, letting go of Ezra as he grinned. "You mean if I try this..." He scooped water in his hands.

Ezra gasped. "If you even try...!" He reflexively shoved a handful of water at Rusty as he scrambled backward.

"Would I?" Rusty gave him an innocent smile. But just when Ezra got his footing, he shook the handful of water across Ezra's chest.

Ezra gasped at the sudden cold shock against hot, sensitive skin. "You sly little asstrumpet!"

Rusty's laugh only provoked him more. Oh, it was on. Rusty didn't know who he was messing with. Ezra hadn't been king of the water park for nothing as a kid.

He beat both hands through the water toward Rusty, splashing him with a wall of water. All he needed was one well-placed splash to win this round.

The yowl let him know he'd succeeded. "Oh, shit. Okay, okay!" Rusty gasped. It was his turn to run for the shore, but he moved in slow motion. "Mercy!"

That gave Ezra plenty of time to grab that hot little ass with both cold, wet hands. "No mercy, motherfucker."

Rusty yelped and laughed again, reaching back to try to hook Ezra around the waist.

Ezra just escaped in time, lurching sideways and then sprinting through the surf. It was comical how high he had to lift his feet to get clear of the water, and even he was laughing by the time they both made it to the beach.

"Just for that, you're warming me up," Rusty scolded him, bracing his hands on his thighs and shaking off like a dog.

Ezra giggled, dancing out of the way. "You started it. But I'll happily warm up any body part I cooled off."

"I hope you mean that," Rusty growled quietly. He grabbed Ezra's hand and towed him up the beach toward the tent, his stride long and purposeful. That lack of hesitation, the utter confidence he showed, just made Ezra's knees melt just like his feet melted into the sand.

The mood couldn't be more different from how they'd gone to bed yesterday. Now, they were both full of vigorous energy, desperate to warm up, and more than that—desperate for each other.

Nobody and nothing else to distract them, just the chemistry that they couldn't seem to escape, and adoring gazes, and eager hands. And all Ezra could do was pray that Rusty wouldn't regret a moment of it later.

RUSTY

"Mmmph—need to—" Rusty tried to talk, but Ezra kissed the words from his mouth. He had to shift Ezra gently, walking him up to the tent and reaching out one-handed to fumble for the zipper.

Ezra finally pulled back, his breathing thin and quick as he grinned. "You first."

"You just want the view," Rusty teased, ducking inside. It was a lot warmer in here now that they'd been properly chilled.

Ezra followed, dropping onto his knees with ease. Oh, that made Rusty's brain go a mile a minute.

"Quick, zip up," Rusty urged, and Ezra fumbled but drew the zipper across. Instantly, even with one thin layer between them and the outside world, it felt like their own private cocoon.

"Don't get the whole place wet, though." Rusty grinned, grabbing towels and tossing one at Ezra. They wiped the water off themselves, their gazes still raking over each other's body. The atmosphere was thick with tension, and Rusty kind of wanted to draw it out.

His boner was still rock-hard and ready for whatever was coming. He wrapped one hand around it, squeezing gently and watching Ezra.

Ezra moaned. "Oh, that's a great view. If I'd known you were into that, I'd have plopped my ass in a banana floaty in the harbor weeks ago."

Rusty laughed as he laid his towel out along the sleeping bag so he could sit down. "You look like a merman swimming in the ocean. I love it." All he wanted to see was Ezra floating placidly on the waves, that gorgeous red hair fanned out around him as he fluttered his tail.

Ezra paused as he squeezed the ends of his hair in his towel. "Huh?"

"No, just your long, red hair, and... I don't know, you'd look at home stretched out on a rock with shells in your hair." Rusty blushed, suddenly embarrassed at how vividly he daydreamed about Ezra. Maybe he shouldn't have said anything.

But Ezra smiled and winked. "A-blrrr-blub-blub?" Ezra tilted his head and widened his eyes innocently, playing along like he could only speak... Mermish? He ran one hand down his own chest toward his cock, fluttering his lashes.

Rusty snickered. "I'm glad you let this sailor lure you ashore." He pretended to think about it. "Or did I get lured by a siren...?"

"You don't want to hear me sing about anal," Ezra said with a soft snort. "Or maybe you do. I can't think of a rhyme for *my tight hole* that isn't *your thick pole*."

Rusty cracked up again. "Is *that* my deepest desire?" His cock was aching at the dirty words, and he jerked one hand slowly along it, his heart racing at his own boldness. "Your tight hole?"

"If it isn't yet, it will be." Ezra glanced at Rusty from under his lashes, kneeling primly next to him.

Goddamn, even knowing it was a setup to make him even hungrier for Ezra, it worked. It was as natural as breathing to grab Ezra around the waist and pull him in sharply, until he tumbled on top of Rusty.

"Oh, no! I'm being kidnapped by a sexy sailor." Ezra swooned onto Rusty's lap. "He might take advantage of me."

Rusty grinned and slapped Ezra's ass. He gasped just as deeply as Ezra did at the gorgeous, sharp sound that rang through the air. "Don't play innocent now, you."

Ezra's facade of innocence dropped moments later. "I can't even pretend. I'm more the devil on your shoulder than the angel. It's the redhead gene. I can't help it." He squirmed closer to Rusty, spreading his knees so their cocks bumped against one another's.

Their faces were just inches apart. From here, he could admire Ezra's freckles, the pout of his lips, the curve of his neck. God, he looked gorgeous like this.

Rusty couldn't resist him for a moment longer, and he didn't want to. He might not fully understand what he was doing, but his instincts guided him. That, and the sneaky gay porn videos he'd downloaded over the last week, just in case they became relevant.

They'd been all right, but so... scripted. There was no playful, flirty back-and-forth and no sensual, slow element to what had unfolded. Maybe he needed help to find better porn. Or maybe he just needed Ezra to teach him in person.

Just do what feels good, Rusty told himself. Ezra would correct him if need be.

Rusty pulled Ezra in with an arm looped around his

shoulders. They kissed languidly at first, like they had all the time in the world. In here, it felt like they did.

"I love seeing you naked," Ezra whispered against his lips. "That was the perfect sight to wake up to. Well, no. I woke up earlier this morning and saw you still asleep, which was hella cute, but problematic for my morning wood."

"You had it, too, huh?" Rusty's throat went dry. "Wish you'd woken me up. We could have taken care of it at the same time."

Ezra pressed their foreheads together. "But then I might not have gotten you like this, horny and desperate for my touch." He walked his fingers down Rusty's side. "Feel my cock against yours?"

Rusty jerked his head in the tiniest of nods. Ezra would feel it anyway, pressed together as they were. "I love it."

"You'll love this even more." Ezra slid his hand between their bodies. It was cool, but at least not freezing anymore. That coolness felt incredibly good in its own way.

Long, slender fingers wrapped around Rusty's shaft, and Ezra pressed his own erection against Rusty's, squeezing them together in his hand. "When you can feel my shaft pulsing against yours, me spilling my hot load across you..."

With this man straddling his lap, bold and dirty, Rusty growled quietly. He pressed hot kisses from Ezra's lips to that spot by his ear. When he flicked against Ezra's earlobe with his tongue and then pressed a long kiss behind his ear, he was rewarded with a quick series of moans and whimpers.

Ezra's grip tightened, and he started stroking their cocks together. Rusty thrust lightly, the slickness between their shafts lubricating the way, and grabbed Ezra's hips to keep him still as he did so.

Fuck, he could already imagine how hot it would be to be buried balls-deep inside Ezra, making him throw his head back and bare his throat. He wanted to grab Ezra, fucking him hard and fast just like this.

Ezra's quiet moans were joined by grunts of pleasure as Rusty's imagination took over and ran wild. He kissed Ezra's neck and throat, enjoying finding new spots that made Ezra squirm on top of him.

"You're imagining it, aren't you?" Ezra breathed out. "Me taking your great big cock inside me until you stretch me open." He squeezed their cocks together for emphasis, his grip just perfectly tight.

Sparks of heat tickled Rusty's shaft and ran deep into his belly. His head was so sensitive to each brush of Ezra's ridge sliding across his own. How had nobody told him how fucking incredible this would feel?

Rusty jerkily nodded. "Can't stop picturing it now."

"I want to blow you first, though," Ezra whispered. He loosened his grip, and Rusty groaned. The brief protest from his cock was worth it for the heat of Ezra's mouth.

He'd never felt this before, but he'd imagined it plenty of times.

"Yes, please," Rusty gasped.

Ezra grinned and slid down the sleeping bag in one fluid motion, until he stretched out—his head in Rusty's lap, toes brushing the tent door.

"Now, uh... bad time to be asking, but were you tested recently?" Ezra asked, his gaze flicking to Rusty's.

Rusty gulped. He wanted to lie and say yes to spare himself the embarrassment, but he also didn't want to lie to Ezra's face.

Ezra could clearly see the conflict going through his eyes, because he propped himself up on his elbows. "It's okay if you're not negative. We'll figure it out."

"N-No, I... I don't need testing." Ezra gave him a side-eye

that looked like it came with a lecture, so Rusty hurried on before he could waste his breath on words instead of sucking him off. "I mean I got it done once, in case. But I've never done... this. With anyone."

Ezra's expression shifted from surprise to disbelief and then—not amusement, as Rusty had feared, but delight. "Really?"

"Yeah," Rusty mumbled. "Never got that far with women, never wanted to... and you're the first guy... so..."

"I get to give you your first blowjob? Oh, hon! Let's stop wasting time!" Ezra beamed at him. In a rush of breath, like he couldn't wait to suck Rusty's cock, he added, "I'm tested, all negative, good to go, ready to lick your Tootsie Pop."

He was already staring down at Rusty, too, his tongue darting along his lower lip.

Fuck, Rusty was hard and wet already. He twitched under the gaze, his breath coming in a shaky laugh. "Do whatever you want to me."

Ezra winked. "Oh, I will." He gently curled his fingers around the length, holding the weight in his palm like he was admiring it. Then, his tongue darted out.

It was strange, the sparks that flew through Rusty's whole body when Ezra's tongue dragged from base to tip. He'd never imagined it like *this*—so good that he instantly needed more.

Now, he saw what all the appeal was. "Yes," Rusty gasped, curling his toes into the sleeping bag. There wasn't much room to squirm around in here, but he wanted to grab something. With no headboard, he settled on Ezra's shoulders.

Ezra giggled. "You ain't felt nothing yet. Grab my hair, babe."

"Are you sure?" Rusty's voice cracked. "Your..." Ezra's

hooded gaze flicked up, and he nodded once when Rusty started to ask. "Yes? Awesome. Tell me if I'm hurting you," Rusty whispered. He stroked his fingers through the hair at the back of Ezra's head, then gently wound a fistful around his fingers.

"That's the point." Ezra cast a fond look up at him before he kissed the head of his cock again. "Didn't I tell you I want you to use me?"

Fuck. Rusty's hands were shaking, he was so turned on. It took all he had to restrain himself from just thrusting into Ezra's mouth, and he suspected that Ezra was trying to entice him to do just that.

But instead, he dealt with Ezra's teasing kisses and licks along his shaft, even if his grunts became more pleading and desperate with every passing minute. Ezra kept moaning, too, sending little vibrations through him.

Finally, without warning, Ezra took him in whole, those gorgeous lips stretching around the head of his cock and plunging down to the base. The wet heat made him blush as his breath caught in his throat. Better yet, tightness wrapped around the head of his cock.

The cry Rusty gave must have been heard all the way over in Hart's Bay. He tightened his grip instinctively, and Ezra grunted. He kept his head still, gaze flicking up to meet Rusty's.

Ezra grunted once, and then it became obvious that he was waiting.

Waiting for Rusty to fuck his mouth.

Oh, I've died and gone to heaven, Rusty thought. His fingers curled harder into the loop of hair around his hand, and he grinned as Ezra moaned and squirmed. He started pushing up with his hips, watching and feeling those smooth lips drag along the length of his shaft.

It was too fucking hot, watching his thick cock disappearing into that gorgeous mouth. Ezra had never looked prettier than he did now, hazy eyes and swollen lips and hair floating everywhere. Ezra's hard-on bumped against his shin every time Rusty pulled Ezra in toward him.

Rusty was so turned on he could hardly think. Or, more importantly, hold back the orgasm that was approaching at a hundred miles an hour.

This was a thousand times more intense than his own hand, and Rusty had never felt anything like it. But he *could* tell when that cliff edge was crashing near. It was just far higher, more dizzying, than it had ever been before.

"Fuck." Rusty gulped for breath. "I think I'm—watch out, baby." He tried to loosen his grip, but Ezra's hand slammed down on top of his own, holding it there.

Oh, fuck. Ezra was going to swallow Rusty's load.

That was the last thing Rusty thought before bliss vibrated through every tense muscle in his body.

It was like searching in the corners of his living room for every piece of a broken glass when Rusty tried to compose his thoughts again. Everything was sharp and vivid. Adrenaline pumped through him, yet he felt weirdly relaxed at the same time. Sleepy, even.

Contented. That was the word he was trying to put his finger on. As Ezra scooted up onto his lap again, Rusty automatically looped one arm around his waist and rubbed his back with the other hand.

Staying skin to skin came automatically, as did Rusty's smile. He didn't even realize he was doing it until Ezra beamed back at him and touched his cheek. "I like that smile on you."

Rusty's cheeks flushed with pleasure at the compliment.

He could hardly take his eyes off Ezra, knowing where those lips had just been. "Th-Thanks."

"God, you're hot," Ezra murmured. "Was that really your first time?"

"Cross my heart." Rusty swallowed as he pressed his palm into Ezra's chest and dragged it down slowly, admiring the thin trail of red hairs that led up just past his belly button.

But when Rusty reached Ezra's stomach, Ezra caught his hand and stopped it, twining their fingers together.

"Hm?" Rusty glanced up again, those deep brown eyes piercing him once more.

"Don't feel obligated to reciprocate," Ezra murmured. "It was my pleasure to treat you. Orgasms aren't always tit-for-tat."

"No, but I want to." Rusty couldn't explain the desperation in his chest. He tried to untangle their fingers, but Ezra's grip was strong. "You deserve to come just as hard as I just did. I might not know what I'm doing, but I'm not going to let you settle for less than you deserve."

Ezra had made Rusty feel like the most desirable man alive for a few minutes. It wasn't just about reciprocation. He needed to make Ezra feel cherished—as beautiful as the image of the merman he'd just seen.

"Well." Ezra gave a breathy laugh and tossed his hair, finally letting go of Rusty's hand. He looped his arms around Rusty's neck, his knees lazily splayed to either side. "What a gentleman. I'm not sure if you're getting my dick or hopes up more."

"Hope springs eternal in the hard-on?" Rusty grinned as he peered between their bodies at the throbbing length that poked up between their stomachs.

It was something else, touching another man's cock—

stroking, even. The warm, velvet length wasn't unfamiliar, but the shape was a little different. Thinner, with a sharper head and higher nuts.

Ezra cried out quietly when Rusty ran his fingertips across his balls, and Rusty grinned, cataloguing it in his growing list of ways to get a reaction from him.

As he gingerly wrapped his fingers around the shaft, he stroked about as hard as he liked and hoped that was right.

Ezra made it clear. "Yes, good," Ezra breathed. "Faster."

It felt backward, but it was too late to switch hands now. Rusty had Ezra squirming on his lap, his hips bucking whenever his strokes slowed. It was hypnotic.

Best of all was watching his pale lashes flutter closed, lines appearing around his eyes as he scrunched his face up adorably. Ezra bit his lip, so rather than kiss him, Rusty leaned in, pressing kisses slowly along his jaw to the throbbing pulse point in his neck.

Slowly, Rusty's confidence grew. He'd had years of practice on himself. Applying that to another guy wasn't hard—especially when he was rewarded with these beautiful sounds.

He even slowed his pace, running his fingertips down along Ezra's balls again and tickling gently. He wanted to draw it out so it would feel even better for Ezra in the end.

"Fuck," Ezra gasped. "How'd you get so good at this?"

Rusty chuckled quietly. "Intuition. I've been waiting a long time for this," he whispered. "Also, a lot of jerking off after fucking up on dates."

Ezra laughed breathlessly.

It was a thought that hadn't even privately occurred to him until this moment, but the moment he said it, he knew it was true.

How long had he dismissed stray thoughts as the product

of too much porn or too little sex? How many times had he watched videos and focused just on the guys in them? How many times had he come to their moans, ignoring the supposed stars of the videos?

Fuck, it was like ripping a blindfold off after stumbling around a maze for years. The light was painful, yet he drank it in without pause, desperate for every experience he'd missed until now.

"Yes, baby. You're so perfect," Ezra whispered. His voice crackled with pleasure, but Rusty never doubted the sincerity in his words.

Rusty put the exciting discovery of his thoughts aside for later. Instead, he focused on the hottest fucking sight he'd seen in his life: Ezra close to the edge of orgasm right here on his lap, skin shining with sweat and hair falling into his face.

"You're gorgeous. I love watching you," Rusty murmured, pressing his lips against Ezra's neck and nuzzling behind his ear. He kept his other arm firmly around Ezra's back, supporting him.

Every flick of his palm up the warm, thick shaft made Ezra gasp. Rusty wanted to explore more, but he'd found something that worked. Stopping to try anything fancy now would only get an elbow in his ribs.

Rusty was already halfway to hard again with how fucking hot this was. They could easily spend the whole day taking turns shooting their loads. Which sounded awesome, but they *did* have work to get to in town.

"I'm so close," Ezra gasped. "Don't stop. Please."

The desperation in his voice made Rusty's grip tighten. He crushed Ezra's chest against his, burying his face in Ezra's neck. "Never," he whispered, kissing his neck and shoulder.

"Yes...!" Ezra couldn't finish the word, losing his voice.

All he had were harsh pants that finished in a long, low growl. The sounds slammed every one of Rusty's buttons at once.

"Come for me," Rusty ordered him, his voice low and commanding. He wanted to wring this pleasure out of Ezra over and over, until he was so spent that he begged for a break.

A cry tore from Ezra's throat as he rode Rusty's lap, making Rusty imagine him squeezed tight around his own cock. Ezra thrust into the tight ring of Rusty's fingers as his hot load splattered between their bodies.

The whole time, Rusty held him close, whispering in his ear. "So gorgeous. That's it. You're so sexy. You feel so good on my lap."

It was filthy and unashamed and glorious, yet strangely, pure and raw and *real*.

Nothing was ever going to be the same.

Rusty grinned as he finally loosened his grip, stroking Ezra until the last droplet squeezed out.

"Oh, God. We're a mess again," Ezra laughed breathily. He was all sweaty and glorious, pushing his hair out of his face, swaying where he knelt over Rusty.

"Mmm." Rusty winked, rubbing Ezra's back before he flopped onto his back. "Next time, we'll save time and do it in the ocean." He wiped himself off with the towel and found the driest patch before handing it to Ezra.

Ezra snorted. "My pipes might freeze. That *would* save on cleanup, but I don't want to test it." He cleaned himself off and bundled up the towel, then finally levered himself off Rusty and lay on his back next to him.

"So, that was awesome." Rusty grinned over at Ezra.

As he got dressed, Ezra watched Rusty with a smile that made something in his chest flip-flop faster than ever. Yeah.

He was pretty sure that was the dopamine and all that stuff talking, but he was glad that he'd shared his first time with Ezra.

"Told you so. And there's so many more things we can try," Ezra said.

A shiver ran through Rusty. Was that a promise? He damn well hoped so. Because there were so many more things he wanted to do with him now.

Instinct hadn't failed him yet.

15

It was too good to be true.

Not only had Ezra successfully camped for an entire night without floods, fires, or calamity, but he'd shared a tent with his crush. And then he'd introduced the not-so-straight man of his dreams to the joys of gay sex for the very first time.

It was hard not to float down to the water's edge in order to wash up the breakfast dishes, while Rusty put out the fire and started taking down the tent. Driftwood and seaweed floated nearby, and the waves were slow but steady. He only had to scramble backward a few times a minute to avoid a big one.

Ezra crouched by the water's edge, swilling sea water across the plates while trying to keep his feet out of the surf. Just because he was barefoot didn't mean he wanted to freeze any more body parts off than he already had today.

He was in a world of his own when Rusty spoke up behind him.

"Just about ready."

"Yah!" Ezra gasped, tipping forward. He flailed for balance and dropped the dishes, then tried to grab for them.

"No!" Just before he hit the water, Rusty grabbed him around the waist and hauled him up, nearly throwing him backward onto the beach. They had to scramble several paces back before they outran the wave and the log it was carrying up toward them surprisingly quickly.

The wave finally pulled the wood back along with it, and it slowly rolled back down. It had been bobbing around just offshore this whole time, looking harmless enough that Ezra had stopped noticing it.

But the plate disappeared along with everything else the tide claimed.

"I was fine," Ezra waved it off, pouting. "Now your plate's gone."

Rusty grunted. "That's called a sneaker wave. It sneaks up on you. They're a lot bigger on some beaches. You can break bones when they pick up logs and dump them on you." His tone was serious, but Ezra was watching the plate bobbing away.

"Oh... ass-crackers," Ezra moaned. The water would definitely soak his jeans if he tried to wade out to knee depth to grab it—and that log was still there.

But Rusty just grinned and looked around, then grabbed a long, black strand of seaweed.

Ezra laughed. "No way." He was *not* going to lasso it.

"Watch and see." Rusty winked. Cool as a cucumber, he held both ends, tossed the middle into the surf in a big loop, and the plate drifted in along with it.

Ezra's jaw dropped. "What? Seriously?"

Rusty grinned and added the stray plate to the net bag and pulled the drawstrings shut. "There." He ushered Ezra away from the edge of the surf like it was nothing.

Ezra cracked into giggles as they walked back up the beach to dry sand, taking Rusty's hand. "You're one of a kind." Ahead of them, the tent was all packed up, their bags in a neat little pile, and Rusty had already hauled the kayak out.

"I hope that's a good thing." Rusty's eyes sparkled playfully as he deposited the bag on top of their other stuff. He didn't let go of Ezra's hand to let him put his shoes on, though.

"It is." Ezra faced Rusty and took his other hand now, too, swinging them back and forth. "I know a good thing when I see it."

"I know a good thing when I feel it." Rusty's grin was suggestive. "And boy, did I feel it today." Then his tone picked up again, sweeter and sparkling. "Thank you for coming with me overnight. This has been a great break."

Ezra bounced up on his toes, fighting the sinking sand to peck Rusty's lips. "You're welcome."

"In fact, I was wondering..." Rusty cleared his throat, his grip on Ezra's hands tightening.

Ezra caught his breath, unable to hide the small gasp he gave. Just reading Rusty's expression told him what he was about to ask. He looked eager, excitable, but nervous—like a puppy trying its best to please him.

"Would you like to date? Make this official?"

Ezra swallowed hard, his mouth suddenly dry as his ears rang. Those exact words—he'd daydreamed about them for weeks, but he hadn't seriously expected to hear them.

And he certainly hadn't thought that he'd react this way. Instead of squealing with delight and bouncing into Rusty's arms, Ezra's fight-or-flight reaction kicked in.

Is this really a good idea? Is it too good to be true? Can it last?

A hundred questions hit him in the span of two or three seconds. Not long enough to think of any answers, but long enough to make it clear to Rusty that Ezra was hesitating.

Worry wrinkled Rusty's brow as he caught his breath. "Oh. If you don't want to—"

"No, I—"

"I mean, I know it's sudden—"

"I like you, I just—"

They were talking over each other, suddenly looking everywhere *but* each other's eyes. And then they both went quiet, waiting for the other to finish.

"You first," Rusty said with a nervous little laugh.

Ezra licked his lips. It was hard to keep his hands from shaking, but he tried to breathe deeply. Rusty stayed quiet now, letting him think, thankfully.

And he had plenty of thoughts.

I got what I wanted, Ezra thought. *I want this. I want him. So why am I shutting down now?*

But it was good to be cautious, wasn't it? It had gotten them this far. He'd rather have the heartache of missed opportunity than the total heartbreak later.

It would be all too easy to lose Rusty, one way or another. Not only was life itself a hazard, but he had so much uncertainty on his plate.

"Penny for your thoughts?" Rusty finally asked.

Ezra gulped. He didn't want to share all of them—like *What happens if you go back to Maine?* He wasn't going to be another naysayer in Rusty's life.

Rusty had enough of those, and they were trying to push him out of Hart's Bay and into a more sensible career. He'd already left for more opportunities once. If he had to, he'd do it again, leaving Ezra alone.

No, not alone. He'd moved here with his best friends

because of just that—his fear of being alone and left behind. His friends would have his back.

"I just think... I don't want to be an experiment." Ezra was almost afraid to breathe. "I don't want you to rush into deciding anything because of me, either."

Rusty's expression shifted from worry to thoughtfulness now. He swung their hands gently and nodded. "Uh-huh? And?"

"I just... I can't date someone closeted." Ezra's breath came out in a rush as he closed his eyes. "I didn't want to admit it before, because I didn't want you rushing into coming out when maybe you're not attracted to men after all and you just wanted to try things and I offered to let you do that anyway so it wouldn't be fair—"

Ezra ran out of breath, his breath ragged as he inhaled, and Rusty took the chance to interrupt. He let go of one hand, pressing a finger against Ezra's lips. "Breathe. It's okay," he murmured.

Ezra *was* awfully dizzy right now. He nodded as Rusty let his hand fall away again, then stepped forward to hug him. "I'm sorry. I didn't want to be that asshole going *come out for me or else.*"

"But you need a boyfriend who's already out?" Rusty's voice didn't sound as harsh as he'd feared.

Ezra nodded once, his heart thumping. God, he was almost sick with worry. Would this be it—the demand that was too much for their relationship to weather?

"That's fair," Rusty said after a few long moments. He pulled away and took Ezra's waist, waiting until Ezra met his gaze. When he did, Ezra couldn't look away. Rusty was so fucking sincere all the time. It was one of the things he loved about him.

"You think?" Ezra blinked. "But I was telling you all

along I don't mind if you experiment with me. It doesn't have to mean anything..."

"And what about *your* needs?" On that word, very gently, Rusty shook Ezra, his expression earnest. "You've told me now, so I'm going to respect that."

Ezra blinked several times, his throat going tight. He rested his hands on Rusty's forearms, trying to clear his mind. His heart and soul were already telling him to hold to that line and not back down. He *wasn't* okay with dating a closeted man, even his dream guy. At last, he nodded. "Thank you."

"Okay." Rusty kissed Ezra's forehead and took a step back, then cupped his cheeks. "Thank you for telling me that."

Ezra could breathe again all of a sudden. Rusty wasn't telling him to go fuck himself, or yelling at him about being straight. He was being *nice* about it all. "You're... welcome?"

He'd never had someone thank him for rejecting them before. If the world had gone topsy-turvy today, it was upside-down and backward now.

Rusty finally let his hands slide away from Ezra's cheeks, tucking them in his pockets. "I can promise you one thing— you're not an experiment, and I'm never going to treat you like one."

Ezra swallowed hard. *It's easy to say that, but we'll see,* he thought. He was afraid of being weighed up against everything else Rusty was doing and found... less important.

If Rusty's parents disapproved as much of him as they did of Rusty's business, he'd be the easiest to give up on.

Still, he managed a quick smile. "Thanks."

Rusty winced as his phone chimed. "Uh... I know the timing's not great, but could we maybe start heading back?

Sorry. That was my phone alarm. I don't want to miss the tide, and the weather's supposed to get worse."

"Oh, yeah. Of course."

Ezra helped Rusty load the gear into the kayak, marveling at how he made it all fit. Then he stepped into the front, holding his breath and thinking light thoughts as Rusty shoved the kayak out into the water and climbed in, too.

They wobbled a bit, but within a few strokes, they were out into the ocean again. After they coordinated their paddling, Ezra waited for the silence to grow awkward before he spoke up.

It was hard when he couldn't see Rusty, but he didn't want to rush this conversation during a five-minute drive when they got back to Hart's Bay, and then say goodbye.

"I hope I didn't, like, just break your heart there." Ezra reminded himself not to twist to look at him. "I'm sorry. It's not that I don't like you—I hope that's obvious. I'm sure my huge crush has been so subtle."

Rusty's chuckle was soft. "Yeah. I hardly knew about it," he teased gently.

Ezra snorted. "But if you were out, I'd have said yes in a heartbeat. I didn't want to pressure you to change your whole life at once. I don't think that's healthy. You have so much going on in your life. New job, new hometown—or coming back to it, really—new sexuality... that would be a lot."

"It would," Rusty said. "But in a good way. I mean it when I say you've changed my life."

Ezra smiled, the tense knot in his chest slowly starting to unwind. "Yeah?"

"There's so many moments that make more sense now." Rusty talked softly, as if speaking to himself. "Like, I just thought it would come with a glaring neon sign. Or everyone else around me would know, but everyone always assumes I'm straight."

Ezra made a face. "Not a problem I've ever had," he muttered. And he was proud of it, but it did make life interesting sometimes.

"I know, that's not always bad," Rusty hurried to continue. "But... I don't know, I just never knew anyone like you. If I had, I probably would have realized way sooner, or at least realized something was up with me. It's impossible *not* to notice you."

"Oh, go on." Ezra tossed his hair playfully, glad he was facing forward so he could hide his blush.

Rusty laughed. "I'm really glad I happened to walk in that day, for more than one reason. Some of them selfish."

"Are my awesome blowjobs one of them?"

Rusty's chuckle was deep. "Oh, yeah." The sudden roughness in his voice made Ezra's skin prickle with pleasure. Goddamn, why couldn't the tide wait for one more round? "But it's more than that. At first I didn't even consider it a possibility, that I might be gay. If I did, I compared myself to like, a stereotype. But then I kinda liked you from the start, but I still thought it must be a passing thing. But meeting your friends made me realize there's all kinds of ways to be gay."

"Good," Ezra murmured, smiling. "You're coming over again, right?"

"I'll bring supper tomorrow after work. It's my turn," Rusty said.

"That would be great," Ezra said, his throat suddenly tight again. He couldn't interrupt his paddling to dab his eyes, so he had to keep on going and tell himself it was sea mist. "Tomorrow's great."

Silence fell for a little while, but it was much more comfortable than before.

Ezra smiled to himself as he dipped his paddle rhythmically, enjoying the glide across the water now that they had momentum. It was a constant fight against the tide, but seeing the scenery from a whole new perspective was rewarding. He could hardly keep his eyes forward, there were so many interesting rocks and trees and potential paintings at every angle.

The waves were indeed getting higher, the wind picking up and whipping Ezra's hair painfully across his cheeks, but Ezra felt perfectly safe with Rusty behind him.

When he recognized the jagged points that separated the sand surfing beach, the rocky beach where the town held its barbecues, and the last point before the marina came in view, Ezra found himself oddly disappointed.

Sure, he could use a real shower and eight pounds of conditioner for his hair, but there was something raw and real about sharing this view with Rusty.

Rusty let him out of the kayak first, and he awkwardly belly-flopped onto the concrete ramp before helping Rusty out. It took some sweat and heavy lifting to get the gear out, then the kayak loaded into Rusty's truck.

After that, when he was peeling off his life jacket and enjoying the familiar view from land, Rusty came to lean against the truck next to him.

"I really hope we can keep doing what we're doing." Rusty's voice was soft but direct and firm. "I like it, and I like you. If you need a boyfriend who's out and proud, I get that. But for now, I don't want to lose this." He looked taut now, worried.

Ezra sucked in a quick breath. The cloud that had hung over Ezra's head since they'd left the beach suddenly lifted.

They could keep going like this? Yeah, maybe it was a bad idea, but he knew what Rusty meant. Losing this would sting.

"Yes," he murmured, smiling at Rusty as he took his hands. Then he glanced toward the boutiques, wondering if anyone could see them. "I'd really like that. As long as you think about where you're going, so I know where I stand with you."

Rusty just tightened his grip on Ezra's hands and smiled slightly. "I won't get anywhere by hiding away. And you're too lovely to be hidden away."

Oh, God. Ezra was breathless again. How was it that a few well-chosen words could make him swoon?

"I'll definitely need time to process everything." Rusty dropped his hands so he could close the tailgate of the truck and dig out his keys. "But I'll keep you posted, yeah?"

"Yeah," Ezra murmured back and waited to climb into the passenger seat. As he did, he bit back the urge to reassure him—to tell him that if he wasn't ready to come out, they could figure things out.

Rusty was right. Damn it, even when he was turning Rusty down, he was the kind of guy who cared about *why*—and reminded Ezra to care.

Which was why Ezra so badly wanted to throw the conversation out the window and say yes instead, ask him to be his boyfriend officially for the converted warehouse's grand opening.

The drive back to Ezra's house was all too quick. "Right, here we are," Rusty announced as he pulled up to the curb in front of the house.

Ezra took a quick glance. No car, but lights on inside. Some of his friends were home, then. Maybe he could avoid them by staying in the shower for three hours. Or hide in the attic until he was ready to talk to them without spilling his heart.

God, it was exhausting having all these feelings. Worst of all, though, wasn't the feelings he *was* having. It was the ones he was ignoring, like the feeling that he was just grasping for new excuses now that Rusty's label wasn't an excuse anymore.

Ezra swallowed hard. "Yeah. Thanks for a great trip." He unbuckled and slid closer, then hesitated.

But Rusty made the decision for him, turning to him and swooping in to press a long, lingering kiss on his mouth.

Tingling warmth replaced all the fluttery anxiety that had filled his stomach moments ago. Ezra was solid and grounded again, and all he wanted was to grab Rusty and drink in that feeling in deep, ravenous gulps.

If they'd been standing, Ezra might have swooned straight to the ground. As it was, he turned to jelly right here on the truck seat.

Rusty had to tap his knee to bring him back to life when he pulled away for breath. Ezra giggled and slid away at last, then grabbed his bag. "Thanks for the ride. I'm sure we'll do it again soon. See you for supper tomorrow."

"You're w—welcome," Rusty stuttered as the second meaning clearly occurred to him.

Ezra gave a wink and slid out, trotting up the path with a grin on his face. He loved taking Rusty by surprise, making him blush, and best of all, giving him something to remember.

It was almost enough to make him forget the dizzy, feverish uncertainty that had taken root deep in Ezra's belly.

Because as incredible as the day had been, and as understanding as Rusty had been, the decision about where to go from here wasn't in his hands.

It was all up to Rusty, and Ezra had placed it squarely there. He was dizzy with fear and hope and a thousand emotions bundled into one.

Hell, Ezra was even a bit proud of himself. He'd set up a boundary instead of taking Rusty's emotions on board first and foremost.

If Rusty came out for him, Ezra would be over the moon. But in the back of his mind, that fear would still linger—what if this didn't last? What if the pressure proved to be too much in the end?

All he could hope was that Rusty's broad shoulders were strong enough to carry Ezra's needs as well as his own.

16

RUSTY

Rusty had the perfect solution to all his problems. It had come to him while he was unloading the tent and gear from his truck, daydreaming about Ezra and their trip away.

Taking on another partner was obviously out of the question. He already had one, and Pascal—well, Rusty was fond of him because of their history as friends, but Pascal really did nothing for the business itself. Rusty was on his own as far as the grunt work.

But he also needed security before he could promise his heart to Ezra. And that security could be provided by finding an investor to fund his first few years of experiments. If things went wrong this winter and he didn't get government funding for another year, it would give him a chance to make it work on his own—and he wouldn't have to leave Hart's Bay to do so.

And not leaving Hart's Bay meant not leaving Ezra, and he could better support him. Not that they were moving in together yet, but Rusty felt like he *should* be able to guarantee his own stability.

The only problem was that he needed an investor.

Land was easy to get, especially now that Rain seemed to own a lot of it around town. Money, though? That was tougher.

There *was* one person who did have that, but talking to him meant making a bargain with the devil.

Rumor had it he was only in town every couple of weeks —his big mansion just a few minutes' walk from the harbor sat empty most days. He was probably living in one of his luxury villas somewhere in California now. On the other hand, he was one of the few people in town who had money to burn.

On the other, other hand... his parents would be livid if they found out he was working with Floyd. Rusty could break it to them as a way of making up for suddenly firing them all those years ago. And it might be a moot point anyway, if Floyd said no. But if he didn't ask, he wouldn't get. Any port in a storm.

And if he didn't figure out a way to convince Ezra, his parents, and everyone else who mattered to him that he could make this business work...

No. He had to pull himself out of the self-doubt that had plagued him since Ezra's rejection. It had started out straightforward, but the doubts had crept in.

Did he really know what he was doing? Could he promise Ezra not just his heart, but his future? How could he do that while his business was so unstable?

So Rusty was going to prove his commitment, however he could, and he was going to move fast. He couldn't afford the risk of losing Ezra.

On the way past the town square, driving Ezra home, he'd spotted the familiar sight of a fancy car, which probably belonged to either Floyd or the son he was still on good terms with.

As soon as he'd gotten home, Rusty had called the one person who knew where anyone in town was at at any given time: Cher. And as it turned out, just a day later, Floyd Hart was at her bar, having a drink and glaring at most people who walked in.

"Whatever you want him for, show up fast and make the elevator pitch snappy," she advised him and hung up.

So Rusty strode for the door without hesitation. Minutes later, he pulled up alongside the art gallery and jumped out of the truck.

The wind tugged at his clothes, and he paused to glance up at the sky. The weather was getting nasty, and he was glad not to be on the ocean today.

Rusty couldn't help peeking in the front window of the art gallery on the way past. It looked like the shop was closed, but he saw light coming from the workshop at the back of the place.

After Rusty headed into Cher's End Table, he glanced around the bar to take in the scene.

Only about half a dozen people—the stalwarts, including Gregory—were here. The guys from the art gallery weren't here, as he'd expected they might be. Probably because at the end of the bar, sitting side-on to the bar so he could face the door, was Floyd.

Just as predicted, he glared at Rusty when he walked through it. But Rusty didn't let that stop him. He strode right up to him.

"Hi," he greeted. "Nice seeing you around."

He wasn't dumb—he'd heard that Floyd had tried to mess with the art gallery and the boutiques just for daring to exist.

But this was different. He wasn't messing with the family dynamics, and he wasn't someone coming in from another town. Rusty had grown up here, his parents had worked for Floyd, and he hoped that was enough to get his foot in the door.

Floyd's bushy brows knit together in an amusing mix of confusion and skepticism. He clearly hadn't expected Rusty to talk to him, let alone to be so friendly.

"What do you want from me?" Floyd correctly guessed at his intentions, his expression clearing up.

Rusty took the stool next to him. "I have a business proposal. I know you keep tabs on everything here, so you already know what I'm doing."

Floyd was silent, but his expression was shrewd. Rusty took that as a yes and kept going.

"I'm looking for an investor to grow my business." Rusty had no idea how this stuff worked. He hadn't run his own business before, and he sure as hell hadn't used anyone else's money. "I'm willing to pay good interest."

"What do you want my money for?" Floyd's eyes narrowed, the frown lines permanently etched into his face deepening.

"To invest in different seaweed species so I can figure out the hardiest for these conditions. And to buy a better boat, so I can harvest everything when the time comes. My funding from the government covered the permits, but not much else."

Floyd eyed him for a moment and then snorted. "No." The syllable was curt, and Floyd didn't soften the blow. "It's a stupid idea."

Okay, this wasn't the best idea he'd ever had. If making a living from the sea was a sensitive subject for his parents, it had to be even more so for the owner of the business that had folded.

Cher was perfectly still behind the bar, a towel over her shoulder, feet spread in a wide stance and arms folded like she expected to have to throw one of them out of the place.

"Fine," Rusty said simply and stood up. "You don't believe in it. Lots of people don't." He turned for the door, ready to drive home and figure out another plan. At least he didn't have to worry about Floyd being a dick to him because he was dating Ezra.

Floyd wasn't done. "I'd sooner invest in a luxury spa for all the wealthy yuppies around here who'd buy your so-called product. Oh, wait. There aren't any." His voice was an ugly sneer. "You want to improve this place? Good luck. People here will bite the hand that feeds 'em."

The bar was perfectly quiet as people strained to hear every word.

A chill ran down Rusty's spine. "You were the hand that fed us, until you took the food out of our mouths," he said, fighting to keep his voice quiet. "You know what it's like to choose between milk and bread?"

"I don't owe you a thing." Floyd cast an arm around to take in the whole place. "None of you. Not a damn one. I only gotta look out for me and mine. And if I wanna be stinking rich, that's my business."

For the first time, Cher stepped forward, swinging the towel down and around in one hand like she was about to smack him. "You wanna keep pretending you got money, honey? Show it. Go to the boutiques' opening, buy up what they're selling. Try doing *some* good, if you can."

Floyd sucked in a quick breath and whirled to glare at her. "That's—you swore you wouldn't say anything."

"And you've had chance after chance to stop being a

windy bag of dicks." Cher snapped her towel in his direction, hitting the bar top just in front of his arm. He jumped and sat backward, quickly drawing his arm off the counter. "I told you: get gone, stay gone. But you keep coming back every couple weeks, because outside this town, you ain't shit, and you better hope nobody here finds that out."

Floyd was pale now. "You don't know what you're saying," he snapped, standing up so fast he nearly kicked the stool over.

"I know what demons you're fighting," Cher retorted. She folded the towel and laid it on the counter, then leaned toward him, folding her arms on the bar. "I'm not biting my tongue for *your* sake. I didn't want it to come to this, Floyd, but here it is. Get out."

"What—but—you can't kick me out!" Floyd sputtered. "This is the—the—the living room of the town! And it's Thanksgiving season!"

"Yeah, and if you came and took a dump in the middle of my living room, I'd smack you with a rolled-up newspaper. Or a turkey leg." Cher's gaze hardened. "Now, you want me to keep going, or are you leaving?"

Floyd stared at her for a few long moments before sneering and turning on his heel to stride out.

The door banged shut, and slowly, whispers started up again in the corners. A few more people had come in since the argument began, and no doubt they had to find out the whole scoop from the others.

"God," Cher muttered. "I could use a drink now. Look at all those busybodies. I might just close and kick 'em all out."

But Rusty just smiled. "Yeah, but you won't." She talked meaner than she bit—or at least, he'd always thought that. He was starting to wonder, hearing her talk just then.

Cher puffed out her lips and sighed. "Suppose so. What can I get you?"

"An unseasonably calm winter and a couple grand?"

"That doesn't require blood sacrifice?"

"Coke, I guess," Rusty said, slowly sitting down again. She looked frazzled. "Are you okay?"

She looked surprised that he'd asked. As she flipped the cap off the bottle and slid it over, she finally sighed. "Not really. It's hard seeing what's become of him."

"Yeah." Rusty frowned. He'd always thought the guy was the backbone of the town. Sure, his parents had never liked or respected him, but Floyd was like the statue in the center of a town square—the guy who never changed, never concerned himself with lowly people's business. But being important wasn't the same as being a force for good. Seeing the real—and real ugly—man under the veneer was rattling.

"He could've been a decent person. He was, once." Cher sighed, gazing into the distance.

Rusty paid and stayed quiet, wondering what else she might say. "Yeah?"

"Guess you'd be too young to know about all that." Cher gave him a small, sad smile. "You know right after his wife died, he proposed to me?"

What the shit? Rusty spat his Coke out, spraying it across the counter in front of him as he coughed. "What?"

Cher tossed him the towel and nodded down at the counter, so he wiped up after himself with a muttered apology and handed it back.

"I don't run around telling people that. It's like being invited onto the schoolyard bully's dodgeball team." Cher wrinkled her nose.

"Ew," Rusty groaned, rubbing his eyes. Cher had to be twenty years younger than Floyd, and she was actually a decent human being as opposed to a pile of shit in a human-shaped body. "I'm glad you said no. Assuming you *did* say no." Were they secretly married? Nothing that came out of her mouth could surprise him after hearing that.

"Of course I said no, in stronger terms." Cher scoffed. "I was only twenty-five, and I'd just bought this place. No way in hell was I letting some guy closing in on fifty muscle his way in. Especially a heartbeat after poor Miriam passed away."

"Was that what it was about? Getting part of your business?" Rusty leaned in.

Cher eyed him for a few moments and then flapped her towel at him. It wasn't the menacing snap she'd given Floyd, just a playful one. "Oh, check you out, fishing for gossip." Rusty blushed, and she winked. "I'm just reminiscing about the old times. No matter now. So, you can't get money from him. What are you gonna do?"

"I'll just take the chance that this year's harvest will be good." Rusty nibbled his lip. "If not, I'll figure it out then."

"The government didn't fund this?"

"Hell, no. Like I told him, their grant basically covered the permits. Millions of miles of paperwork." Rusty rolled his eyes. "And maybe a couple of ropes. That was about it."

Cher hummed and nodded. "Well... ignore that old fogey and figure out a way to get to what you want. And make sure you know what that is."

It was clearcut, wasn't it? Rusty wanted to stay here, to make his own way in the world without relying on others, and to give back to his town. And he wanted Ezra by his side while he did all that.

The picture formed in his head, crystal clear: Ezra on the boat, leaning back and keeping Rusty laughing with his running commentary and flirtation while Rusty hauled in soaking, heavy lines and picked the algae off his precious crop.

God, Rusty's chest almost ached with the visual. He could taste the salt spray now.

"You've gone a funny shade of red. I'd say you've figured out what that is," Cher added, smirking at him as she tossed the towel in a basket in the corner and dug out another.

"Y-Yeah." Rusty shook his head.

Ezra had made it clear what he had to do, and it wasn't about his business. That was just his own worries playing on his mind. Ezra had never once told him that his business was a problem. That was Rusty's insecurity talking.

What Ezra wanted was Rusty being public about who he loved, and that meant a tough conversation. Tougher in some ways than approaching some asshole on the slim chance he'd work with him, and with nothing to lose if he said no.

"I think I know what I've gotta do," Rusty murmured, pushing himself to his feet and heading for the door. "Thanks, Cher."

As with driving anywhere in this town, it took just a few minutes to reach his parents' house. By now, they'd both be home and maybe settling in to cook supper while they read out articles from the newspaper to each other.

It made him smile, because he couldn't help but picture himself and Ezra in that situation.

Oh, goddamn, he was smitten.

Rusty knocked before he entered, then stepped inside and wandered through the front hall. "Hi Mom, Dad!"

"In the kitchen, dear." When he made his way there, Mom greeted him with a kiss on the cheek. She was wearing an apron, while his father had flour-covered hands. "This is an unexpected surprise. Don't worry. We're making enough for three."

"It's okay, I wasn't going to stay," Rusty said. "I just wanted to drop by and share the news."

Dad cleared his throat. "We have a bit of news for you, too."

"You go first." As sure as Rusty was that they would be on his side, putting it off for another few seconds felt good.

"Well, we've negotiated a deal on Gregory's boat. He's an old friend of your father's, so he's willing to sell it to you cheap. And he'll help you make sure it's seaworthy, too." Mom smiled at him, the expression tentative.

It made Rusty's heart soar. Not only did they give a shit about his business, but they clearly cared about his feelings. If this was their way of making up for the near-argument before, he'd take it. "Really?"

"Really. We can see it this weekend," Dad confirmed. "And there's one other thing." He cleared his throat and looked at Mom, but she nodded back at him, giving him a turn to share the news. "Well, we were talking about eventualities. If—*if*—this first year's harvest doesn't go well, we want to make sure you have a fair chance. We'll fund you for the second year, if need be."

Rusty blinked several times, not sure he'd heard that right. But he definitely had. Not only did they believe in him, but they seemed to have had enough of a change in heart to put their money on the line.

And given their fear of the sea failing him the way it had them, that was huge.

"Oh," Rusty breathed out, clearing his throat a few times. "Oh, wow. That's... you guys. I don't know what to say."

"Just hug me and help me cut up these apples while you tell us your news." Mom smiled and then gasped when he picked her up off the ground. "Rusty!"

He laughed and put her down. "Sorry. Couldn't resist." He picked up the apple corer and grabbed a few apples, pushing the corer down on them to split them. "So, uh, my news."

No, he couldn't do this without looking at them. So Rusty turned to them, drew a breath, and swallowed hard. "I'm gay." He tried to say it as casually as possible, like an interesting fact he'd read on Twitter.

The next few seconds were the longest moments of his life. His parents exchanged a look, and then...

Mom smiled at him. "Have you met someone you want to introduce us to?"

Rusty opened and closed his mouth a few times. "Have—what? I mean, yes. I think. Maybe. We'll see what happens with us."

Dad just clapped a floury hand on his shoulder, with a tiny puff of white powder. "I'm glad you told us, son. It doesn't change a thing. I hope you know that."

Rusty let his breath out and nodded. "Yeah. I thought so, but I wanted you to know first." At the sly look they exchanged, he groaned. "Or close to first, anyway. Who told you what?"

"Well, a few people said they've seen you hanging around that art gallery a lot. That's all." His mom winked. "Is he from Hart's Bay? What do his parents do?"

Rusty let a breathy laugh of relief escape. Just like he'd thought, they were more worried about who he was than what he was.

"I'll let you ask him yourself. He's coming to the grand

opening. And... thanks," he said after a few moments, even if that word didn't feel quite adequate. "For everything."

There was a knock on the door, and he cleared his throat. "I'll get that," he told them. It would give him a few seconds for his eyes to stop burning quite so much and his throat to clear.

It was the next-door neighbor, Mrs. Kane—or Lori, as he knew her now. If anyone had more gossip than his parents, it was Mrs. Lori "oh, did you know" Kane.

"Oh, Rusty! Hello. I was hoping that was your truck. Did you know there's been a log boom accident? Two or three days ago, some rookie set a whole boom loose. Logs drifting all over the place! I thought your seaweed might be in danger and you should know."

Rusty's heart rose into his throat, and he swallowed hard. Shit. This wasn't just idle gossip. "Thanks," he murmured, and he meant it.

That explained the log that had nearly smashed into Ezra's legs in the sneaker wave, and the amount of timber he'd seen floating on their kayak trip back. In stormy weather like this, all it took was one or two logs getting caught up in the lines and a few heavy days of waves to destroy the whole damn setup.

"I gotta go," he announced to his parents as he strode back to the kitchen. Better not to tell them where, or why. They'd only worry for him, out alone in the boat. As long as he left now, before the storm really set in, he'd be fine.

"Is everything all right?" Mom frowned at him.

"Oh, yeah." Rusty managed a smile for her. As long as he did what had to be done, things would turn out just fine. Especially now that he knew they had his back. "Never been better."

EZRA

"I'm sure he'll be here any minute." Ezra kept his voice as cheery as he could, but it was impossible to hide the waver of uncertainty.

It was also impossible not to notice the skepticism and sympathy on his roommates' faces as Ezra lingered near the entryway of their house. Thankfully, they knew better than to say anything.

It was getting a little late to be putting on supper, but maybe Rusty was bringing over a precooked meal like a casserole. Ezra resisted the urge to keep checking his watch. He perched on the arm of the couch so he could look out the living room window at the driveway.

No truck, no handsome hunk carrying trays of casseroles.

"What happened?" Aaron murmured, gliding into the living room to sit on the couch next to Ezra.

Ezra huffed and shrugged. "Nothing." The last thing he wanted to do was go over their last conversation with a fine-toothed comb.

He hadn't heard from Rusty since then. No text yesterday night or this morning. That wasn't so unusual—they didn't always text, especially when Rusty was up at four to catch the tide and didn't want to disturb Ezra.

But it weighed on his mind now that Rusty was late for the first time ever.

"Mmm." Aaron put his hand on Ezra's knee, drawing his gaze. He looked like he hadn't slept since before Ezra left for his trip.

"What's up?" Ezra asked instead, trying to distract himself. They had time to figure out supper. The guys down at the art gallery—Beau and Ross—weren't yet here. As far as Ezra knew, Ross was busy hanging the last few photos on the walls of the boutique units. He could text him to pick up ingredients if need be.

"I think we're ready for the opening on Friday. As long as the weather doesn't change," Aaron murmured, chewing on his lip. "The storm should let up by then."

Ezra knocked on Aaron's head gently. "Knock on wood."

"Dick." Aaron flicked Ezra's ear with a tired smile.

"You like it. Need any help?"

"I've got Yolanda coming in early. I think I'm all right. I'm sure Rain and Colt wouldn't turn down the help, but watch out. I nearly walked in on a hot moment a few days ago," he snorted. "Stress relief comes in all kinds of forms."

Ezra laughed. "Can't blame them. Young love, right?" With that, he cast another glance out the window and then blushed. Of course his mind went to Rusty first of all.

"Apparently." Aaron tapped Ezra's knee. "Well, I'm happy one of us is getting laid, at least. Well, you and Rusty, Jesse and Finn, Rain and Colt..." He counted on his fingers. "Even if you had to, like, *commit.*"

"No," Ezra muttered under his breath, biting his lip.

Aaron waited for a few moments and then reached toward Ezra's ribs as if to tickle him. "No?"

Ezra yelped and smacked away his hand. "Fine. Busybody," he complained. "He wants to go out. I said no."

"What? *What?*" Aaron reeled backward, his usual spark of energy suddenly returning to him at a good bit of gossip. "*You* turned *him* down?"

Ezra folded his arms, rubbing his biceps where they still ached from so much paddling. "Yeah. I don't think he's ready."

The silence stretched out until he couldn't resist looking at Aaron. When he did, Aaron had his lips pursed and brows raised, his own arms folded.

"What?"

"I'm just saying," Aaron drawled, reaching out to tuck Ezra's hair behind his ear. "Maybe... just maybe... *you're* the one who's not ready, if you're trying to hold him back."

Ezra's cheeks flushed and he stood up abruptly. That made something deep inside his chest twist into a knot, and he didn't like it. "I'm going outside to text him."

The prickly Aaron he'd seen lately might have made a sarcastic comment about there being phone service in the house, but Ezra got a pat on the arm. Good. His friend must be feeling ready for the opening after all, if his stress was lifting.

When he got to the front porch, Ezra pecked out a quick message. *Hey. On your way now?* Then he stared at his phone, waiting for the bubbles that meant Rusty was responding.

No sign of them yet, so he finally sighed, pocketed his phone, and leaned on the railing. It was nice to get a minute to himself to think, but he couldn't avoid the anxiety bubbling in his chest.

Only one thing could fix that.

He shaded his eyes to peer down the street. The wind was picking up, the first few fat drops of rain coming down. This would be a quick, fierce storm, blowing away by tomorrow morning. Or so they hoped.

Darkness was setting in early and fast with the clouds hanging low in the sky, but still no sign of Rusty. The purr of a motor approaching was a car, not a truck—and a familiar car, at that. Jesse's car pulled up and he got out, along with Beau and Ross.

A small piece of Ezra had hoped that Rusty was just catching a ride with them. That would be kinda neat, if he felt comfortable enough with Ezra's friends to do that.

But instead, nothing.

"Is supper on yet?" The way Jesse asked made Ezra suspect he knew more than he let on.

"Dunno yet," Ezra said, trying to keep it casual. "Waiting for Rusty. He must be running late." They paused and exchanged looks as they approached the porch, making Ezra fold his arms. "What?"

"He was heading out in his boat when we left the parking lot." The words hung in the air before Jesse continued, his cheery voice forced. "But dude, you'll never guess whose car we saw outside Cher's earlier today!"

"Who?" Ezra's heart was only half in it. Rusty was going out in his boat? Now? Was he trying to catch them their supper or something? But he hadn't seen any fishing gear on board the boat, and it would be way too late to try that.

Fuck, he was being stood up. Worse than that, they were all being stood up.

"Floyd!"

Ezra blinked. "That asshole? He's back?" Shit, was he going to try some stunt tomorrow?

"I don't think so. He stormed out of there like he had a fire lit under his ass." Beau cackled. "I talked to Cher and she says he's not staying around for the grand opening, don't worry."

As Ross climbed the porch steps, he lifted his bags of groceries. "We're making teriyaki salmon and green beans. The salmon was on sale. We've got supper covered."

"Cool," Ezra responded automatically, listening to Beau bang his way into the house and announce his news at top volume. He held the door for Ross and waved him inside.

The chaos followed Beau inside. When the front door shut, he was left in the peace and quiet of the front porch—but with a heavy heart.

Suddenly the droplets splashing on the path reflected his mood.

Ezra could feel it creeping in, the whisper in his mind that he was too much for Rusty to handle. Had his ultimatum backfired? Had Rusty been pissed off at Ezra demanding that he come out?

Worse, was he right to be angry?

Ezra's mind flashed back to that painting, messy but finished, drying in the corner of the workshop—his self-portrait of the ugly, insecure, emotional monster creeping out from under his skin.

He sank onto the top porch step, where he'd be sheltered by the awning, watching the droplets ricochet off the ground and explode into a thousand tiny molecules.

Kind of like his heart right now.

Rusty hadn't even bothered letting him know he

wouldn't be there. If it were just Ezra he was blowing off, that would be one thing. But it was him and all his friends.

Thankfully his friends were acting like it wasn't a big deal, picking up emergency supper ingredients and throwing something together. Still, Rusty had let him down.

As he stared down the street, part of him hoped for Rusty to tear up the street, park, jump out, and apologize for being late. That would be a very Rusty thing to do—not being late, but being mortified about it.

But there was still nothing.

Ezra didn't know how long he sat there, his clothes steadily growing more damp even if he was sheltered. The air was thick with humidity, making him shiver, but he refused to go inside for a jacket. He just hunched into his sweater and put his hands into his pockets.

"Hey, dude." Benji stood in the doorway, his voice careful. "Supper's just about ready."

"Thanks." Ezra made himself stand up at last, stiff. "I'll be right in."

Benji lingered for a moment more, like he wanted to say something, but Ezra didn't look at him. The door thumped gently again, and Ezra finally glanced back to find it closed.

He took a deep breath and let it out, steeling himself to apologize for Rusty. He already knew he was going to feel upset and let down the moment any of his friends did. Taking on board everyone's feelings at once was an exhausting job.

"You're gonna have some explaining to do, mister," Ezra muttered. He finally headed inside, reveling in the warm rush of air as he headed through to the kitchen.

"Hey." Benji scooted along the bench seat that stretched along one side of the kitchen table to make room for him. All the roommates were there, but no sign of Jesse, who still had honorary roommate status even if he lived next door with Finn.

"Where's Jesse?"

"Headed over to his place through the gate." Beau gestured with his fork toward the backyard. "He wanted to meet Finn for a romantic meal or something."

"Ew, romance," Aaron snickered. He grabbed the bowl of green beans, served himself some, and passed it on.

Benji sighed and smiled, his eyes starry. "I think it's sweet. And it's nice they still come over so much."

"It's nice that they cook sometimes," Ross said. "They don't just come over and mooch."

Which brought the conversation to a grinding halt. Ezra was glad his hair shielded him as he glared toward Ross.

Ross stuttered. "I-I mean, Rusty will take his turn sometime. I'm sure he just forgot."

Beau shushed him quietly, but the damage was done. Ezra's gut was already tight. He calmly took green beans, but his hands shook as he handed the bowl to Benji.

"I'm sorry Rusty didn't come over. I swear, he said he'd bring supper. Not sure what's going on with him."

"It happens." Beau gave him a big, cheery smile that only looked somewhat forced. "Don't sweat it."

"And supper's delicious," Aaron said, nodding. "Thanks for picking up the salmon, guys."

Ross was eating some kind of tofu covered in the same teriyaki sauce as the rest of them. "The sauce is great."

Still, Ezra's shoulders were heavy with worry. He stayed silent as the conversation moved on, not feeling like participating. It was noticeable with fewer guys around their table than usual—without Rain and Colt, who were probably pulling a late one to finish their boutique building before it opened, and without Jesse and Finn, and without Rusty...

"You guys didn't fight, did you?" Benji bit his lip. "Did he get tired of us? Straight guys, right?" He rolled his eyes.

Ezra stood up abruptly. He didn't want to admit how much that rattled him, but he also couldn't hide his feelings. "Fuck that. Anyone who gets tired of us can go suck his own dick."

A ripple of laughter went through them all—nervous but affectionate. "That's right," Beau agreed, reaching out to touch Ezra's arm.

But Ezra didn't want to be comforted. He didn't want them to hand him a glass of wine and sympathize about how men were jerks who used them like toys until they got boring or inconvenient or pushed them into too much self-discovery.

"No. It's not right. It's not fair, and it sucks, and it hurts." Ezra's voice shook. He stepped clear of the bench and headed for the backyard, blinking as his vision swam all of a sudden.

Two chairs sat under the back awning, the rest drenched by the rain. Ezra picked one of them and slumped down into it, shivering as the cold bit into him once more.

Ezra had only had half his dinner. He'd regret it later, but right now he wasn't hungry, and he'd hardly tasted it. All he wanted was one damn apology from Rusty—by text, if need be.

Or at least some explanation.

Sorry, I can't come out for you. That's too much for me right now.

Anything to explain this sudden absence. Anything but the gaping, Rusty-shaped hole that was starting to open in Ezra's life without sense or explanation.

A minute later, the back door rattled and Ezra's chest burned with indignation. Couldn't he come out here and cry by himself for two seconds without someone coming to give him well-meaning advice?

But it was Benji, and his tears dried up. He hardly knew the guy, and they hadn't gotten off on a great foot with Benji trying to steal his man.

Maybe he should have let him have him. Then Benji would be the one sulking out here alone, while Rusty took a fun spin in his boat and broke promises and hearts.

"Sorry for what I said." Benji approached slowly and then sank into the chair next to Ezra. "I wasn't really thinking things were serious."

"They *were*. I thought." Ezra folded his arms over his chest, wishing that simple move could pull all the emotions back into his chest and lock them down tightly.

"I totally misread things at dinner that first time with him, then. Sorry about that, too." Ezra glanced over, and Benji gave him a guilty smile.

Damn it, Ezra couldn't afford to burn bridges with everyone just because one guy was being a dick. He sighed and let his arms drop, then reached out for a brief hug.

Benji rocked forward in his chair to hug him back for a few seconds before he pulled away. "If you want to vent, I can shut up and listen."

Ezra wasn't going to. He even planned to say *no, that's fine*. But then the words came.

"He let all of you guys down, and I feel shitty about that. And he hasn't talked to me in a day and a half, and I think I said something wrong, but I meant it. I told him what I need. That's not wrong, is it?"

"No," Benji said softly, his hand on the arm of Ezra's chair.

Ezra blew a sigh and closed his eyes, dabbing at them with his thumb again. "It's stupid, how much it hurts. Maybe he just forgot. And he's not answering my text because he's driving a damn boat, and I don't want him to crash on the rocks and die."

Oh, wow. Ezra's gut lurched as the words spilled out of his mouth. One after another, the pieces clicked into place.

"I don't want to get attached to him and then lose him." Ezra doubled over, bracing his elbows on his knees. "Damn it, I can't go through that again."

Bless him, Benji didn't ask questions. He just rested his hand on Ezra's back, his thumb rubbing gently.

"I thought I'd be too much and scare him off before now, but I wasn't. So I got my hopes up that maybe he was changing. Going gay for me." Ezra swallowed a bitter laugh. "Now I wish I hadn't, because if he's just going to ghost me, that's the worst thing ever. The worst. He has to know how it looks, right? Getting me to sleep with him and then dropping off the face of the earth and all because I couldn't date him because he wasn't out and I can't—" Ezra ran out of breath. Every ounce of his insecurity was hanging there now, but Benji just kept stroking the ends of his hair.

"It's okay," Benji whispered. "Catch your breath. You're with friends. If he *is* using you, we can get even with him later. We'll egg his boat for you." Ezra managed a little smile, and Benji smiled back at him. "Any man who's man enough for you will do what it takes to keep you. If he's not right for you, if he's not ready, that's nobody's fault."

Ezra groaned quietly. "I wish it were. That'd be easier."

"Yeah," Benji agreed. He patted Ezra's back. "This storm is getting bad, though. Hey. So. Wanna see something cool?"

Ezra was desperate for distraction. He didn't want to go inside and have more people fuss over him yet. "Sure." As Benji rummaged around in his lap, Ezra snorted. "It better not be your dick."

Benji grinned back. "I'll wait at least three seconds before offering consolation sex." He took his keychain out and unclipped the laser attached to it.

Ezra wiped his eyes and straightened up, watching as Benji shone the thin beam of green light out through the raindrops.

Instead of steadily shining on the fence at the back of the property, the light beam appeared in midair in broken stops and starts. The dot on the fence flickered wildly about.

"Oh, of course," Ezra murmured, weirdly hypnotized by the flickering. "The rain drops. That's cool."

Benji smiled at him. "Isn't it? I like using this on a clear day to trace the constellations, but it's fun in the rain, too."

Ezra took it from Benji and took a turn shining it around, pointing at different objects—the barbecue, the trees, the fence—and watching the beam flickering about in midair.

When he tried to hand it back, Benji shook his head. "Keep it. Just don't point it at planes or I'll come throat-punch you. My best friend in high school became a pilot."

Ezra laughed abruptly. "I won't," he promised. "Thanks."

It was a little token, a dollar store keychain, but it was a sign that things were okay between him and Benji now. At least he had that going.

As Benji headed inside, Ezra stayed outside for another few minutes, letting the simple action of watching the flickering light soothe his racing thoughts.

The colors and angles it made were fascinating to his artistic brain, and it made him think of more ideas for his art. Like a painting of Rusty, cold and sharp and outlined in thin green lines.

And that was Ezra's cue to go to bed and sleep. This

weekend was the boutique opening, and he had no idea if Rusty would be on his arm anymore.

If he didn't hear from him by morning, he might just not get out of bed tomorrow. What a Thanksgiving that would be.

18

RUSTY

Rusty wasn't sure whether the wave that sloshed into his face came from the wide-open rain clouds or the ocean. It didn't matter either way. He was already soaked from head to toe, water sloshing around inside his boots.

He braced himself against the swell as the nose of the boat came up and down again, spinning the boat away from the line for the hundredth time.

The curse words came fast and furious. His palms ached as he gripped the rough fiber, keeping himself close to the buoy.

Conditions out here had worsened faster than he'd thought. It had been a race to get out here from his parents' house, and now—stomach grumbling, arms aching—he wished he'd stayed for apple pie.

But there was no question his choice to come out here had been the right one. No logs tangled up in the lines close to the surface, thankfully, but he'd discovered a raft of bull kelp tangling two of them. Some seedlings had already been ripped out, too delicate this early in the growing season to wrap around the rope.

Without diving, the only way to handle it was to haul the heavy line out hand-over-hand, cutting away the bull kelp and throwing it in the back of his boat to cart away.

It was exhausting work even on a sunny day, and with the wave swells growing rapidly, steadily more so. With a better boat—like Gregory's—he wouldn't be tipping around so much with every wave, but he couldn't do anything about that right now.

Rusty groaned with relief as he cut away the final piece of slippery black kelp and let the line down into the water again.

It was pitch-black out here, his only light the ones he'd clamped onto the boat in a moment of foresight. Often while gathering early in the morning from a tiny, bobbing dinghy in Maine, he'd cursed the low light. He'd taken those lessons back home with him.

It was close to high tide, and the lines were taut. Ideally, he'd check out beaches nearby for any washed-up logs that he could haul out of the surf, where they wouldn't roll back into the water and drift over toward his little enterprise.

But conditions were rough enough that the nose of the boat hung in the air a moment before crashing down, sending another jolt up his neck. He was going to have a pounding headache later from that.

Definitely not weather to hang around in, then. Things were fine for now, and there was nothing more he could do until the morning. Hopefully he'd escaped the worst of the log boom bust already.

Rusty staggered as another wave crashed over the bow and canopy, straight into his face. Blinded by the water, he grabbed the edge of the canopy and spat out the salt water, then rubbed his eyes into the crook of his arm and ducked underneath.

Thankfully the boat was closed at the front, at least. A pain in the ass for setting lines, but a blessing now. The surface under him rolled from side to side, slowly, making Rusty send a prayer to anyone listening that the boat wouldn't roll over. Even Rusty's sea legs wobbled for a moment as his heart lurched.

It was past time to head back to shore.

"Fuck—" Rusty had to haul on the wheel to get control of the boat again, steering at an angle into the waves. Once he was sure the boat wasn't going to flip, he breathed out deeply to calm himself down.

It wasn't easy going to get back to the harbor. The waves breaking across the bow wanted to drive him into the shore. Only the knowledge he'd carefully cultivated of the shoreline kept him steering safely around the rocky outcroppings.

It was like night and day to steer past the breakwater and into the harbor, and Rusty suddenly remembered how to breathe.

This was one of those days he'd prefer Ezra not witness. It was all fun and laid-back when the water was flat and forgiving, but days like today, even Rusty doubted himself. He couldn't blame others for doubting him, too.

It *was* a lot of change all at once: him moving to Hart's Bay, starting a new business, making new friends, and dating a guy. If Rusty weren't so hardheaded, he might decide the stormy days and tough conversations weren't worth it.

Rusty was so tired he could hardly think as he shut off the engine and coasted toward the dock. It must be late out here now. His watch said it was only eight thirty. The art gallery was dark, and all but one of the little shops overlooking the marina had their lights off, too.

Rusty had to try two or three times before he got the loop of rope around the cleat and hauled his boat close. He left it looser than he otherwise would and put down the bumpers in case the waves grew higher in here, too, and rattled the boat around.

He didn't bother trying to strip out of his wet clothes. It was too cold to risk that kind of exposure, and he'd need to throw everything in the washing machine anyway.

Instead, Rusty plodded up the ramp toward the truck, his stomach fighting his exhaustion to growl something fierce. Even reaching up to slide the key into the truck ignition was a lot of work. At least he'd thought to line the seat with a towel before he'd left, but he soaked through that before he even made it home.

He'd left his phone in the truck so it wouldn't get wrecked, which had been the right choice. Even now, Rusty was still dripping wet, so he wrapped it in the spare shirt he kept behind the seat of his truck.

When he was inside, the miserable weather kept safely out by a strong front door and walls that still seemed to bob up and down, he dropped everything on the tiled floor by the entrance and headed straight to the shower, shivering even in there.

The heat helped revive him just enough to think clearly again. Once he'd wrapped himself in a towel and went back to the front door to retrieve his phone, he finally checked the messages.

And his stomach dropped.

Shit. Shit, shit, *shit*.

A single text had never made his heart drop the way this one did. It wasn't just the message—it was the lack of follow-up. No *Are you okay?* or *What happened?* or anything.

Like a single light blinking in the dark, then going out.

Rusty fumbled to dial Ezra instead of texting him back. He crossed his fingers that he could find the right words to say. Saying sorry for letting Ezra and all the guys down didn't feel like enough.

His fear took over: they all hated him now.

"Hello?" Ezra's voice was a mumble, and for a moment Rusty couldn't decide if it was sleepy or drunk.

"Hey, it's Rusty. Ez, I'm sorry. Shit. I just forgot."

The rustling static in the background sounded like Ezra rolling over in bed. The way his voice crackled confirmed it —he'd woken him up. What was he doing in bed this early?

"It's okay." Ezra's voice was small and quiet, though. Like he had been at the bar, that very first night.

"No." Rusty scooped up the soaking wet laundry in one arm and carried it to the bathroom, dumping it in the basket along with his towel. "It's really not. I went out in the boat. There was a log boom break up north, and I had to check the lines. But I should have put it on my calendar or something, and I didn't."

Ezra's voice was more alert now. "Was it dangerous out there?"

Rusty sighed. "Yeah. It wasn't fun, but everything's fine."

"You could have texted me or stopped by the gallery or something." Now Ezra sounded annoyed, which was kind of confusing. Rusty was explaining himself the best he could. Hadn't he just said he'd forgotten?

"I—I would have, if I'd remembered. I know, that's a dick move. I promised for days to cook for you all, and I didn't show."

"No, I don't give a shit about supper," Ezra said suddenly. "We improvised. It's fine. I care about you going out into a storm without telling me."

This was new. He'd never been prickly this way before,

and Rusty wasn't sure what to make of it. "I... It's part of my job, babe. I had to get some bull kelp off the lines before it ripped the whole line of seedlings out."

"Did you have anyone there to help?"

"Well, no." Rusty sighed. "Pascal doesn't do shit—he just throws money at me sometimes. And I wasn't going to tell my parents. They're only just coming around to the idea in the first place."

"Would you go out on a hike to the backcountry by yourself without telling anyone?" Ezra's tone was sharp, cutting through the line, and Rusty suddenly recognized it—fear.

"No." Rusty bit his lip. "No, you're right. It was a dumbass move. I should've told you."

"If we're gonna do this..." Ezra trailed off, then cleared his throat. "I need you to tell me when you're about to do something dumb. I won't stop you, but I need to know. And I need to be able to send a search party. Or maybe find a better partner who can help. I don't know what the answer is. I just can't listen to you casually telling me you were out there by yourself without telling anyone because a job needed to be done. You need to accept help sometimes. We all do."

Rusty drew a breath and let it out. Just like their last conversation, Ezra was giving him an ultimatum—putting conditions on their potential future relationship. "I'm a grown-ass man, Ezra. I can make a stupid decision sometimes. I don't need the lecture."

"I'm not lecturing. I'm just telling you that I need some warning before you maybe go drown. I can't lose you, understand?"

Rusty froze. Like another bucket of sea water or cold rain in the face, he suddenly realized where Ezra's words came from: fear, and loss. Of course he was being a little bit overprotective. "Yeah," he rasped, running a hand down his face. "I'm sorry I worried you. I'll be a lot more careful."

"Thank you," Ezra murmured, drawing a breath. "Sorry I'm nagging. I just..."

"No, I get it," Rusty said.

"Just, please, get some help. If you were alone out there and something happened... I couldn't handle it."

"There's nobody else *to* help me," Rusty burst out with, sinking onto the couch and covering his face with his hand. "I can't afford to take on a partner, and nobody would want that much risk. I can't even find an investor." He wasn't about to admit that Floyd had shot him down.

"There's always a way," Ezra countered. "Have you told Pascal that you need more help?"

Rusty opened his mouth and then closed it again. They'd barely talked in the last few weeks. "Well, no."

"Fucking straight men," Ezra sighed, his tone creeping up. "Allergic to talking."

There it was, slipping out sideways in Ezra's tone.

Rusty's gut rolled, and he swallowed once, hard. "You still think I'm straight." Of all the people he'd expected to believe in him, Ezra was at the top of the list.

"N-No," Ezra stumbled over the word, but the uncertainty gave it all away.

Rusty's nails dug into his thigh instead of the phone. "I don't know how much more gay I could get than our trip away. If you don't believe me, spit it out." Heat pricked the corners of his eyes. "I don't know what I'm doing yet. I'm just trying my best, Ez."

"And then you dropped off the map," Ezra responded quietly. "You didn't text me for two days, and then you went out in the boat instead of coming to supper. I'm sorry. I shouldn't label you when you've made it pretty clear, but you just disappeared. What am I supposed to think?"

"That I just got what I wanted and left?" Rusty's exhaustion frayed his temper. "I wanted to date you. You're the one who said no."

"So then I figured you'll go find some guy who *will* date you under the table." Ezra's laugh was quiet and bitter. "Lots of us out there will."

Rusty growled quietly. How could he show Ezra what he meant to him? He didn't have the art skills to be able to paint him floating on the waves, giggling as his hair splayed around him and his elegant fingers flicked water toward Rusty. He couldn't craft words to describe the vision of Ezra that came to him every night, softly smiling and nestled into the pillow next to him.

And most frustrating of all, he sure as hell couldn't hug him good night, pull him into his body, and let his hands do the talking.

"I don't *want* any of them, Ez. I want *you*. I came out to my parents today."

Ezra was quiet for a few long moments. "You what?"

"I came out. They took it well. They want to know what your parents do and where you're from, and probably your high school transcript. You're lucky they aren't chasing you to come over for Thanksgiving tomorrow."

Ezra managed a quick laugh. "You—seriously came out a day later?"

"That's how serious I am," Rusty responded, his heart racing. Ezra obviously hadn't expected that. "And how ready I am."

Ezra chuckled softly. "Wow. Okay. Sorry, I really knee-jerk reacted. Congratulations."

"Thanks," Rusty answered, smiling to himself. "It's nice to have it out there."

"Are you coming to the grand opening on Friday?"

"Yeah." Rusty gulped, his mouth dry. He was suddenly afraid that Ezra was about to tell him not to show up. "Ez. Do you want *me?*"

Ezra's laugh was shaky. "More than I can say."

"Then come with me, as my date. Open, out, and proud," Rusty said. "I'm not great with words, so let me show you. Let's stop with the accidental dates. Come with me tomorrow as my date, and then we'll decide if we're ready for labels."

Ezra sighed. His voice was steadier now. "I'd like that. I was worried you wouldn't want to come with me. That I'm asking too much from you. I didn't know you'd come out so fast."

"It is a lot," Rusty admitted. "But at the same time, it's easy. All I have to do is follow my heart."

"And talk to me, damn it," Ezra added. "And Pascal, and your parents. Don't keep it all bottled up. You're not going it alone. You're so strong, but if you don't accept help sooner or later, you're going to end up crumbling. I won't watch you do that to yourself."

He still felt pretty damn alone, and he wasn't sure Ezra understood the reality—the whole big, wet, cold, bitterly exhausting reality—of his job. But Rusty wanted to leave Ezra smiling this time, so he agreed.

"Sure. Okay, so I'll see you Friday, huh? Be ready for the big day."

"I'm ready as ever," Ezra said. "Are you?"

Rusty gave a shaky little laugh. Half the town was going to be there, and they'd see him with Ezra at once. His parents might know now, but there was a difference between *knowing* and *meeting* the guy he hoped to date.

"I sure hope so. Okay, I'd better get ready for bed. I'm beat. I'll get in touch tomorrow and we'll figure out a plan."

"Sounds good," Ezra answered, yawning. "Sleep well. And congratulations again."

"Thanks." Rusty's chest was warm with pride that he'd passed that milestone. "Good night, hon." The word was coming off his tongue easier every time he tried it.

Ezra's voice was soft and fond again, the edge gone. No more claws—he just got the soft purr. "Good night, baby."

All Rusty could do was drag himself to bed. His eyes closed the moment he hit the pillow, and he could swear he felt the bed sway back and forth in his dreams. It felt about as unsteady as his whole future right now.

Who knew what the weekend would hold?

19

EZRA

It was a strange helplessness in Ezra's chest that left him smiling one moment, and on tenterhooks the next.

However hard he tried to hold himself back, his heart was on the line. No wonder he'd thrown up so many roadblocks, trying his best to escape Rusty's encircling arms.

Easier to avoid the safety that could be shattered at any moment than let himself indulge. But in that avoidance, he might be hurting both of them.

Why didn't life, grief, or love come with an instruction manual?

Ezra wiped his eyes with his sleeve and cleared his throat, then muttered a curse. The paint on his sleeve would be streaked on his forehead now. At least it hadn't gotten in his eyes.

"You need any coffee?" Aaron asked from the side door of the workshop. "Yolanda and I picked the winning roast for tonight, but we've got test batches to get rid of."

"Sure," Ezra murmured, but he was barely paying attention. Instead of lying in bed all day on Thanksgiving, he'd sprung up early, ready to channel his feelings into art.

He was back at it again today. Aided by Aaron running through the house at six in the morning on his way to the shower, shouting, "It's clearing up, motherfuckers!"

Ezra rolled his eyes. It was impossible to know if the clear weather would hold all evening, but at least it would be all right for the opening ceremony. The storm had blown through, leaving changes in its wake.

He'd painted all morning—started one piece, finished another, and now this one. The new ones taking shape were the most exciting, because they didn't feel like the same scene all over again.

There was a different palette at work in them, and it was oddly hypnotic. Ezra had started with the bright, almost lime green of the laser pointer, and the deep, rich blue of the sea while kayaking. Then he'd added stormy blue gray, and mixed up a deep, night blue.

"Thanks," Ezra murmured when Aaron pressed a cup into his spare hand.

Aaron knew better than to stick around while he was in this mood. "I left a thermos up front with the other guys. See you later," he said and hightailed it out of there.

Ezra barely noticed, his gaze intent on the picture taking shape in front of him. It couldn't have looked more different than he'd envisioned it originally, yet that made it all the richer.

Rusty was front and center, the hard lines of his body outlined in that bright green—just the right shade of green to signal danger, even though it should have been a *go*. The wave crashing toward him was edged in deep blue, and the scene was night, not day.

Nothing about it looked the same as it had a few days ago

in Ezra's mind's eye, but it was so compelling that it drove him onward. He drained the coffee, set the cup on the floor, and kept working to dot the dark night sky with bright green stars.

This time, he was surrounded by phosphorescent, blue strands of kelp drifting on the tide. Ezra squinted over every careful jag of fronds and the angle of Rusty's arm, fingers trailing through the seaweed instead of the water like his reference photo.

It was otherworldly, alluring and yet whispering a dark secret.

Don't step in too far. You'll never get free.

A soft throat-clearing behind him made him frown with annoyance, but he ignored it and dotted a few more stars, then stepped back.

"Is this a bad time?"

Rusty's voice made him whirl on the spot, his heart rising into his throat.

"No," Ezra said, immediately defensive. How was he going to explain this one?

But Rusty didn't ask him to. He just walked closer, his gaze already on the wet canvas.

Damn, he looked good in faded jeans that did wonders for his ass, and rolled-up sleeves that did wonders for his arms. He'd clearly just come in from the water, because his hair was all ruffled in that sea-spray way.

But Ezra's attention was on his face, rather than his sexy figure. The creative flood ebbed away under the anxiety.

"Who's this?"

Ezra swallowed hard. "Um... you?" He glanced down at the chair where his phone still sat, reference photo and all.

Rusty followed the gaze and then scooped the phone up, squinting. "Hold on. Is that...?"

"Yeah." Ezra laughed slightly. "Told you you're my muse."

Rusty blinked a few times, but he was frowning as he went to offer Ezra the phone, spotted his paint-covered hands, and put it back where he'd found it.

Shit. He'd said something wrong.

"It's... that feels like a romantic thing, taking nude photos. Right?" Rusty leaned on the counter nearby, and Ezra had never been more aware of the distance between them.

Or how much he wanted Rusty to close that distance and hug him, paint and all.

"Yeah. It's pretty romantic." Ezra dunked his brush in cleaner and grabbed a towel to dab his hands. "I'm sorry. I should have asked afterward, but I forgot. Don't you like it?"

"Well, it... I don't know," Rusty admitted. "I figured out what's bugging me last night. It feels like you're offering me little bread crumbs of your heart, instead of the whole thing. I want it all. And I want to give it all."

Ezra blinked several times, his mouth opening and closing with surprise.

"Well, good morning to you, too," Ezra finally answered, managing a laugh. But his hands were shaky and his belly was suddenly tight, pointing toward an uncomfortable truth.

Just like Benji's uncomfortable truth—that he was afraid he'd gotten to be too much for Rusty too quickly. Only this time, it was Rusty watching him steadily, his hands tucked in his pockets.

Ezra stepped closer, into Rusty's personal space bubble. He breathed a sigh of relief when Rusty let him, and they were almost toe-to-toe. Rusty took his hands easily when he reached for them, but he still wasn't saying anything.

"I think you're right," Ezra murmured. "But I don't know

if I have anything more to give. I've already tried." He let go of Rusty's hands so he could pace, gesturing with his hands naturally. "I can't get you out of my head. You were wondering if I like you. God, I hope it's obvious that I do. It has been from the start, to me. But..."

"But?" Rusty asked, his lips pressed together. Ezra couldn't tell if it was annoyance or nervousness.

"But I've tied my heart to yours, and it's scaring me." Ezra underscored it with a sharp gesture and then turned around and kicked one of his empty metal easels.

It clattered loudly as it hit the floor, and he instantly regretted it, mumbling an apology and scooping it off the floor. He folded his arms, turning this way and that, trying to find a way to get rid of the nervous tension that flooded his body.

Rusty was there, wrapping his arms around Ezra, and damn if Ezra's heart didn't ease like he'd just breathed in a gulp of sea air after a long day in a paint-fume-filled studio.

Wait—he had. Rusty smelled like the ocean, and Ezra sniffed again to enjoy it. Then the tears spilled, and it was an altogether different kind of sniffle as Ezra flung his arms around Rusty.

"Shh," Rusty whispered, rocking him gently. "Thank you for opening up to me."

"I'm just scared," Ezra whispered. "Scared that you'll leave, ultimately. Whether it's to work in Maine, or to date a woman who suits you better, or to date a man who suits you better, or to marry your boat and only ever see me in passing..."

Rusty's grip tightened, and the pressure made the tension slowly drain from Ezra's shoulders.

"I'm not leaving you," Rusty said, his voice reassuring in its low and firm tone. "I'm sorry I scared you and made you doubt that. I fucked up yesterday. And I should have texted you after our great few days together. But I'm sticking around to fix things."

Ezra breathed out as the tears subsided, rubbing Rusty's back and gulping a few times. "God. I'm full of too many feelings. My own feelings and everyone else's feelings and random feelings that are floating by..."

Rusty chuckled gently. "I like that about you," he murmured. "You're teaching me to talk about mine. And you know what?" He pulled back, his gaze on Ezra's face. "I did a lot of thinking this morning."

"Oh?" Ezra's heart skipped, and that anxiety was instantly back. This better not be the *let's fix the relationship by just being friends* talk.

Rusty squeezed Ezra's shoulders. "'Tis the season to be merry and bright and gay." The corners of his eyes crinkled with his smile. "I'm ready to come out to everyone later today."

The rush of relief made Ezra almost want to sit down. "Don't do that again," he scolded, finally sliding his phone into his pocket so he could do so. "I thought you were going to be all *and I'm actually straight* on me." He winced apologetically. "I know, I keep using that label for you. And I'm sorry. That's my fear talking."

Rusty hummed and nodded. "I did a hell of a good job pretending to be straight. I didn't even question it myself for too long." His hands rested on Ezra's shoulders as he circled around to stand behind him, thumbs kneading at the tension there. "I called myself that more than anyone, but it wasn't true."

Ezra swallowed hard, craning his neck to look back and up at Rusty. "And 'gay' is okay with you?"

"Gay is *great* with me." Rusty grinned down at him.

"Hope you're ready to make out with me tonight. That'll save me a lot of conversations."

Ezra laughed and reached up to lay his hands on top of Rusty's. "I can't wait," he assured him.

"Now... tell me about that, if you want," Rusty murmured, nodding toward the easel.

Ezra's gaze flitted toward it again. "It's... well, it's you. But not. It's my fears again, I think."

"It kind of matches the self-portrait you did after that hike."

Ezra blinked a few times and then stood up, Rusty's hands sliding off his shoulders, to find the canvas standing in the corner.

Damn. Rusty was right. The same blues were the base tone for everything else, though without the vivid green tones. That had been a new inspiration, thanks to Benji and the little pointer that was now attached to his own keychain.

"The side of me that doesn't want to be tamed and boxed up, and the side of you that's afraid to admit how much you care," Rusty said.

Ezra lost his breath for a moment as he looked up at Rusty. Finally, he managed a grin. "You're writing all the labels for my next showing."

Rusty laughed. "Goddamn it. That was my one deep thought for the day, that's all."

Ezra shook his head. He set down the painting nearby and glanced between the two of them. "Actually, there's a thought. With a little extra tweaking, they'd match really well."

"We do," Rusty said softly, which knocked Ezra's concentration clean out of the water again. Ezra looked up at him and stared, and Rusty just smiled sheepishly. "I mean, I think so, anyway?" he offered.

Ezra smiled back at him. He was right, of course. "We sure do," he said. "And it's high time we let everyone else see that."

"Tonight," Rusty promised and then kissed Ezra so deep that he forgot all about dates, grand openings, and art shows.

"First, we need to get showered and cleaned up. I'll pick you up tonight?"

Ezra didn't have to think about it. He just followed his heart, and his heart told him to say yes.

And not just that—but *fuck* yes.

2 0

RUSTY

"There you are, Rusty. I was starting to think you drowned."

Ah, shit. Not only had Rusty's dad found him, but he was wearing the scowl that meant he was in deep trouble.

Rusty swallowed his sigh as he turned away from the group that had formed outside the coffee shop. He didn't even have Ezra by his side to distract him.

Why had he thought he could get away with it?

"That's right. I heard—from reputable sources—that you were out in the boat during that storm. You want to explain yourself, son?"

"Not really," Rusty said with a sigh, rubbing his face. The grand opening was going really well so far—the editor of the one-man town newsletter for Hart's Bay was here taking photos and interviewing people, and all the shops seemed to be doing a brisk business.

His dad pulled him out of the crowd and around the neat wooden planters with their little stubby trees. He led him to the wrought iron archway over the ramp to the wharf, and Rusty knew he was in for a real telling-off.

"First of all, never go out in those conditions again." Rusty tried to speak up and protest, but his dad wasn't done. He held up a hand. "And second, if you're going out, for God's sake, tell us."

"Dad—I was fine," Rusty snapped.

In a moment of calm clarity, he saw the change in himself. He was done with people trying to tell him he wasn't doing his life the right way, or treating him like he didn't know his own mind.

The anger subsided and he stood up straight, the force of conviction behind his words. "I made the decision that had to be made, and it's a good thing I did. There was a whole nasty raft of bull kelp. It tore up half a line, and it would have taken the whole line out—maybe several lines."

"You don't know the sea around here. If you run aground on that point in bad weather, you'll never get out of that boat in time."

"I will. You learned by experience, too. And I stayed safe. I've already learned where the dangerous spots are."

His mom was approaching now, Ezra by her side and walking with a bouncing stride and big smile.

Time to play it cool. "Hey, guys," Rusty said, and then laughed. "I see you've already met Ezra."

"I have. Rumor has it you need to introduce us properly," his mom said, and Rusty could have died with relief and gratitude for the distraction.

"Mom, Dad, this is Ezra. We've... been dating." He didn't want to use the word *boyfriend* until Ezra okayed it, but that seemed safe enough. A sideways glance at Ezra reassured him, because Ezra smiled and took his hand.

"Good to meet you," his dad said gruffly and shook hands with Ezra, while his mom leaned in to kiss Ezra's cheek.

"Now, we were just talking about this harebrained boat trip of his."

Oh, God. They'd already cut the ribbon and eaten the cake. Could they just slip off now?

But movement from the other corner of the boutiques' shared front sitting area, Colt and Rain striding in, caught his eye. There was a cheer going up, and applause, and someone shouting.

Aaron spotted Rusty looking and grinned, giving him a thumbs-up. "They got engaged!"

"No way!" Rusty grinned at Ezra. "You want to congratulate them?"

"We'll let the first crush of people pass," Ezra laughed.

"How wonderful for them." Mom smiled before looking back at Rusty. "So, your father told you how upset we were to hear about you taking out the boat?"

"Oh, God." If *that* didn't distract them, nothing would. Rusty braced himself. "Yeah. Mom, I've been boating for the last five years in Maine. I'm not a kid anymore."

"You're not," his dad agreed solemnly. "At your age, I had you to worry about. Every day when I went out with the men, I just wanted two things. A good catch, but more importantly, to make it home to you."

Rusty's throat went tight. He squeezed Ezra's hand hard. "I know." He didn't remember much about that time, and his parents rarely talked about it, but the snippets he'd caught had stuck in his mind.

"Maybe having Ezra here will make you more cautious."

"And if I'm too cautious and something takes out the harvest, you won't tell me it's *the sea giving and taking away,* or *a sign that I should look at more sensible careers?*" Rusty countered, frustration welling up again. They paused and glanced between each other, and Rusty sighed. "That's what I thought."

Ezra was shifting from side to side, his eyes wide and one hand resting lightly on his chest. He was clearly feeling awkward as hell right now.

"I won't lie, it worries us," Mom finally said. "But it's nice you've found a man who doesn't mind your unusual choice."

That was Ezra's cue to say something. Rusty felt bad, and he wondered if there were a way to smuggle him out of this conversation. But the man just tucked his hair behind his ear and shyly smiled. "It sure won't be easy, but I like that he doesn't take the easy way out. It's a good sign for the future."

It was a great answer. Not taking sides and annoying anyone, but also not leaving Rusty to fend for himself. It even subtly reminded them that they were meeting for the first time and were supposed to be on their best behavior.

Oh, God, Rusty could kiss him right there.

"That's good," Dad said after a moment. "He's a good kid, our boy." He patted Rusty's shoulder and then took Mom's hand. "Come on, let's offer our congratulations and get home. Looks like Cher's opening up, so the party will be moving over there soon."

Mom laughed and nodded. "Tonight's for you young folks. We've got a crossword waiting for us."

But no sooner had they left than Rusty spotted Pascal with his new girlfriend, Laura. She'd come into the picture sometime in the last few weeks, and he'd barely seen his old friend since then.

"Pascal! Hey, over here."

Pascal looked around until he spotted them, then smiled and let go of Laura's hand to head over to them. "Hey, man. How's it going?"

Rusty let go of Ezra's hand and half hugged his friend. "Great, great. The line check didn't go well, but... we only lost half a line. For that bad a storm, that's all right. And the log boom broke."

"Yeah." Pascal looked like he hadn't listened to any of that. He was glancing curiously at Ezra.

"This is Ezra," Rusty added, and he took his hand again. His heart flip-flopped with an anxiety he hadn't expected.

Sure, he might not talk to Pascal much anymore, but he was still his oldest friend. They'd known each other when they chased each other around Hart Square with sticks, hiding in the long grass and pretending to be warriors.

Pascal's jaw dropped for a second before he glanced back to Rusty and then Ezra again. "Oh. Hi. Um, I'm Pascal. Old buddy of his. I'm an accountant over at Keynes."

Rusty cast him a confused look. "And my business partner..." he cued him.

Pascal smiled. Once, he might have leaped on that and talked Ezra's ear off about their businesses as kids—lemonade stands and all. Now, he just shrugged. "Yeah. I suppose. You're still all in on this?"

Rusty blinked a few times. Was this some alternate universe where he had another job? "Uh... yes? You haven't been answering my texts, man."

"Ah, you know." Pascal smiled and looked back at Laura, who was busy talking to another friend outside Aaron's coffee shop. "Life gets busy. I'm surprised new love isn't distracting you, too!" He laughed.

"Do you let new love stop you getting to work on time?" Rusty glanced at Ezra, glad to see him looking as confused as he felt.

Pascal just shrugged. "No, but what you're doing... that's hard work. Look, man, I've been thinking."

Ezra's grip tightened on Rusty's hand, and a second later, he realized what Ezra had heard in Pascal's voice. This was the breakup talk.

"Yeah?" Rusty asked.

"I'm just not cut out for hard work, or keeping track of everything like you do. You're the tough guy here, not me. I'm just dead weight. If you want to cut me out of it and buy back my share when the crop comes in... you're welcome to."

That was less subtle than a brick to the balls.

"Cool." Rusty managed to smile, trying to quell the rising panic in his chest at the casual *when*. At least Pascal was confident that he'd succeed, even if he was bored of playing investor now. "It might be summer by the time that cash flow happens," he warned.

"Oh, no problem." Pascal waved it off and smiled. "It's all just spare money anyway, right?"

Rusty knew his friend had been making good money in the years he'd been scrambling over sharp rocks, palms bleeding and stinging in the salt water, but not *that* good.

"Great," he managed, gritting a smile at Pascal. Laura was waving him over, so he pointed her out. "Looks like new love calls. See you around, man."

He was still dazed as Ezra led him toward Cher's. Ezra didn't ask if he was okay—he just stuck him on a barstool and handed him a beer.

A few sips later, Rusty finally managed to get his thoughts in order. "What the hell?"

Ezra had pulled up the stool next to him and had a hand on his thigh. "I know. That seemed kind of... sorry, I know you were friends. But that was kind of harsh?"

"Super harsh." Rusty shook his head slowly. "Definitely can't afford to hire help, then..." he mumbled.

If he had to use his profit at the harvest—*if* that

happened—to buy out Pascal's investment, then that meant less money for next year. Did nobody understand that this was a serious enterprise? That he'd gone through thousands of pages of paperwork and thousands of dollars of permits? He was going to give this all he had, because it *was* all he had.

Well, no. That and Ezra, if he were really lucky.

The thought pulled Rusty out of the numbers and worries running through his head, and he took Ezra's hand. "Thanks. Wow, I was out of it there, sorry."

Ezra just laughed softly, his eyes crinkling in that beautiful little smile of his. "No problem. You got parented *and* unpartnered in like ten minutes there."

"Okay, thank you. Glad it's not just me feeling like that was a *lot* all at once," Rusty said, laughing as he took another sip of beer.

Then he had an idea. "Hey, is everyone in here now?"

The place was packed, but most people were in the front corner with the tables, and it looked like that was where Colt and Rain were holding their impromptu reception. Champagne bottles were definitely floating around out there.

"Looks like it. People were just starting to lock up as the party moved over here. Why?"

Rusty smiled and glanced over at Cher, making eye contact. "Could you be a doll and keep these back there?" He slid their bottles over the counter. He wasn't sure they'd come back to get them, but she probably knew that.

She winked and took them, then strode off to get someone else's order.

"Before I have too much of that, I'd like to take you out again." Rusty smiled at Ezra. "May I treat you to another romantic evening cruise?" Just like the day they'd met.

Nothing but the open water, the hum of the engine, and Ezra's enthusiastic squeaks.

Ezra perked up immediately. "Sure." He grinned, twisting his hands together as he stood up.

But Rusty wasn't done. He had one more thing he needed to do before they left the bar.

He led Ezra to the middle of the bar and then stopped, spinning on the spot to take his hands. "Love's in the air tonight. You think it's contagious?"

"Yeah...?" Ezra couldn't hide the hope on his face. It was adorable.

"Good. Me too." Rusty grinned and dropped Ezra's hand, cupping his cheeks instead. He drew his lover in, and Ezra went easily, rising onto tiptoe and resting his hands on Rusty's chest.

And then they kissed. Rusty ignored the catcalling and cheers nearby, just enjoying Ezra's soft, warm lips.

There was no better way to come out than making out in front of a crowded bar of people who'd known him his whole life. That would remove any trace of a doubt about who he really was.

And Ezra was glowing again. He looked like his little rust-colored sunshine right now. When he finally pulled back for breath, Ezra laughed and swayed into Rusty, leaning heavily into him. "Oh, my. That's a boyfriend power move."

"Is it?" Rusty beamed, his spirits soaring. "Well, I'm happy to be your boyfriend. Worth the wait?" Rusty murmured into his ear, smoothing his hair and tucking it behind his ear for him.

"Oh, yes." Ezra beamed at him and then around at everyone else. "Thank you for waiting for me to be ready."

Rusty beamed at him, trying to find words to express the

rightness that hit him all at once. "No, thank you for waiting. Now, may I accompany you to your sea-based chariot?"

Ezra giggled and hooked his arm through Rusty's. "Of course."

On the way out, they stopped to wish Colt and Rain a happy engagement and fended off more than one *so, are you next?* comment for their display.

When they finally made it to the dock together, hand in hand, Rusty grinned. He paused under the iron arch. "I should carry you over the threshold, but I think the only safe way to get you down the ramp would be the fireman's carry."

Ezra gasped and backed away. "If you try that, I will call you every name under the sun, and maybe pants you."

Rusty burst out laughing and took it slowly down the ramp instead, letting Ezra walk on the section with better tread. They made it to his boat, and he unzipped the canopy, then helped his boyfriend inside and grabbed life jackets.

His *boyfriend.*

Oh, man. That was the first time he'd thought of Ezra using that word, and Rusty just lit up inside and out—he could feel it.

"You look like the cat who got the cream," Ezra said.

He wriggled into his life jacket before even noticing what Rusty had done. Last trip to the boating supply store, Rusty had picked up an orange camo life jacket. It suited Ezra even worse than the plain, bright orange one.

"Oh, God," Ezra laughed, but he sounded giddy. "I'm glad nobody's here to see this but you."

"I won't tell if you don't," Rusty murmured, letting his voice shift to a low rumble as he sidled up close. "Maybe that turns me on—oof!" Their life jackets bumped before he could get anywhere close enough to Ezra to breathe it against his lips like he'd planned.

Ezra giggled and chest-bumped him in return. "Maybe I'm turned on by you being all sexy and boaterly."

"Boaterly," Rusty repeated, squinting. "Nautical?"

Ezra drew himself up and tilted his chin up proudly. "No, boaterly. I made that bed. I'm lying in it."

Rusty started the motor and cast off, guiding Ezra to sit down until he made it out to open water.

"Hold on!" He grinned as Ezra clutched the canopy, then opened up the throttle far more than he had last time.

Ezra whooped with surprise, his jaw dropping.

Rusty laughed. "You want me to slow down?" he called over the noise of the engine and the crashing of the hull against each little wave. They were barely white-tipped, but at this speed, the ride was never going to be smooth.

"No!" Ezra gestured forward, his gaze bright with delight and approval. "Faster!"

Rusty took them past the point and looped around, grinning as Ezra held on for dear life. His hair shook free, whipping around his face and getting in his mouth, but Ezra just kept tucking it into the back of his life jacket.

With Ezra bouncing happily in his seat, Rusty did a tight loop and then slowed down, laughing as he got to a nice bit of open water with no rocks nearby. "You want a turn?"

Ezra's gaze popped open wide. "Really? I'd love to!" He slid in as Rusty made room for him, then showed him the throttle and steering wheel.

"It's pretty simple," Rusty said, standing up and holding the edge of the canopy. "I'll keep an eye out for driftwood. Not many of those logs seem to have made it down here, luckily. They must have gotten washed out instead."

Ezra was tentative at first, barely puttering through the water, but then he rapidly gained speed and confidence. Before Rusty knew it, he was doing at least three-quarters the speed that Rusty had been, and his grin was a mile wide.

God, it was adorable seeing his boyfriend enjoy himself. Rusty even forgot to look out for driftwood until a piece thumped the underside of the boat on their way over.

"Oops. Sorry!" Ezra covered his mouth, his eyes wide.

Rusty laughed. "No, my bad." He had to tear his eyes off that beautifully sheepish look to look at the water ahead. "That was my job. You're doing great. I'm seriously impressed. I'd let you drive it more. Maybe I've found my new partner after all."

"Am I distracting you?" Ezra giggled. He fluttered his lashes and pretended not to know what Rusty meant, playing innocent.

Rusty gave him a roguish wink as Ezra looked over. "You always distract me. It's terrible for my focus, you know."

"Why don't you take over driving again and I'll distract you some more?" Ezra asked, slowing down the throttle.

But Rusty's throttle was speeding up with those words. His heart thumped as Ezra lifted himself out of the seat and leaned against the dashboard, still facing Rusty.

"What did you have in mind?" Rusty asked, sliding past him to sit.

Even this brush of their bodies made him catch his breath. He gripped the throttle hard, trying not to accelerate too quickly, even if that was what his heartbeat was doing.

"Well," Ezra purred over the motor, "that depends if we stay nice and far from prying eyes." He squeezed onto Rusty's lap with a mischievous grin, wedging himself between Rusty and the wheel.

They might have had more room without the life jackets, but Rusty wasn't about to suggest they take them off. He sucked in a quick breath as caution whispered to him. He could still see over Ezra's shoulder, just about, and there was no boat traffic around here anyway.

He wasn't sure he could stop Ezra, even if he wanted to. His boyfriend was kissing spots on his neck that made him see stars despite the steadily building cloud cover overhead.

"Nnh!" Rusty grunted sharply, his whole body shivering when Ezra's groin lined up with his.

Ezra started to rock his body in sinuous, slow rolls, and those clever lips and teeth found a spot on Rusty's earlobe that made him whimper. He was hard now—and so was Ezra, judging by the firm bulge rubbing against his.

Rusty kept the speed down and one hand on the wheel, trying his best to pay attention to his surroundings and not the gorgeous redhead who was slipping the button open and zipper down on his jeans.

"Fuck—" he grunted, his cry cutting his voice short. Just the brush of Ezra's long fingers into his underwear and against his cock got him the rest of the way hard.

"Make all the noise you want, baby," Ezra breathed out, hot and warm against his ear. His tongue trailed down to the corner of Rusty's jaw, where he placed one openmouthed kiss. "I want to hear it."

Rusty swallowed hard and spread his legs, shifting around to help Ezra work his cock free from his jeans.

Then Ezra did the same to himself, and it took all Rusty had not to break his concentration on driving the boat to look down. Their life jackets obstructed the sight of their groins pressed together, but they didn't get in the way of the action. That was the important part.

The firm heat of the shaft pressing against every sensitive spot he had was indescribably satisfying. It felt right when Ezra took them both in one hand, squeezing them together as he ran his hand up and down the shafts.

"I love how bold you are," Rusty managed to grit through his teeth while struggling for breath.

Every nerve in his shaft was hypersensitive, and thank God their hot bodies were crushed close together. It gave them shelter against the cold breeze that tickled the back of his neck.

Ezra's other arm drooped lazily around his shoulders, and his fingers walked up from the back of his neck to grip the hair at the back of Rusty's head. "I love that you take it all in your stride."

"We're going to have to run to the car if we make a mess," Rusty warned with a laugh.

Ezra clicked his tongue. "Good. It's not the walk of shame, it's the run of pride. It's character building."

Rusty wasn't prepared to argue that one while Ezra's fingers danced over the head of his shaft, sending sparks dancing straight down into his belly. He grunted and then relaxed, letting himself moan again freely.

The sound carried over open water, even over the engine. It made him grin and blush at the same time.

"Frotting feels amazing," Ezra breathed out, beaming at him. "Especially against a nice, big, juicy dick. But you know what feels better? Me riding you right here, bouncing up and down on your hungry cock until you shoot your load deep inside me..."

Rusty's mind whirled. He raked his nails down Ezra's back and then worked his hand under his life jacket, trying to clutch him as close as he possibly could. "Fuck, yes," he whispered.

Every visual Ezra painted with his words was burned into his mind now. He needed this.

"You better invite me over," Ezra giggled. "Because I'm taking the day off, and I'm going to make you do the same thing."

Rusty nodded hard. He could spare the time when his boyfriend asked him to in *this* tone of voice. "Yeah. Please," he whispered. "I've been fantasizing for so long."

Ezra moaned into his ear. "And I've been wanting you, too, baby." He started thrusting into his fist, his length sliding back and forth over Rusty's with each quick jerk of his hips.

Rusty growled, his nails biting into the wheel cover until they left marks. He had enough leverage to pin Ezra here, so he started to thrust, too.

Ezra kept his fingers tight around them both, and each quick jerk of Rusty's hips made them both gasp for breath. The climax built between them in a rush of heat and need, but Rusty fought it for as long as he could.

Finally, he let go of the wheel and grabbed both of Ezra's shoulders, crushing Ezra into his chest and crying his name at the top of his lungs. No holding back, no second-guessing himself.

Just raw, untamed, wild need coursing through every inch of him—body and soul.

Ezra fit him in every way he could ever ask for, and Rusty was so grateful they could both see that now.

Ezra came moments later, whimpering and pressing his face into Rusty's neck as his hips stuttered, losing their steady rhythm.

Wet heat spilled between them both, making their last thrusts slick and tingly until Ezra finally let go and peeled himself away.

With a breathless laugh, he landed on his butt on the boat floor, messy and flushed as red as his hair and beaming. "Aaah-mazing," he proclaimed.

Rusty laughed as he turned the boat toward the harbor and dug in his jeans for tissues. "You can say that again."

Time seemed to blur until the all-important moment: when Rusty climbed into his bed alongside Ezra. His new boyfriend immediately cuddled into him, wrapping his arms around him and pressing his face into his chest.

Rusty chuckled gently and stroked Ezra's hair as his eyes drifted closed. "Good night, babe."

"G'night, love." Ezra's voice was sleepy, but Rusty could still make out that word.

Oh, it made him smile. No need to have a great big talk about it. They were both on the same page at last.

"Sleep well, love," Rusty echoed, his heart thumping with excitement for a solid minute before he managed to settle down again.

He'd finally won over Ezra's head and heart, and come to peace with his own. All was well right now. They could deal with the rest of the world in the morning.

21

EZRA

It was almost eerie how silent the world was when Ezra woke.

He wasn't used to getting up with the sun, but the unfamiliar surroundings made him stir to life. That, and the bicep he'd been nuzzling had just been drawn away from him gently.

He pouted and glanced up at Rusty, but Rusty seemed to be fast asleep, his arm now flung over his head.

Though Ezra closed his eyes, the excitement had already crept in. No way could he get back to sleep now, thinking about his new relationship status.

Oh my God, I'll have to update Facebook, he thought, grinning. His closest friends had all seen that wonderful, show-stopping, earth-shaking public kiss yesterday. But he still had plenty of acquaintances and family members to make jealous.

He'd never been able to lie still when he was awake. After a few minutes of squirming, enjoying the closeness to

Rusty but also trying not to wake him up, he had a better idea: breakfast in bed for his gorgeous new boyfriend.

Ezra drew himself out from under the covers and grabbed his clothing, tiptoed to the door, then slipped out.

He hadn't gotten a chance to have a real look around before now. It was a nice little house, though, and just a few blocks from his own. It looked like there was a guest room and bathroom upstairs.

Down the staircase he headed, shivering even once he was dressed again. It was a little bit cool, but it was the light creeping into the room that made him hold his breath.

Ezra drew aside the living room curtain and blinked. He was pretty sure there was a row of houses opposite Rusty's, but none were in sight. Oh, wait. The wind shifted just a little, and a mirage of a house appeared for a moment before the thick blanket of fog covered it again. At least the storm was well and truly gone. It wasn't raining or anything, just eerily quiet.

A nice love seat and couch set in the living room promised some fun cuddling in the future in front of the TV, but the fridge had Ezra's attention.

Wait, what? No bacon, no eggs, and no milk. How the hell was he supposed to work with that?

Ezra sighed and then checked his phone, grabbing it from the table by the door on the way. Lots of questions and comments from his friends, but he could ignore them.

It was a little past seven, so the grocery store at Hart Square would be open. That was an easy walk, cutting through a few houses' side yards on the path down. He could be there and back with ingredients in fifteen minutes, before Rusty even knew he was gone.

Then an even better idea occurred to Ezra. That would bring him right to the harbor, and Rusty's boat. And however much Rusty had made last night about them and not about work, he'd seen Rusty's worried glances along the coast toward his farm.

Ezra knew how to drive the boat now, and he knew where the farm was. He'd be extra careful and take it slow, but he could zip there and back and check the lines. It wasn't dangerously windy out there—he could barely hear the ocean from here.

He might be a city boy, all flat shoes and hair products, but he could help his wilderness man. He could prove that he *was* a good match, not some Lycra-clad figure he'd invented in his anxiety-fueled bad dreams.

And best of all, Ezra would show Rusty that accepting help wouldn't kill him. Without even having to get out of bed, he could get peace of mind that the farm was okay for today. And then he wouldn't get that vaguely worried, distracted expression on his face halfway through the hot sex Ezra had planned for later.

Perfect.

Just in case Rusty woke up, he scribbled a quick note. *Heading out, back in 30 mins!*

He tucked the note under Rusty's keys, unhooked the boat key from his truck key fob, and slipped out the door.

This. Was. Awesome.

Ezra breathed in deeply, listening to the boat engine purr as he slowly followed the coastline toward the farm.

The fog was heavy, but he could still stay safely far enough away from the rocks, making good use of the navigating thingy on the dashboard that showed him how deep the water was underneath.

The smell was unmistakable: gas, salt, and that certain something of a foggy day. It was a heady mix, and it made him feel like he was heading out on an adventure.

"Whoa!" Ezra twitched with surprise when the floating markers came in view. That had been much faster than kayaking out. He slowed down, steering the boat exactly where they'd been when Rusty brought him here—around the outskirts, so he didn't get the propeller caught.

Nothing seemed to be amiss at all. Ezra cut the engine and scrambled to the back, shading his eyes to peer down into the depths.

It occurred to him now that he wasn't entirely sure what he was looking *for*, but it all looked the same as before to him. Except one line, close to the surface, was totally bare. Farther down he could just make out dark tendrils, so that must be the line that got stripped by the bull kelp.

No logs, no more kelp, and all the buoys were firmly attached.

Ezra snapped a few photos, then pocketed his phone. "Done."

Turning the boat around was hard, but he waited for the tide to help. As it tugged the bow gently around, he applied a little power until he'd gotten the rest of the way.

That meant keeping the shore on his left now. Easy.

Being alone out here, with just nature and his own thoughts, was strange. Ezra was used to being alone for short periods of time—painting, for example. But relying on himself, this exposed to the elements?

He could see how healing it would be, and why Rusty liked it so much. Maybe he needed to do that healing—if not with solitary boating, with something else.

He'd held Rusty off for much too long, afraid of losing him, and even afraid of admitting to his own fears. And damn it, he carried that ugly, angry, emotional, needy self around inside him. He had since his brother died—angry, irrationally, at Jon, and at the driver who'd killed him, and at the world for letting it happen. He'd never been able to quite see past that to a world where he didn't hold that piece of himself back again, fearing more loss.

Hell, he'd been afraid of his own anger. For a long time, he'd backed off as soon as real anger touched him—afraid that it might consume him as it had before art saved him.

Ezra caught his breath as he realized the shore had disappeared. He could see water washing over shallow rocks in the direction he *thought* it might be, so he didn't dare go any nearer. He had to just assume it was that way.

But this didn't look familiar at all.

Even when he squinted through the tufts of mist that drifted across the gray shoreline, he wasn't sure it was the shore. The fog was closing in, rather than lifting and burning off.

The sky was dark, too, providing little help. It was hard to see where the sun might even be, and that was his only other landmark.

Instantly, the exhilaration faded, replaced by a growing horror. He'd seriously overestimated his own ability to be a helpful equal partner here.

"Shit," Ezra whispered. He slowed to a crawl and dug his phone out, opening Google Maps.

Ah, shit. It was struggling to locate him, the map turning this way and that. The dot sometimes drifted so close to the shoreline that he gasped and jerked the wheel, looking up and expecting the rocks to be there.

"Not a good time to fuck uuuup," Ezra whined at it. It seemed to have an idea which way he was facing, and it was telling him he'd passed the harbor.

But he hadn't been lost in thought for *that* long. If he turned around now, he might lose track of the coastline altogether. He had to be close to the harbor, right?

"Well, fuck me sideways," Ezra muttered, thumping his phone against his forehead when it changed its mind yet again and located him in the nearby national park.

His signal was shit, but there was one other thing he ought to try next. He gulped and dialed Rusty's number. The phone just beeped and he cursed, resisting the urge to toss it overboard. That wouldn't help anything.

Shit, how was he going to explain this? He was only supposed to be out for a few minutes, and here he was taking a joyride in his boyfriend's boat, which he probably needed some kind of license to drive, and lost.

And he didn't even know how much fuel it had. What if he drifted out into the Pacific Ocean and nobody ever found him?

Ezra choked back a sob and pressed his hand to his chest. He didn't want to die in a tiny little boat when some great big container ship ran him over!

His phone vibrated. "Signal!" Ezra lunged for it, fumbling to press the answer button.

"Babe, where the hell are you? I got the note, but my boat keys are missing."

"So, um." Ezra's voice wavered. "I took the boat out to check the farm."

"In the *fog*?"

"Yes," Ezra whimpered. "I'm sorry. I wanted to take the stress off you and help, and I got there fine, but then I turned back and now I'm lost and I can't see the shore and the signal will probably drop any minute now...!"

"I'm on my way. Take it slow, keep an ear out for any boats nearby," Rusty instructed, his voice instantly in a tone

Ezra had only heard once before—the very first time they'd met. It was commanding and knowledgeable and *safe*.

Ezra clutched the phone tight. "Okay. How will you get to me?"

"We'll figure that out in a sec. Do you have the fish finder?"

"Yeah. That's what it is? Are those fish under me?" Ezra squinted at the little triangles.

He might not be totally screwed. If he got stranded, he could fish for his supper until the Coast Guard could track him down. He stifled the sobbing laugh.

"If they look like—never mind. Just, if you see the bottom rising, don't run aground. Where does your phone say you are?"

"It's really confused right now. It says I went past the harbor, and I might have, but I don't want to turn around and get even more lost. I can't see the shore anymore..."

Now he couldn't even see the flickers of mist parting across deep gray rocks.

"Stay on the line. If we get cut off, redial me as soon as you have signal." Ezra could hear Rusty's truck starting in the background. "I have to make one stop before I come to the harbor. How far ahead can you see? Jesus, it's thick here on land."

"Maybe..." Ezra squinted at the water. "Six feet?"

Rusty was silent for a few moments, which was actually worse than if he'd cursed or something. "Okay," he finally said. "I'm only a minute away from Gregory's. When we—"

The line crackled and warbled, then cut out.

Ezra whimpered and stabbed at the screen. The fucking thing had cut out.

Okay, but if he turned around, maybe he could stay within the zone where he'd gotten signal...

It was a risk, but he was no longer sure he'd been going straight at all.

Ezra took the boat in as quick a circle as he dared, finding his own wake to line himself up with. Now he was at least going the opposite direction he had been, so if that was more or less along the coast, he'd be heading back toward the harbor.

The map was probably right. He'd overshot it, because he'd been puttering along for way too long now.

"Fuck," Ezra moaned, his grip ironclad on the wheel. At least his panic helped keep him from feeling *quite* so guilty, stupid, and downright shitty.

It was a stupid plan, he was stupid for thinking he could try to help Rusty, and he was utterly, monumentally stupid for actually trying to do so without telling anyone. In trying to make Rusty accept help, he'd just done exactly what he'd told Rusty off for doing.

Ezra swiped the tears away from the side of his nose, cursing under his breath at himself.

"If I get back safe, no more *great ideas* about helping him out. Leave him to do what he's good at. Just painting for me. Painting, and maybe a kayak trip, with constant supervision."

A laugh bubbled from him. Talking helped keep him calm.

The purr of the boat engine was his only company as Ezra kept his gaze fixed on the horizon, tears trickling down his cheeks no matter how much he willed them not to.

I'm sorry, Rusty. I'm just a dumb city boy after all.

RUSTY

Rusty's heart sank when the line cut off. Fuck, this was a lot worse than he wanted to let on to Ezra.

Running aground was a very real possibility, or drifting into the open sea—and the path of much larger ships with so little visibility and no radio.

Most people didn't know how to steer in fog, either. They looked straight ahead and felt like they were going straight, instead of focusing on the farthest water they could see. It was almost guaranteed Ezra had been going in circles.

The biggest relief was that he'd had phone signal until a minute ago. That meant he was in reach of cell towers, and not miles out in the ocean. *Yet*, his brain added, and he cursed under his breath as he parked in front of Gregory's house, flung himself out, and trotted up to the front door.

"Sorry, man," Rusty mumbled under his breath before knocking on the door hard. He rang the doorbell, too, and listened hard for movement. As he waited for what felt like forever, he shifted from foot to foot, phone clutched tightly in his hand in case Ezra called back.

Gregory was one of a few guys around town who'd been on deck with Rusty's dad. He'd no doubt forgotten more about the sea than Rusty had learned yet. And most importantly, he had a functioning boat at the marina—with radar that would help Rusty get back to land.

After the second knock, the door flung open and Gregory stood there, bleary and scowling in checked pajamas and a fuzzy bathrobe.

"Where's the fire?" His Irish accent was faint until he'd reached the bottom of a pint glass, but apparently being half-asleep did the trick, too.

"I need your help. There's been an incident. Ezra took my boat out to check on the lines, and now he's lost."

"Jesus," Gregory cursed, glancing over Rusty's shoulder. "In this fog?"

"Yep. And he's only driven my boat once."

Gregory groaned and swiped a hand over his face, looking more awake now. "The daft fucker. Here. Take the keys. I'll meet you down at the dock. I'll wait on land in case someone's gotta call the Coast Guard. If I don't hear from you in half an hour, I'm calling them."

"Gotcha." Rusty caught the keys Gregory tossed him and saluted him with them. "Thanks, man."

Gregory made surprising speed out of the house. By the time Rusty was climbing out of his truck, Gregory had sped through the town square and pulled up next to him.

He climbed out bundled up in a sweater and thick jeans, his expression grim as he led the way down to the boat. "You better know what you're doing in my baby. God Almighty. Promised your parents I'd talk sense into you when you got 'round to buying her. Didn't think I'd have to knock sense into that eejit lad's pretty little head, too," Gregory grumbled. "And it's bloody cold and dark out here. No sun to burn off the mist. A man could get hypothermia. Nobody with sense would be out on a day like today." He launched into a steady stream of complaints and doomsaying on their way down the ramp.

By the time they reached the boat and Rusty jumped in to start the engine, Gregory was halfway through one of his stories. Someone he knew in a trawler had run up on rocks in thick fog, and the crew had nearly drowned.

"But I'm sure Ezra will be fine," Gregory said, much too cheerily, shoving a life jacket at Rusty before unmooring the front lines. "Don't wreck it before you buy it."

Rusty gulped and nodded. "I'll try not to. Thanks again, man."

Gregory pushed the boat out and nodded. "Remember: half an hour. And you don't want the fine the Coast Guard will slap on you. Especially if your boy's not got his license."

"Gotcha." Rusty hadn't thought of that, but it was a concern that paled in comparison to his fear for Ezra's life. If they needed professional rescuers, he'd get them.

He'd give anything in the world to make sure Ezra was okay.

The man standing on the dock, hands in his pockets, quickly disappeared into the fog. Rusty could still barely hear his mumbled complaints for a minute longer over the engine before that disappeared, too, muffled by the thick blanket of mist.

As Rusty kept one eye on his phone, waiting for it to ring, he steered toward the mouth of the harbor. God, this fog was thicker now than half an hour ago, wasn't it?

Knowing Ezra's way of taking on other people's problems, he should have seen where this was going when Ezra kept insisting he needed help. Instead, Rusty gave him a damn driving lesson. He might as well have handed him the keys himself.

Rusty's chest was tight with fear, and he couldn't stop running through the *what ifs*. If they got out of this unscathed, he was going to count it as a miracle, then listen to Ezra and partner up with someone who knew what the fuck he was doing.

Maybe Gregory himself. He had the gear, the knowledge, and a fondness for the underdog. He'd hauled himself out of bed without a second thought for Rusty and Ezra and handed him the keys. His dad knew and trusted him.

Planning helped Rusty not think about what he was going to do next, and what could happen to Ezra while they were out of touch.

The loud, abrupt chime nearly startled him into dropping the phone, but he cheered as he picked up. "Ezra!"

"Yep, it's me." His boyfriend sounded rattled but determined. "I turned around and got within signal range again, so I must be doing something right."

"You're doing great, baby," Rusty assured him. If he were lost out there, alone in the fog, he'd freak out. "I'm in Gregory's boat now. I'm just at the mouth of the harbor. Don't listen to the phone for a moment."

"Huh? Okay." There was a rustle and muffled sound that indicated Ezra had done so.

Then, Rusty blew the horn.

It was impossible to tell from his end whether he was hearing himself through the line or not, but Ezra whooped. "I hear you!"

"Great. Okay, you're close by," Rusty said. "Take it super slowly. Last thing we want is to crash the boats together. This ain't bumper boats."

Ezra managed a small giggle. "Going as slow as it'll let

me. It's not as easy as it looks." His breathing was shallow and quick, betraying his real feelings. Rusty had never been prouder of him for keeping it together. If Ezra had fallen apart, it would have been so much harder to save him. But he was the kind of guy who could save himself, too.

He just needed a helping hand, and it was Rusty's job to be that man for him. Not just his job—his pleasure, and his greatest wish.

"No, it's not." Rusty's lips quirked into a small smile. "Right, so I just need to work out how to go in a loop. If I keep blowing the horn, and you tell me if it sounds louder or softer..."

"No, wait. I have a better idea." A moment later, Ezra said, "Anything?"

Rusty tilted his head. He didn't hear a thing, but then he saw it—a little green line cutting through the fog. The laser light swept around.

"Yes! Good thinking, hon. I see you," Rusty praised, his heart leaping to his throat. "Just keep doing that. I'm coming for you."

"Please," Ezra moaned, the cracks finally showing in his forced calmness.

Rusty's heart squeezed tight with the desire to hug his boyfriend so tightly he could hardly breathe. He wanted to wrap Ezra up and take every ounce of anxiety away from him. "You're gonna be fine," he murmured, his hand twitching on the wheel to line himself up with the line the laser cut through the fog. "I'm almost there, hon."

"I'm never, ever, ever getting in a boat again."

Rusty chuckled softly. "I don't blame you, babe."

"I'm sorry I took the boat out," Ezra said, and Rusty could hear him gulping back tears. "I had no right to do that. I was just trying to help, and I didn't think."

Rusty blew a quick *pffft* sound. Now wasn't the time to make Ezra feel worse than he already did. He wasn't going to let Ezra upset himself even more. "I practically set you up for it," he told Ezra, keeping his eyes peeled as the laser light grew stronger. "I should have looked for help before now. I appreciate you trying to help me, though. The idea was sweet." Going it alone was a foolish idea, especially when he wasn't familiar with this ocean. Ezra could have paid dearly for Rusty's pride.

Ezra gulped. "Idea sweet, execution less than ideal." Rusty laughed loudly at the understatement, and Ezra gasped. The laser swept around in a semicircle. "I heard you!"

Rusty cut the engine and listened for the purr of his own boat. When he heard it, he followed the sound and the thin green light, and then the clouds in front of him parted, and there it was.

His boat, and his Ezra there in the orange camo life jacket, waving frantically to him.

Rusty wanted to cry with relief. He'd never been so glad to see his boyfriend. Part of him wanted to swim over to his boat just so he could grab Ezra and never let go. But letting Gregory's boat drift off into the fog wasn't a smart idea, so the hug would have to wait.

Rusty started up the motor again and waved back, grinning as he steered carefully alongside Ezra. "Come on. This way, love." He couldn't quite reach out and touch him, but his boat—and his words—were as close as he dared get.

Ezra beamed, his blush visible through the mist as he ducked under the canopy to get to the steering wheel.

Slowly, glancing at the radar and compass, Rusty led Ezra back to port. Ezra had been a good half mile south of the harbor mouth, so he'd definitely gone past it. Worse yet, he'd been steering toward it, so if he hadn't turned around...

Rusty shivered and focused on getting them back in one piece, blowing his horn at two-minute intervals. He hoped that Gregory could hear them from land, too, and hold off calling the authorities.

The wharf loomed into view, a dark shape that must have been Lucy slipping into the water at the sound of their approaching engines.

Rusty cast a worried look in Ezra's direction. Steering up to a wharf wasn't always easy even in calm conditions, but Gregory ignored Rusty and strode to the end of the wharf, waving Ezra over to the other side.

Sending a silent thanks his way, Rusty focused on maneuvering close enough to grab the rope and moor himself, while Gregory caught the rope Ezra threw him.

Rusty had no sooner climbed onto the dock than Ezra was skidding toward him, flinging his arms around Rusty. With both their life jackets on, Ezra nearly bounced clear off him.

Rusty caught his arms and held tight, running his hand through Ezra's hair and cupping the back of his neck. "I've got you, hon," he murmured.

"I'm such a city boy," Ezra breathed out, pressing his face into Rusty's shoulder. "I only wanted to prove myself, and it was dumb. I wanted to be useful."

Rusty nearly pulled back from Ezra and stared. Prove himself? Why would he need to do that? He shook his head. "You didn't need to," he told Ezra, taking hold of his arms. "I love you for who you are, my sweet city boy. I was so worried for you. Don't ever do that to me again. You scared the daylights out of me." His chest was tight as the full impact of what could have happened started to sink in.

It was hard not to panic, but clinging to Ezra helped.

Ezra went still for a moment, and then his hold tightened. "I know. I'm sorry," he whispered. "I love you, too."

That was one good thing to come out of this. They weren't dancing around the bond they'd built.

"This is all touching," Gregory muttered from nearby, "but some of us would like to go back to bed, if you don't mind."

Rusty laughed and pulled away from Ezra, then held out the boat keys to Gregory. "Thank you. I actually had a question."

Gregory took the keys, looking wary. "Yeees?"

"Would you consider becoming a business partner? I need help—I can't do it alone, that much I know now. And I can't do it with someone who's just in it for the money and doesn't care about what I'm doing."

"Ah, you've got me there," Gregory said, tossing the keys up and down in his hand before he pocketed them. "Still love the sea. I shouldn't, treacherous lady she is. But I've never quite been able to give her up." He squinted at them both, then shrugged. "Ach, why not. Someone has to keep you daft gobshites from washing up in pieces. Like my old buddy. By the time the Coast Guard got there—"

"Okay-thanks-bye!" Ezra let go of Rusty's hand and briskly strode up the wharf, life jacket on and all.

Rusty laughed, turning to follow him. He didn't blame him one bit for wanting to escape that story. "Thanks again, Gregory."

"Don't mention it. I owed your dad one, I'm sure. How about my boat, then? You like her?"

"She's great," Rusty admitted, glancing up at Ezra to make sure he made it up the ramp.

"She is. She'll do us well for the first few years." Gregory held out a hand, and Rusty shook it firmly. "Can't wait to get started. Well, in this weather, I can. You go chase your lad."

Rusty grinned, shrugging off his life jacket and handing it back to Gregory. "Thanks."

Then he trotted up the ramp, joining Ezra at the top under the iron arch. He glanced back and watched Gregory puttering about, adjusting the knot on the line, patting the side of his boat. He could swear he heard him talking to her.

After all the what-ifs that had been running through his head, all had turned out well. The adrenaline was finally ebbing, leaving Rusty tired out but grateful.

"He's a good one," Ezra said, then looked up at Rusty, his eyes shining. Pure adoration was written over his face, making Rusty go all hot and flushed. "And so are you. Now let's get back to your place. I have plans for you."

"Do I get a say in them?"

"You'll think you do," Ezra promised. He grinned. "But first, we'll stop by the store. We still need bacon and eggs to fuel us later."

Rusty grinned and tugged on Ezra's life jacket. "You wanna take this off?"

"Oh!" Ezra laughed and shook his head, then wriggled out of it. After Rusty tossed it into his truck, Ezra took his hand and squeezed. "I don't want to float anymore. I want to let the tide carry me wherever you go."

Rusty leaned in for a gentle kiss, then squeezed his hand. "And I'm lucky to have you by my side. Come on. Breakfast waits for no man."

EZRA

"That was really good." Rusty grinned as he looked up at Ezra, mopping up the last of his egg yolk with a slice of toast. He winked. "You can stay."

Ezra laughed, melting into his chair. "Phew." Rusty's seal of approval meant even more after he'd been so reckless this morning. He'd insisted on cooking, the action giving him something to do with his hands that calmed him. This was a way of being useful that didn't involve endangering everyone. "I hope I get to, quite a lot."

"Me too." Rusty smiled at him over their empty plates. When Ezra tried to clear the dishes, Rusty waved him off. "No, no. Get to the living room. I've got these."

When Rusty joined Ezra in the living room, he had a fuzzy blanket over his arm. He settled down next to him and wrapped it around both of their shoulders.

Ezra smiled, nuzzling into Rusty's shoulder and drawing his end of the blanket tight. "So, I guess we should talk."

They'd already checked in to make sure they were okay

before cooking breakfast. By mutual silent agreement, they hadn't had the bigger conversation about it yet.

Rusty nodded, his arm draped around Ezra's shoulders. It felt less scary with him already giving Ezra warm looks. "Are you okay? Not in shock or anything?"

"Fine," Ezra murmured and then grimaced. "Well, mostly fine. Kind of embarrassed about it all."

"It all worked out," Rusty assured him, but then he sighed. "And I'm so glad. Even I didn't like that fog. You must have been scared witless."

Ezra snuggled into Rusty, pressing his forehead into his shoulder and working his knees up onto Rusty's lap. "I was. I was planning what supplies to save if I washed up on a desert island and had to make a raft to get back home."

Rusty chuckled deeply, but it wasn't unkind. "I'd pick you on my desert island team."

"Really?" Ezra quirked a brow. "I can't even steer a boat in a straight line."

Rusty squeezed him. "Babe, nobody can. The trick is to look at the farthest patch of water you can see so you can calculate the current and adjust."

"Oh." Ezra made a mental note, then snorted. "Like I'm planning on leaving the house when it's foggy ever again."

"Can I coax you back onto a boat someday?" Rusty kissed the top of his head. "I really liked our little cruises."

Ezra's chest drew tight, but he nodded. He didn't want to let his fears hold him back anymore. "And I won't steal her for any more joyrides."

"You can, on a clear day, after I make you get your license, and I've checked it over for you..."

Ezra laughed. "Okay, so, never ever."

After a moment, Rusty pulled back to look at him. "Why did you do it? Aside from just wanting to help me? You said you wanted to prove yourself. But... we're already dating." He tilted his head. "What's to prove?"

Ezra blushed and fidgeted. He looked away, then back at Rusty, steeling himself. "Remember my self-portrait?" When Rusty nodded, he went on. "It brought up a lot of ugly parts of me. Desperate for attention, for love. Willing to take on board everyone else's feelings before mine. I want to be better than that. This decision came from that place, too. A little piece of me wanted to be useful, just to make sure you... you need me."

Ezra's throat went tight, and tears pricked at the corners of his eyes.

"I need you so much it hurts," Rusty murmured, pulling him into his chest and cradling him. Those big hands were gentle as they rubbed his back and fidgeted with his hair. "I was so scared about losing you."

"Same here," Ezra whispered, closing his eyes. "And I feel awful about making you worry for my safety. That's, like, my biggest fear. That's why I yelled at you the other day. Then I did the same thing. God, I'm a dumbass." He gave a small laugh.

Rusty nuzzled Ezra gently, making all the stress bleed from him. "You're not a dumbass. And I'll try harder to stay safe," he promised. "But I'm not going anywhere."

Ezra nodded, letting the words sink into his bones. For the first time, he started to believe it. "You came for me, even though it was dangerous for you, too." He pulled back enough to kiss Rusty's cheek. "That's really... you're my big damn hero, you know that?"

From the first time they'd met, when he'd approached that asshole like an avenging angel, through to this morning when the lights on his boat had broken through the fog...

He really was Ezra's hero.

As he'd expected, Rusty snorted and waved it off. "I just did what had to be done. But I'll get better at asking for help doing it."

Ezra smiled to himself, running his hand up Rusty's stomach to rest on his chest. "And I'm going to get better at handling my fears. You can look after yourself—way better than I can out there. I can't keep you safe, and trying will only hurt us both."

When he stopped to think about it, maybe that was why he'd moved out here in the first place. All his friends had been so jazzed for it that he'd just gone along with them, even if he'd known it would wreck his love life. He just hadn't wanted to lose them to distance.

"Proud of you," Rusty murmured, tucking Ezra's hair behind his ear and cupping his cheek. "Not a lot of people could have kept it together like that, not knowing a thing about what they were doing."

Ezra wanted to deflect the compliment, but instead he let it sink in. Maybe he wasn't an exact match for Rusty, but maybe he just filled in Rusty's gaps, and vice versa.

Rusty didn't need someone in Lycra or waterproof over-alls. He needed Ezra, as he was.

Ezra's smile slowly grew, and he leaned in to kiss Rusty. "Thanks," he finally said.

Rusty pecked his lips in return. "And I'm not going to abandon you," he told Ezra. "I just want you to know that I'm in it to win it. I'm making up for lost time now. I want to keep you safe and happy, and be your muse, for years to come."

"Yeah?" Ezra glowed with pleasure. "My big mouth is that good on your dick?"

Rusty laughed, but he didn't let the comment go. "Because of your big heart, Ezra."

Ezra opened his mouth for a second and then closed it. Rusty had blown straight through his defenses, as usual, with his openness. How had he ever doubted his commitment?

"That's why I wanted to wait so long. Not because I'm ashamed of you, or of being gay," Rusty said quietly. He tugged at the blanket, pulling it around Ezra's shoulders a little more. "But I wanted to make sure I can give you what you need for a long time to come. I don't want just an exploratory fling. I don't do that kind of stuff."

"No," Ezra managed, dizzy with relief and pleasure. "No, you don't. See also a certain farm."

"I hope you're okay with my wild ideas." Rusty chuckled.

Ezra smiled. "One of those wild ideas was me. So I can't exactly complain," he said with a wink. "Whatever happens with it, we'll make it work."

"Both feet first is the best way to jump."

Ezra snorted. "How about tipping in sideways? Or dancing in up to the ankles and then shrieking about the cold?"

"Well, sometimes you need someone to throw you in the deep end." Rusty grinned. "Even if it will wreck your hair."

Ezra leaned in and kissed him deeply, melting into the warm comfort of his strong arms. "Especially if it'll wreck my hair," he murmured back.

Rusty growled and nipped his lip. "You're giving me ideas now."

"What kind of ideas? Hair mask ideas?" Ezra widened his eyes innocently, playful. "Cum's supposed to be good for the skin. I wonder if it could help with split ends."

Rusty laughed, but his hand stayed on Ezra's neck just above his shoulder, his thumb rubbing gently against the spot on Ezra's neck that made his skin dance and jump with sparks.

"I'm so proud of you," Ezra whispered, walking his fingers up to Rusty's cheek. "You've come out and asked Gregory for help and all kinds of stuff in just a few days."

"You were right about all of that stuff. It was about time," Rusty murmured, catching his hand and kissing the back. Then he turned it over, kissing Ezra's palm. "There's a lot I've been waiting a lifetime for."

Ezra gave a breathless giggle as heat rushed to his cheeks. "Yeah? Like the chance to rescue a clueless city boy and redeem those bonus blowjobs?"

Rusty stared. "Wait, what bonus blowjobs?"

"Did I not tell you about them?" Ezra gasped. "For rescuing me from that awful date? Oh, right. I didn't. I thought you wouldn't want to redeem them."

Rusty growled playfully. "If only I'd known *bonus blowjobs* were available."

"I'm pretty sure I made that clear with every other word," Ezra giggled. Then, he held up a finger. "That reminds me. I have one more demand."

"What's that?" Rusty looked earnest, like he was about to spring to his feet and do whatever Ezra asked.

The power was heady, but Ezra stayed focused on the end goal. "Make love to me, my sexy sailor."

Relief flashed across Rusty's face, and he grinned. "I'd be honored, my gorgeous wild-hearted merman. But there's better spots than right here. Will you come back to bed with me?"

He stood and offered Ezra a hand, so Ezra let the blanket fall and took it. "There's nothing I'd rather do except... each other."

"In fact, while we're making demands, I have a new

rule," Rusty said and flashed him a grin. "Fog days are for fucking."

Ezra beamed at him. "It's a deal."

Then, Rusty scooped him up in a fireman's carry and Ezra squealed, but however much he protested, Rusty carried him straight up the stairs with ease.

And goddamn if it didn't make Ezra melt across his shoulder—especially when Rusty slapped his ass and whispered the dirty things he was going to do to it in just a minute.

There was no mistaking it: Rusty was the man for him.

2 4

RUSTY

"You're lucky I didn't pants you there, mister," Ezra gasped when Rusty dumped him on the bed.

Rusty mournfully shook his head. "Lost opportunity. Don't worry. There'll be others." He sat on the edge of the bed, running his hand down to Ezra's palm and tracing along each finger.

Ezra sat up, spreading his legs. "Only because I want to strip you slowly and savor every moment. Come here," he ordered and took Rusty's hand, pulling him closer.

Rusty straddled Ezra, shifting until he found a comfortable way to kneel. He locked his arms around Ezra's back, holding him tight and close as he gazed at him.

The hint of a shy smile that flickered over Ezra's face, and the freckles that dusted his cheeks, and those beautiful lashes that fluttered as Ezra gazed up at him... Rusty wanted to memorize every detail.

"What?" Ezra giggled, his cheeks turning steadily pinker until they almost matched his hair. "You're looking at me like..."

"Like the most precious thing I've ever seen?" Rusty asked softly, one hand sliding up Ezra's back and over his shoulder until he could cup his cheek. "Because you are."

Ezra squeezed his eyes shut, wrinkled his nose, and made the most adorable squeaking noise.

Rusty burst out laughing. "What was that?"

"My heart bursting with happiness." Ezra's eyes were shimmering with wetness now.

"Ah, shit." Rusty swiped his thumb along Ezra's cheek when the happy tears spilled over. "Sorry...?"

"It's okay," Ezra whispered, closing his eyes. "I like having feelings of my own. Especially this feeling." He ran his fingers through Rusty's hair, combing it back. "I could live in it forever."

"Can you? Let's do it," Rusty murmured. He wasn't even joking, but Ezra giggled.

"Deal. As long as the fog-fucking rule stays in place."

Rusty smirked. "We're not fucking the fog though, right? It's pretty chilly."

"Have you tried?" Ezra's eyes were drying up now, his smile cheeky.

Rusty pulled his lips into a mock frown. "No comment. Desperate times, man. Desperate times."

Ezra laughed again, the sound a light shimmer. "I love your sense of humor. You make me laugh every day."

"At me or with me?" Rusty scrunched up his face, making Ezra keep laughing.

"Both." Ezra pecked his lips, then rested his head on Rusty's shoulder as he worked his hands up under his shirt. "Arms up."

"Oooh." Rusty raised his arms and let Ezra pull his shirt and sweater off in one move. He fought his way out until his head was clear.

Then Ezra tossed his shirt aside, and it landed on the edge of the laundry basket. "Victory!" He raised his arms again. "More sports successes! Your sportiness must be rubbing off on me."

"Something's rubbing off on you," Rusty growled, grinding against Ezra's lap.

"I knew sportiness was hard, but I didn't know it was that big." Ezra bit his lower lip, looking Rusty up and down.

God, Ezra was delicious. He knew just what to say and do to wind Rusty up and set him loose.

Rusty pulled Ezra's shirt over his head and kissed his neck, reveling in the heat of his skin against Ezra's. His new boyfriend was smooth and lithe, and he arched toward Rusty with every touch.

It was easy to make Ezra moan. As Rusty kissed down his neck, he found more hot buttons. The lightest touch along Ezra's back made his whole body shiver as he gave the sexiest whimpers.

"I'm never going to get tired of this," Rusty whispered, his eyes wide. He couldn't think how he'd lived without it all this time.

Ezra's nails dug into his shoulders. "Wait 'til we're naked. Speaking of which, hurry up."

"Oh, okay," Rusty laughed. "No slow and gentle?"

"There's time for slow and gentle later. I need wild, you-just-rescued-me sex," Ezra moaned.

"How about *I-just-rescued-you* blowjobs?" Rusty asked, lowering Ezra to the bed so he could kiss those small, perky nipples.

"Yeah," Ezra whispered hoarsely, which was about the only word he could manage between his groans.

When Rusty trailed his tongue down toward Ezra's hip,

he gasped and half sat before he flopped back again. "Oh my God, you meant me."

"Yeah, I did." Rusty grinned. "I need to learn how to do this so I can wake you up in the morning." He kissed the hollow just above Ezra's hip.

Ezra whimpered, his hands rising to clutch at the headboard. "C-Cool. That sounds great. Yep," he panted.

Rusty kept pressing openmouthed kisses along every inch of skin he could find, taking note of what made Ezra cry out the loudest.

When he couldn't ignore the tent any longer without feeling really cruel, he slid his hand to Ezra's jeans and popped the button, then slid the zipper down as slowly as he dared.

"Rusty motherfucking Campbell, you *are* a tease!" Ezra exclaimed, his eyes wide.

Rusty tried to look innocent. "I don't know enough to be a tease."

"Then it comes naturally. Get my damn pants off before I take matters into my own hands," Ezra ordered.

Rusty grinned and hooked his thumbs into Ezra's jeans, dragging them down along with his underwear. He scooted down the bed, pulling them off his feet and dumping the socks, too.

"There," he murmured, admiring the view.

Ezra was spread-eagle now, his hard cock flat against his stomach and achingly pink. His toes curled into the bed as he pushed his hair out of his face and tucked it over one shoulder, then grabbed the headboard again.

"God, you're hot," Rusty whispered. His whole body ached with the need to be on top of Ezra, inside him, claiming him with every kiss and every slow thrust.

Rusty shucked his own clothes without preamble, tossing them out of the way and running his hand along his hard-on.

Just a little longer, he told himself, moaning quietly at even this much contact. It was torture to keep his hands off himself, but Ezra was waiting so patiently. His gorgeous cock was wet, precum trickling from the head.

It was his turn first.

Rusty knelt between Ezra's legs again, dropping to all fours and pressing his lips against that shaft like he was licking the drippings from a Popsicle on a hot summer's day.

"Yes!" Ezra panted, his thighs quivering. Rusty ran his hands up them, parting them farther so he could kiss along his balls, then back up to the tip.

As his palms glided over Ezra's stomach, every muscle was taut under his hands.

Rusty grinned and wrapped his fingers around that gorgeous shaft, licking the tip experimentally. It had a sharp, musky tang, but it was sweet, too.

Ezra was whimpering quietly. "You're so hot I can't *even*."

"I don't want you to *even*," Rusty retorted before lapping at his head. He wanted Ezra to lose his mind.

So he took the plunge, wrapping his lips around the tip and swallowing him slowly. The warm, thick shaft was unfamiliar at first, but the act already turned him on so much he could hardly think straight.

Rusty bobbed his head, wrapping his fingers around the base of Ezra's shaft to stroke as he did so. He figured out what he was doing quickly and sucked in his cheeks, flicking his tongue around the ridges of Ezra's cock.

Ezra's cries started quiet and increased quickly in both volume and pitch.

"You're so good," Ezra whispered. "Already."

Imagine when you have me trained up, Rusty thought, but his mouth was a little too full to say it out loud. He'd save that for later. Instead he just moaned, then choked for a moment on the length.

Ezra gasped. "Fuck, that's hot." One hand snuck down from the headboard, running through Rusty's hair. He gripped tightly, sending a shower of sparks over Rusty's scalp and straight down to his cock.

Suddenly, he could see the appeal from this end: the idea of handing Ezra control for a moment, and just as Ezra had once said, letting himself be used for his partner's pleasure.

The idea of Ezra uncontrollably fucking his mouth, spilling his load down his throat while squirming and moaning and talking dirty to the last second...

Rusty's spare hand slipped down to his own cock and he stroked himself, moaning again around Ezra's cock.

"I see you there. Time to fuck me now?" Ezra breathed out. He made it sound like a plea, like he needed Rusty and he was just waiting for his every move. "I hope you have lube. No condom, though. I want to feel you without one. Is that all right?"

Like Rusty was in charge, even though he was just figuring it out, and like Ezra didn't notice any inexperience that showed through.

Rusty slowly pulled his mouth off Ezra, leaving him wet and flushed. Then, he kissed the tip of his cock once before he knelt upright again. He grinned, his confidence building. "Perfect. Lube's on the bedside table. Get it."

"Oooh," Ezra breathed and scrambled for it, nearly flopping right off the bed as he threw himself in that direction.

Rusty reached to grab him just in case, then laughed. "You can take a second longer if it keeps you from knocking a tooth out on the corner of the table, please."

Ezra snorted. "What's a little dental trauma in the name of a nice, deep pounding?" He came up with the lube and flopped on his back again, brandishing it like a trophy.

"Now finger yourself," Rusty ordered calmly. He kept stroking himself slowly, luxuriating in the feeling as Ezra watched him hungrily. He ran one hand up Ezra's thigh. "Show me how you like it."

"Fuckity fucking fuck." Ezra's voice was choked as even his creative insults failed him. "Yes!"

Rusty brushed his fingers along Ezra's body as he watched his slick fingers slide into him one and two at a time. Ezra was even blushing every time he made eye contact.

"You like putting on a show for me?" Rusty growled quietly. "And vice versa?" He moved his arm so Ezra could see him stroking himself.

"Oh, yes," Ezra breathed out. "I could watch that all day."

Rusty grinned. "One day, yeah. But for today... under the terms of the inaugural Fog Agreement, I'd better fuck you."

Ezra squeaked quietly and pulled his fingers out, spreading his long limbs at an impressive angle.

But Rusty had another idea. He grinned and crawled over the bed until he sat next to Ezra. "I think I'm long overdue a ride, Ezra Carter."

Ezra gasped. "Did I ever tell you how much I like your ideas?" He straddled Rusty's lap and grabbed the headboard to steady himself, his hair already in his face and going astray everywhere.

Rusty grinned, gently finger-combing it out of his face and behind his ears.

Ezra blew out a regretful laugh—and another few strands from his lips. "It won't stay there," he sighed.

"It will if I do this." Rusty carefully wound the locks

through one hand, watching Ezra for his approval as he pulled it taut.

He got more than his approval. Ezra gasped, rocking forward into him. "*Yes!* He learns fast. Oh, thank you, whatever power sent me this gorgeous boyfriend."

"The power of shitty Grindr dates, I think," Rusty chuckled. "Weird how life works out."

Ezra moaned. "It was *so* worth the wait for this," he whispered, pressing himself down against Rusty. Then Rusty gasped as he slid inside, and suddenly Ezra enveloped him in a tight heat.

It was tighter than his own fingers, and hotter than he'd imagined. Their bodies were locked together now, and Ezra was gasping for breath as he lowered himself slowly onto Rusty. In turn, Rusty gave a muffled grunt of pleasure as Ezra rose and sank on him, taking him in an inch at a time.

Ezra's voice was raw when he spoke again. "God, you're perfect. Save a boat, ride a Rusty." He melted into Rusty, his chest pressed against the wall of muscle that was Rusty's body. "Your turn. Give it a try."

It was a pleasure to hold the man in place and thrust slowly up into him, his hips moving slowly at first.

Ezra's steady moans of encouragement drove him onward. When he found a rhythm, Ezra joined in, pushing down at the same time.

Each thrust became sharper and deeper, and the hunger between them only built.

He wanted to plunge deep into Ezra with every thrust, pin him in place and make his eyes squeeze shut in that same ecstatic pleasure he'd seen just minutes earlier.

If Ezra's heart had burst with emotions before, Rusty wanted to overwhelm his body with erotic pleasure now.

"I've been waiting so long," Ezra gasped, his breath sharp

and quick. "Wanting you to fuck me senseless with that great big, hard, gorgeous dick."

"Senseless?" Rusty tightened his hold on Ezra's hair, pulling it back so he could kiss his throat.

"Yes!" Ezra squeaked. "Please!"

"Doesn't sound like making love to me," Rusty growled, flicking his tongue against Ezra's earlobe to make him squirm. As he did, the circular motions of Rusty's hardness against his prostate made them both jolt and shiver with pleasure.

"That's the best thing about love," Ezra whispered. "We get to define what it is for ourselves. And that can change every day if we want it to."

For a moment, Rusty stopped on the spot, his lips parting. Ezra was right, of course. How was he always right? Suddenly, he couldn't wait to find out how many definitions of love Ezra had.

"Don't stop!" Ezra begged. "I need you, baby. More than anything." His skin shone with sweat now, his breath ragged as his movements slowed.

If he was out of energy, Rusty was filled with it. The words only spurred him on. He dug his nails into Ezra's shoulders and flipped them over, rolling him onto his back.

When he was settled between Ezra's legs, he slid into him, tangling his hand in Ezra's hair again to tug it back as he started pushing into Ezra.

He could go a lot harder now, and when Ezra squirmed, he could pin him down with a hand in the middle of his chest.

The heat flaring deep within Rusty's belly wouldn't be held back much longer. "I'm going to come inside you so quick if you keep being this hot."

"Yes!" Ezra gasped. "Kiss me, please. I'm so close, too. I need you."

Rusty bent over, draping his body along Ezra's. He caught Ezra's hands and dragged them above his head, lacing their fingers as they kissed in a hot, wet, openmouthed clash of lips and tongues.

Rusty let his weight do the work, slamming into Ezra at a pace that made them both cry out through the kiss.

"I'm so—don't stop—I need...!" Ezra lost his words and just clutched at Rusty's hands, squeezing them hard. His ass was squeezing, too, tightness rippling along Rusty's throbbing length.

It was so hard to hold back at this impossibly hot sight, but Ezra was so close. Rusty gritted his teeth and redoubled his pace. "Come, baby. You're so hot, and you're all mine. Show me you're mine."

Ezra gasped and cried out in an escalating series of *yes* sounds, and then he rolled his head back, his body arching as he squeezed tight around Rusty.

Rusty lipped at his throat and the pulse point on his neck, still thrusting where he could, but Ezra was too far gone to stop now.

"Rusty!" Ezra came undone around him and under him, falling to pieces. Gorgeous, glowing, ginger pieces that Rusty wanted to scoop up, put back together, and make love to again and again.

"Ez..." Rusty let go of one of Ezra's hands and grabbed the headboard. Some of Ezra's wildly splayed hair caught in his grip, but Ezra only gave a series of pleased whimpers.

And then he came, his hips stuttering in a rapid-fire rhythm he couldn't quite control. His world narrowed to Ezra—just Ezra—and the joy of their bodies wrapped around each other.

Like it was just the two of them, forever and ever, standing against the storm.

Pleasure raced up and down his spine, centered on their joined bodies. It flushed his cheeks, his climax squeezing every one of his muscles.

Then it swept away as fast as it had come, leaving his skin sparking with a strange contentment. Every damn drop of energy gone, Rusty gasped for breath and slowly levered himself onto his side.

Ezra giggled and cuddled into his chest, tucking his head under Rusty's chin. "Good?"

Rusty could only give an enthusiastic grunt at first, which made Ezra laugh. When he summoned up words again, he managed, "Perfect."

"Mmm." Ezra hummed, kissing his neck gently. "You have tissues?"

"Mmhmm." It was hard to peel himself away, since Ezra kept a hold on Rusty even when he rolled onto his other side.

He had to laugh as Ezra yanked a handful of tissues one after another before he turned onto his back again. "Did I make a mess?"

"You filled me to the brim, baby," Ezra giggled. When he was done, he sprawled there, casting his gaze down at his own mess, which still coated his stomach.

Rusty smirked and grabbed more tissues, gently dabbing Ezra's stomach clean. "There," he murmured at last, tossing everything into the garbage can.

As soon as he lay down, Ezra rolled down and spooned him again, nuzzling his shoulder. He might as well have purred. "That was so hot. How was your first time?"

"You're so damn sexy it made it easy," Rusty laughed quietly, shaking his head. "That was... wow. Everything I could've hoped for."

"It's not always this easy," Ezra warned with a laugh. "Sometimes the dental trauma actually happens. Careful when we do it against the wall."

Rusty laughed. "I won't drop you into any walls," he promised, kissing Ezra's forehead. "God, I can't wait." He wanted to try everything Ezra knew and then some.

"Still love me for my big heart?" Ezra teased.

"Your ass is ranking pretty high on the list now," Rusty said, smacking it lightly. "Or maybe your mouth. I have to test this extensively to figure out the order."

Ezra squealed and squirmed against him, but he was laughing. "I'll wake you up with a blowjob next time, then. Better than a very delayed breakfast and minor panic."

Rusty laughed, but a prickle of pleasure crept through his body. "You'd better be staying tonight if you're going to make promises like that."

"Mmhmm." Ezra batted his lashes. "I hoped I would. After all, I need all the time with my muse that I can get."

Rusty ran his hand gently along Ezra's hair, smoothing it down along his back. "You can have all the time you ever want."

Ezra hummed, a low noise of contentment, and kissed him once before he nuzzled into his neck.

Rusty closed his eyes, but whatever he did, he couldn't stop smiling. He'd finally landed himself the catch of a lifetime, and he knew it.

The engine purred softly as Ezra huddled into his fluffiest jacket, his gloved hands wrapped around the thermos between his knees.

It was so completely worth the evening cruise to enjoy the stars overhead on a clear, crisp Christmas Eve. But he was also glad he'd thought to bring hot chocolate to enjoy as they took a spin tonight.

And that was quite literal. Rusty had done donuts for them until Ezra had tears running down his face from the wind and from giggling with him, hollering for more.

Then they'd had a quiet run up and down the coast, just enjoying the stars on one side and the moonlit shore on the other. They were close to the beach where they'd camped a few weeks ago; Ezra recognized the scenery just enough to be able to tell.

"I love this part of the coast," Rusty murmured, reaching across the aisle of the boat for Ezra's hand. "It's a calm night. Let's cut the engine and watch the stars some more."

That painting was finally finished—the drawing of

Heaven that Ezra had started a long time ago. And it was never going to be for sale.

Inside the cottage, a candle now burned in the window as evening fell. Lots of pairs of boots dried on the front porch, kicked this way and that in haste to get inside. Ezra could smell the wood fire that trailed from the chimney, and the hot supper being shared among loved ones. For miles beyond the little home, the shore stretched out, a familiar scattering of dark green pines leaning over rocky cliffs—just like this stretch of the beach.

When he moved in with Rusty, this piece of art was the first thing Ezra wanted to bring over. Not that they'd settled on a plan yet, but it was coming soon. Ezra could sense it.

Ezra smiled as Rusty cut the engine, got up, and took Ezra by the hand. He went happily as Rusty led him to the back of the boat, then cuddled up close. They sat on the edge, with Rusty's arm wrapped around him.

"I love seeing the stars on a clear night. There's something so different about seeing it from the water."

Ezra gasped. "Oh! I have a story." Benji had told him about a few constellations, and he'd even remembered one story. "See that? That's Andromeda." Rusty squinted and shook his head, and Ezra beamed. "Hold on." He dug out his keys and detached the little green laser pointer that he was going to carry with him until it died.

He pointed it up, circling the stars he meant.

"So, Andromeda got sent to this sea monster as a sacrifice, but Perseus rescued her and killed the sea monster. So, you know. Romantic? I'll be Andromeda if you be Perseus tonight," he giggled.

"Okay," Rusty chuckled. He rubbed Ezra's shoulder gently. "But I feel like you're the one who slayed my demons." He rested the sides of their heads together.

"We rescued each other," Ezra murmured with a firm nod.

"Before you, I had no idea that love felt like this." Rusty's voice was quiet and honest as he peered up at first and then over at Ezra. "Or that I deserved to feel it."

"Oh, hon," Ezra whispered. "You deserve the world."

Every day just confirmed that they fit together perfectly, now that they weren't holding themselves back from what was right.

"I don't know if I deserved you, but I'm glad you stuck around while I figured things out. I'll work every day to make sure I deserve you." Rusty shifted his jacket around, squirming on the spot and pulling Ezra tight into him.

"You've already got me, once and for all," Ezra whispered. He kissed Rusty, soft and warm and lingering, the chill forgotten.

Ezra had gotten to know him in this month—better than he would have thought possible. They'd spent practically every waking moment together. Rusty had made up for letting his friends down by bringing supper over several times—different seaweed-based dishes, and all tasty. Ezra's favorite was a mushroom pilaf with flakes of seaweed.

Mmm. His mouth watered at the thought. Maybe he could sweet-talk Rusty into cooking it for a second time this week.

Rusty chuckled softly against his lips. "I sure hope so." He pulled away from the kiss and bit his glove, pulling it off and pocketing it.

"I know so," Ezra said, grinning at him. He'd only called him *my future husband*, like, half a dozen times in the past couple of weeks to all of his friends, whether or not Rusty was around.

If there was one thing he was, it was up-front about his

intentions. And thank God, or they might never have fallen together so perfectly.

"I know it's pretty early," Rusty murmured, "but I knew it, too. Even back when we first met... God, it sounds crazy, but I just knew we had something special. You showed me your whole heart right from the start. There are a thousand reasons I love you, and I found them all within days of knowing each other. You're just so *you*," Rusty said.

Ezra blushed, a mile-wide grin spreading across his lips. If this was his Christmas present—a list of compliments he'd never forget—he'd count himself lucky.

But Rusty wasn't done.

"I can't afford much right now, but when the harvest comes in... and I finish buying out Pascal, and all that other crap, you know the drill," Rusty laughed, "we'll pick up something."

Ezra blinked at Rusty's free hand. He was offering him a box, so Ezra took it and opened it.

His jaw dropped. It was a ring—a plain, shiny, silver band.

And the way Rusty was looking at him, everything made sense now.

Ezra squealed as he flew to his feet, then nearly tripped backward over the side of the boat.

But Rusty's arm was still there, bracing him as he grinned. "Good thing I knew you were going to do that."

"Oh, fuck." Ezra clutched the box to his chest, tears already welling up. "Are you—is this—really happening?"

"You have to give me that so I can do it properly," Rusty told him with a gentle grin.

"Yes, but—you're—this is—it's happening!"

Rusty chuckled and pried the box out of Ezra's hand when he just kept rubbing it against his heart and squeaking happily. "It's happening," he promised, taking Ezra by the hand and leading him to the middle of the boat before he knelt down. "Safer for Ezras here."

Ezra giggled, covering his face as the world spun around him. He was giddy with joy. "Baby, I... I don't know what to say."

"Then just say yes." Rusty beamed up at him as he took the ring out.

"You bet your ass I'm saying yes," Ezra breathed out, finally getting his thoughts in order as he held out his hand.

Rusty peeled Ezra's glove off. "I'll make it quick and spare you from the cold," he said with a grin up at him.

"Oh, right. That would help. I don't think I feel cold anymore." Ezra was aglow with a fire he couldn't describe.

"Be mine, baby," Rusty murmured, gazing up at Ezra and the stars beyond.

"Yes," Ezra whispered, his hand shaking as Rusty slid the ring on, then his glove.

He clutched his hand to his chest, feeling the ring through the fabric, and only then became dimly aware that he was squeaking with joy again.

"I love you," Rusty chuckled fondly, rising to his feet and cupping Ezra's cheeks for a lingering kiss that drove away any hint of cold from Ezra's bones.

Then the boat bumped something gently, making them both stumble while Rusty cursed. "Oh, shit. I better steer us."

Ezra clutched the edge of the canopy. "Yeah, let's not make Gregory rescue us again," he agreed as Rusty started the engine.

"He might start charging a fine himself," Rusty said with a laugh.

Ezra just gazed up and around at the night stars while

Rusty backed the boat carefully away from the shoreline where they'd drifted, too caught up in each other to notice a thing.

Then he ducked under the canopy again, crowding onto the driver's seat next to Rusty. Ezra rested his forehead on Rusty's shoulder and slid his arms around his waist.

"I love you, baby. And your tasty mushroom seaweed pilaf. And your impeccable boaterly skills." His stomach growled. "Did I mention the pilaf?"

"Yes, I'll make it for you tomorrow, sweetheart." Rusty laughed, a sound swallowed by the vast, deep sky and the ocean that stretched into forever, and the purr of the engine as they made their way home together, aglow from a moment Ezra would never forget.

At least this time, it was a dry moment, thanks to Rusty's careful planning. It made Ezra giggle softly, and Rusty chuckled, too, without saying a word. They didn't need to in order to share this vision of the future—so full of limitless possibilities.

AFTERWORD

Dear reader,

Thank you for reading *Wild Hart*, the third book in the cozy, heartwarming world of Hart's Bay!

It was a real treat to get up close and personal to a different facet of Hart's Bay than before. My kayaking research was less wet than Ezra and Rusty's, but just as fun... and the seaweed research was tasty! Thanks to Grand Manaan for inspiring me, and to my patient family who waited for me to document every type of seaweed on the store shelves.

I can't wait to show you what happens next as Hart's Bay keeps bubbling to life, and the guys around town keep finding their perfect matches!

Thanks again to Amy, Sandra, Meg, and Kitti for making me look less typo-prone than I am. And, of course, my love always to my Facebook group Petals for taking these guys into their hearts. You asked for Ezra, and I hope you loved him as much as me! And I couldn't do this without my

Cheesebags, whose first response to "seaweed farmer?" was "YES!"

Of all the men patiently waiting for their stories, it's impossible to miss one in particular... the next Hart's Bay novel is coming in January 2020! *Stolen Hart* will be Aaron's story.

Wild Hart will be brought to life as an audiobook narrated by Greg Boudreaux in January 2020!

In the meantime, if you haven't already, sign up to my newsletter to be the first to know when it comes out: edaviesbooks.com/subscribe

You'll also hear about: exclusive Hart's Bay Bites; freebies and deals; new releases in ebook, audio, and print; preorder alerts; sneak peeks at upcoming books; event appearances; and other exciting news as it happens!

I also have a reader group on Facebook if you want to chat about your favorite parts of *Wild Hart*, see cute bee photos and good news stories, and keep on top of my upcoming releases with a whole bunch of lovely readers: facebook.com/groups/edavies

Last but not least: always be you!

~Ed

E. Davies grew up moving constantly, which taught him what people have in common, the ways relationships are formed, and the dangers of "miscellaneous" boxes. As a young gay author, Ed prefers to tell feel-good stories that are brimming with hope.

He writes full-time, goes on long nature walks, tries to fill his passport, drinks piña coladas on the beach, flees from cute guys, coos over fuzzy animals (especially bees), and is liable to tilt his head and click his tongue if you don't use your turn signal.

facebook.com/edaviesbooks

twitter.com/edaviesauthor

instagram.com/thisboyisstrange

bookbub.com/authors/e-davies

Brooklyn Boys

Electric Sunshine

Live Wire

Boiling Point

F-Word

Flaunt

Freak

Faux

Forever

After

Afterburn

Afterglow

Aftermath

Men of Hidden Creek

Shelter

Adore

Miracle

Redemption

Audiobooks

You can see all my books available in audio here: www.edaviesbooks.com/audiobooks